"Lady, you can stay out there until you turn into lawn furniture."

Alex could hear Hunter Garrett perfectly. *Now we're getting someplace,* she thought. At least he was talking to her. "I'm not leaving." She rapped smartly on the window.

There were sounds of muffled conversation and movement. Then his voice came through the glass again, hard and flat. "I have a dog. Don't make me turn him loose on you."

Alex jerked back, debating her next move. Irritating the man was one thing, annoying his dog was another. Then she realized that not once had she heard a bark or a growl. If he did have a dog, it wasn't much protection. "Stop being ridiculous," she scoffed. "You don't have a dog."

A moment later she jumped as deep-throated barking suddenly came from within. Loud. Like a Baskerville hound eager for fresh blood.

"Look, lady," Hunter Garrett called over the dog's vocalization. "I'm hanging on to the biggest Doberman you've ever seen. Killer's attack-trained. I got him for people just like you. If you're smart, you'll get the hell out of here."

It was, Alex decided, an excellent idea.

ABOUT THE AUTHOR

Although *Hot & Bothered* is Ann Evans's first Harlequin Superromance novel, it's her third published book. She has also won two awards. This talented author started writing in high school and wanted to be the next Mary Stewart. Working the midnight shift on helicopter rescue for a local hospital, she used the long hours between emergencies to write and people watch. "A hospital emergency room is a great place to find quirky characters," she says. Ann lives in Florida, where she now works as administrative manager at an investment company. She is currently writing her second Superromance novel. We are very happy to welcome her to the line.

Ann Evans
HOT & BOTHERED

Harlequin Books

TORONTO • NEW YORK • LONDON
AMSTERDAM • PARIS • SYDNEY • HAMBURG
STOCKHOLM • ATHENS • TOKYO • MILAN
MADRID • WARSAW • BUDAPEST • AUCKLAND

For my sister, Barbara Marsh.
With gratitude and admiration.
Not just family, but my best friend.

ISBN 0-373-70701-0

HOT & BOTHERED

HOT &
BOTHERED

CHAPTER ONE

June 9, 11:17 a.m.

"Hello. You've reached 555-2128. If you'd like to leave a message, please do so at the sound of the tone."

Beep.

"This is Alexandria Sutton of the *Miami Sun Times*. I'm trying to reach Mr. Hunter Garrett to set up an interview. Would you please call me collect at 305-555-4000? Thank you."

June 10, 10:22 a.m.

"Hello. You've reached 555-2128. If you'd like to leave a message, please do so at the sound of the tone."

Beep.

"Mr. Garrett, this is Alexandria Sutton again. My paper's very interested in your thoughts regarding Leo Isaacson's alleged suicide. I know you haven't given any interviews in a long time, but let me assure you, we're not looking to sensationalize his death. You can call collect. My number's 305-555-4000."

June 11, 9:40 a.m.

"*Hello. You've reached 555-2128. If you'd like to leave a message, please do so at the sound of the tone.*"

Beep.

"This is Alex Sutton. I understand your reluctance, Mr. Garrett, and I can't say that I blame you for not wanting to get involved again. But if you don't return my call, sooner or later I'm going to show up on your doorstep. Why don't you make this easy for the both of us ... Hello? Is someone there?"

"How did you get this number?" a curt male voice cut in.

Straightening, Alex fumbled the receiver to her other ear, delighted to have finally reached a human being. "Is this Mr. Garrett?"

"How did you get this number?" the man demanded again. Even across the distance of the state, the annoyed edge to his voice crackled through the telephone loud and clear.

"I'm a reporter. It's my business to track down people."

"Don't call this number again."

The scalpel-sharp tone said her obedience was not only commanded, it was expected. Alex smiled into the receiver, trying to keep the exasperation out of her voice, replacing it with friendly empathy. "Look, I'm not trying to upset you—"

"You don't. That would imply I'm giving your request consideration. Which I'm not."

She swallowed a throat full of possible retorts. "Mr. Garrett, this story can be written with or without your cooperation. But surely, if there's any question in your mind about Leo Isaacson's death you'd like to—"

"No."

"Are you aware that the D.C. police are going to begin a full investigation? Your opinion—"

"Won't bring Leo Isaacson back," the man's voice sliced neatly across her words with indisputable finality. "Write whatever you damned well please, but you're going to write it without my help."

Desperate enough to be reckless, Alex said, "If someone's threatened you not to talk, or you're frightened—"

He muttered something she failed to catch, but clear across the state she sensed his anger. "That approach is a waste of time, lady, and you're not even very good at it."

"Wait!" she begged. His cool contempt threw her off-balance. She bit her lip, casting about for the right words, knowing their exchange would falter entirely if she didn't find some way to keep it alive. Maybe it was time to try a different tack. "Look," she said, her voice primed to encourage confidences, "can I be honest with you?"

Hunter Garrett made an ungentlemanly sound of disbelief. "Probably not." His voice was richly steeped in sarcasm.

"If I don't get this interview, it could mean my job."

"Good luck finding a new one."

"Mr. Garrett—"

Click.

June 12, 8:16 a.m.

"The number you have reached has been changed at the customer's request. The new number is unpublished. If you need directory assistance—"
"Damn!"

ALEX SUTTON STARED out the sixth-floor windows of Ernie Galloway's office. On the street below her editor's cool and carpeted domain, Miami office workers scuttled across hot pavement like colonies of ants. Anxious to escape the Florida heat, its citizens hurried through revolving doors from one air-conditioned building to the next.

She touched the windowpane with her fingertips and felt the warmth outside try to breach the barrier of glass. The air conditioner kept the heat at bay and poured a frosty and surprisingly unpleasant blast down the back of her blouse.

Her first summer in Florida. Not as bad as she'd expected, and certainly not as awful as her family had predicted. Boston summers could be pretty brutal, too, she'd reminded them.

Of course, her family had ignored that observation and had immediately set about knocking down every one of her arguments for relocating to Miami. One thing about the Suttons, they knew how to fight for what they wanted. And what they'd wanted was for Alex to be a good little girl and stay in Boston.

It still amazed her that she'd been able to break through their resistance.

She looked down at the file folder clutched in one hand. What she hadn't been able to break was her editor's determination to saddle her with the worst assignment in the world.

Her brother Mel, expressing high indignation, would have refused it.

Her brother Rio would have turned it into a Pulitzer.

She sighed. Lacking her siblings' talent, she knew what she'd have to do with it. She was stuck.

Alex turned back to Ernie. "Admit it. This is Jessup's way of punishing me for my dog-show piece."

Ernie didn't try to deny he'd been pushed into giving Alex this assignment by the publisher, a man known to have a soggy backbone when it came to arguments with his wife. "Can you blame him? You accused his wife of looking like her dog!"

"I did not. I simply made the observation that some breeders have bone structure similar to the animals they raise."

"Which means they look like their dogs. Helen Jessup raises Pekingese, Alex." Ernie rolled his eyes to the ceiling. "If you had to draw comparisons, why couldn't you have said she looked like something pretty? Like a collie."

"I didn't know she'd be an exhibitor at that show. It was a good piece, Ernie, and you know it. And I'd like to remind you that *you* approved it."

He glared at her. "You tricked me. You told me you'd given it a satirical slant. Now Jessup's wife wants you fired. Of course, if I remind them who your family is..."

His words trailed off and made Alex stiffen. "My family has nothing to do with this," she said sharply.

Ernie waved away her comment with one beefy hand. "Relax. I know how you feel about trading on the Sutton fame."

Shortly after hiring her, Ernie had made the connection between Alex and the Suttons of Boston, one of the biggest names in newspaper publishing. She'd begged him to keep that relationship a secret. A man with a notoriously soft heart, Ernie had agreed, but in the inbred world of the paper, it hadn't been long before everyone in the office knew.

Alex settled into the chair across from the editor's desk. The air-conditioning made the vinyl unpleasantly chilly. No reporter could get too comfortable in a chair that cold.

"I think I'd rather get fired than do this piece on Garrett. He wouldn't return my calls, and when I finally got through to him, he was pretty hostile. Instant dislike, Ernie. He's not going to talk to me."

"Make him talk to you. Exert some sweet Sutton charm."

"I don't think it will work on him."

"Why not?"

She shrugged. "Just a hunch. Reporters are supposed to be able to rely on them, you know."

"Come on, Alex. You can do it. A Sutton can talk a dog down off a meat wagon."

There it was again. The inevitable comparison. The Sutton "nose for news" that had become almost legendary in the newspaper game. Both her parents possessed it. And her brothers, one an investigative reporter with a "killer instinct" and the other a savvy political journalist, were nearly as renowned as the subjects of their stories.

And Alex?

She lowered her gaze, discovering sudden interest in the limp creases of her skirt. Ernie couldn't know, of course, and he probably wouldn't have the patience for her insecurities. But that didn't keep his simple comment from creating an intense, unwelcome reaction in the pit of her stomach.

Snapping her thoughts away from her self-doubts and the fear that had always been edged with resentment, she made a dismissing sound and tapped the file folder in her lap. "I pulled Garrett's jacket off the computer. If you read the Vutext, you'd swear the guy's a few doughnuts short of a dozen."

Ernie dismissed her opinion with the wave of his hand. "Forget the goofy environmental causes he was into before he dropped out of sight. He was still smarting from the slap the government gave him."

Opening the folder, Alex sifted through the printouts from the research computer, reading random blurbs. "Some slap. He lost his job, his wife evidently left him, his research grants dried up. The congressional committee even tried to imply he was a traitor to the country. The man's persona non grata in the scientific community."

The editor's chair snapped forward as he leaned across the desk toward her. "Ah, but who stood as one of Garrett's character witnesses four years ago? Isaacson."

"That's a pretty slim connection. Isaacson was working on protective wraps for the army's M1 tanks. Garrett's research centered on nerve gas antidotes. Granted, both their concerns were chemical and biological warfare—" Alex frowned and plucked another scrap of paper from the file. "But Garrett's claim that the atropine injectors weren't doing their job proved false."

"And now Isaacson, a biochemist who seemed to be a rational, intelligent human being two weeks ago, suddenly decides to swan-dive off a Washington office building. One dead, one discredited. Doesn't that strike you as odd?"

"So let me work with Hawthorne on Isaacson's story. Don't make me track down some sour-grapes biologist to see what he thinks. I feel sorry for the guy, but Garrett is old news. Nobody's heard a peep from him in nine months."

The pencil in Ernie's hand tapped idly against the blotter as the look in his eyes turned speculative. "That in itself is strange, Alex. After the whistle-blowing fiasco, Garrett kept a pretty high profile here. Then suddenly he disappears. No more interviews or environmental causes. Why? Where's he been?" Ernie's eyes widened, the pupils glinting at her like water at the bottom of a well. "Can't you *smell* the story?"

She shut the folder so abruptly that papers in the editor's in-basket fluttered a protest. "What I *smell* is a rat." She sighed, sensing this was one battle she was destined to lose. "Jessup wants me out of the office, doesn't he?"

"He wouldn't mind it if you were...on assignment, shall we say...for a few days."

"Are you sending Hawthorne to D.C.?"

"You know I am."

"Then let me go with him. That will get me out of the office if that's what you want."

"I can't afford two reporters working the same story. It has to be Tony's assignment, Alex. You're developing into a decent reporter, but Hawthorne is..."

"Seasoned."

"Exactly." He stood, pulling his belt up over a stomach that had seen too much pasta lately. It was an indication the meeting had come to an end. "Now, don't pout. You know all about paying your dues in this business." He slid a piece of paper across the desk. "Here's Garrett's address in Fort Myers Beach. Get over there and see what you can stir up."

Resigned, Alex rose, slapping the file folder against her leg. "This is a mistake. The guy already dislikes me."

"What do you care whether he likes you or not? Come back with something great, and you'll be out of the life-styles section in no time."

HUNTER GARRETT'S FINGERS slid down the length of the fiberglass fishing rod. It was an uncomplicated piece of equipment, the kind sold in discount department stores everywhere.

Inexpensive.

Functionally plain.

Treasured beyond cost.

He remembered the look of excitement on his son's face when the boy had given it to him. What Christmas had that been? Five years ago? Six? Eric had been about seven, young enough to believe in Santa Claus, but old enough to take pride in buying a gift for his father with his own money.

Memories drifted over him.

Wrapping paper strewn across the carpet. Julie and Eric sitting cross-legged in front of the fireplace, behind them the flames spreading comforting warmth—the first fire they'd built that year, the first one they'd really needed, Florida winters being what they were.

Most of all, Hunter still held a crystal-clear picture of his own gift to his son that year. A catcher's mitt.

Eric had whooped with delight when he had unwrapped it, and in that exact moment Hunter's eyes had found Julie's over the boy's head. He'd acknowledged her cleverness with a nod, and even now he could see that too, that secret little moment between husband and wife, just before she'd handed him a glass of eggnog. The batch she'd made from her mother's secret recipe.

Yeah, that had been one of the best Christmases ever.

He felt the terrible somersaulting in his gut and knew he was doing it again. Letting the memories seep into his system to bloom in painful pleasure. He recognized it as a mistake, but remembrance was a sweet, treacherous thing and wouldn't be silenced with logic. He closed his eyes, trying to control a sense of dislocation by taking deep breaths.

The rod still lay in his hands, no longer bright and shiny, but faded with age and slightly sticky from sea salt. He ought to get rid of it. Buy a new one. Except it was like an old, favored friend. How could he get rid of something that valuable, even if the memories attached to it brought pain?

He could guess what his doctor would say, the pages of notes he'd scribble on his notepad. *Got to let go of the past, Garrett. Can't carry around all that guilt forever, you know.*

Absolutely right, Doctor.

But the rod still went in the pile of fishing equipment he planned to stow in the boat. Because, when it came right down to it, he just couldn't let the damned thing go.

The bell over the door of the bait shop jangled, calling Hunter back from memories. He turned in time to see his best friend and the owner of the marina, Riley Kincaid, walk in. Behind him trailed another man, someone Hunter recognized, someone he thought he would never see again. Someone who sent his heart into a lunatic fandango. *Oh, God, I don't need this. First that reporter, now Braddock. I don't want this. I can't.*

His belly went acid with anticipation and dread, then a resentful calm bubbled up through his momentary panic. There was nothing Ken Braddock could do or say that would make any difference to him at all.

"Excuse the mess," Riley said as he wove his way around tackle boxes and fishing poles. "My buddy and I are getting ready to go after some snook that have our names on them.''

''Plan to catch a few of them myself this season,'' Braddock replied with a grin of understanding.

Have you ever even seen a snook? Hunter wanted to ask, but didn't. Instead, he just stood there in the gloomy afternoon light, waiting to find out why Braddock had come here, dressed from head to toe like a dyed-in-the-wool fisherman, when anyone could tell his deck shoes were brand-new and the lures on that ridiculous hat of his had never seen use.

Riley stopped in the middle of the room and addressed Hunter for the first time. ''Hunt Garrett, this is Ken Braddock. This fellow says he heard the *Lady Jewel* is up for sale. I told him I didn't think so, but he insisted on talking to you.''

''You were right,'' Hunter said to Riley, then slid a direct look at Braddock. ''It's not for sale.''

Riley turned back to the man and gave him an I-told-you-so shrug. ''If you're serious about a boat, I've got a spanking new Bowrider out there in a slip—''

''To tell the truth,'' Braddock admitted with a sheepish look, ''I'd prefer something that's seen a little use. I'm only trying to develop an interest to make a few points with the boss. But I don't want to spend a fortune doing it.''

''It's not for sale,'' Hunter said again. ''Not now. Not ever.''

The frost in his voice made Riley turn to regard him with a sharpened glance. Hunter sensed the curiosity forming in his friend's mind, but he kept his own eyes focused on Braddock.

"Everything has a price," Braddock replied in a quiet tone.

"I'm sure some things do."

He didn't try to disguise the implication in his words. If Braddock wanted to play games with him, he could look somewhere else. The man shifted uncomfortably under the directness of Hunter's stare, then looked back at Riley.

"Would you mind giving us a few minutes in private? I'd like the opportunity to change your friend's mind."

Riley tossed a quick glance Hunter's way.

Hunter gave him a nod, and Riley left them.

The bell over the door announced an uncomfortable silence. Braddock took a slow turn around the crowded shop, touching displays and leafing through tide charts. Content to wait, Hunter settled one hip and leg against Riley's desk and tried to pick his way through a tangled reel. If Ken Braddock was hesitant now about what he had come here to say, Hunter didn't feel compelled to make it any easier for him.

"How have you been, Garrett?" the man asked at last.

Hunter's eyebrows descended in annoyance. Did Braddock really think they could share limping banalities about each other's lives? He said abruptly, "What's with this charade, Braddock?"

The man had sense enough to get to the point. "I didn't think you'd talk to me on the phone, or let me into your house."

"That's the first true thing you've said."

"But I need to talk to you."

Hunter didn't bother to look up from the nest of knots in his hands. "We were through talking a long time ago."

"Have you been reading the papers? They're saying Isaacson's death may not be suicide."

"Why should that bother you? Four years ago, you didn't mind being part of a family of thieves and murderers."

"The Cavanaughs haven't murdered anyone." The vehemence in the man's voice drew Hunter's attention. He watched Braddock jerk off his hat and rake his hair with an unsteady hand. "My God, do you think if I thought that I wouldn't go to the police? It wasn't murder four years ago."

"Tell that to the boys who were out there in the desert, because we both know it could have been. Cavanaugh Laboratories diluted those vaccines until the antidotes would have been as useless against enemy nerve gas as water."

Braddock shook his head. "You're wrong. They still would have worked. They'd have been a little slower to react maybe—"

Irritated with that line of logic, Hunter tossed the reel onto the desk. "Did Charlie Cavanaugh sell you that bill of goods? Your father-in-law's damned lucky some desert madman didn't put that theory to the test."

Another unfriendly silence descended. Then Braddock said in a low, nearly inaudible voice, "I know I let you down."

"You let yourself down. You perjured yourself in front of the committee. I don't know how—I don't think I even care anymore—but you managed to get rid of the evidence. You became Charlie Cavanaugh's perfect little toad."

Braddock's anger flared at the accusation. "He's my wife's father, for God's sake! How could I put him behind bars? He convinced me I was wrong. I was just the production manager at the plant. It's conceivable I made a mistake."

So neat and tidy. You slimy S.O.B. Did you even think about the consequences? "You've still got it all justified in your head, don't you?"

Braddock flushed and looked away, finding sudden interest in a line of new fishing rods propped against one wall. Hunter sensed the man's discomfort, and suddenly knew the origin of it. "Or maybe you're not so sure anymore. You wouldn't be here if you still believed Cavanaugh's story."

Instead of replying, Braddock reached into the inside pocket of his fishing vest. When he extended his hand toward Hunter, the kit lay on his palm, its precious protection encased behind a wall of cheap plastic. "This is the latest batch from the plant. Same thing they carried in the Persian Gulf—three vials each—atropine citrate and pralidoxime chloride. I'm asking you to take a look at it."

Hunter crossed his arms, refusing to touch the kit. "I don't have access to a lab anymore."

"Please," the man said in a flat tone. He sat the clear box on the desk and with one finger slid it closer to Hunter.

"Why this sudden attack of conscience, Braddock?"

"I saw Dr. Isaacson in Charlie Cavanaugh's office two days before the man...killed himself. I want to believe that was a coincidence."

Hunter's eyebrow lifted. "And if it wasn't?"

"Then it's bound to have something to do with the vaccines the plant is producing."

Their eyes met. Sweat broke out on Hunter's upper lip. He'd trusted this man once before, trusted him with *everything*. And been left twisting in the wind. If he placed his faith in Braddock's hands again, he'd be doubly foolish.

"Four years ago I was scared," Braddock added. "But I'm not a murderer. If you find anything out of the ordinary in those injectors, I'll back you up with the police. I swear it. No matter which or how many members of the Cavanaugh family are involved."

I'm not going to fall for this again. I'm not that big a fool anymore. Hunter shook his head. "I don't have the energy or the interest."

The man withdrew a business card and placed it on top of the kit. "Here's my card. Don't call my office. Richie Cavanaugh works just down the hall and I'm not sure I can trust the phone. Use the number I've written on the back."

"You're wasting your time."

"I don't think so," Braddock said simply as he walked toward the door.

Hunter picked up the card. His mouth shifted into an ironic smile as he flipped it over and caught the Cavanaugh logo on the face, Braddock's position stylishly indicated below the company name. "Brad-dock!" he called. With his hand poised on the door-knob, the man swung his head around. Hunter gestured with the card. "From production manager to senior vice president," he observed in a dry, quiet tone. "I guess crime really does pay, after all."

THE GULF BREEZE that fanned the crowded coastline below Fort Myers did little more than stir the heat. Fifteen minutes ago, the air conditioner in the rental car Alex picked up at the hotel had sputtered to a halt. The interior was stifling already.

She'd been driving aimlessly the last few minutes, absolutely certain now that she was lost. Garrett couldn't live in this part of town. The homes here were sagging with age, the neighborhoods orphaned by freeways that led to newer, more prestigious destinations.

She had to stop and ask directions twice, the first time getting absolutely nowhere with a fellow who *said* he didn't understand the question, but who managed to scrounge up enough English to make a pretty obvious suggestion regarding the two of them. Hot and irritated by Ernie's indecipherable directions, Alex brightened considerably when she finally located Hunter Garrett's bungalow.

The small stucco house was hidden behind over-grown clumps of hibiscus and sea grapes. It needed paint and had the vague, unkempt look of a home that didn't get much loving attention anymore. Garrett might once have been something of an environmentalist, but he no longer seemed too interested in his own.

Alex stood on the porch steps, settling her skirt farther down her hips. The suit had been a mistake. She had wanted to look professional but nonthreatening. Instead, the sticky heat had stolen every bit of starch from the yellow linen, and driving for over two hours had left permanent creases across her lap.

She leaned on the doorbell, but no one answered. She glanced toward the two pickup trucks parked in the driveway. *Someone* was home, and she wasn't about to leave until that someone came to the door.

Reaching out to ring again, her hand flew back to her side when the door suddenly opened. Alex plastered an innocuous smile on her face and found herself staring up at a great-looking man.

It wasn't Hunter Garrett.

She'd spent enough time looking at photographs to know this dark-haired stranger wasn't the fellow she was after. She wished he was. *This* man smiled at her with a natural friendliness, touched with just enough healthy, male interest to make her feel like a woman.

"Can I help you?" he asked.

"I'm looking for Hunter Garrett. I was given this address."

"Just my luck," the man replied with a playful wink, then called over one shoulder, "Hey, Hunt. There's a lady here to see you."

He smiled at her. She smiled back. Then she stood face-to-face with Hunter Garrett.

In spite of her research, she wasn't prepared for the sight of him. He was taller than she expected, and he filled the doorway with a quiet determination that set her back a little.

He didn't say a word. He just stood there, his heavy-lidded gaze stabbing into hers with distrust. His hands were shoved into the pockets of jeans that had been washed so many times they'd lost the right to call themselves denim.

Alex realized her throat had gone dry with nervousness and anticipation. She squared her shoulders and held out a business card. "I'm Alexandria Sutton. We spoke on the phone—"

"Riley," Garrett cut in, addressing his dark-haired friend, "this isn't a lady. This is a news hound."

With that, the door shut firmly in Alex's face.

Well. So much for round one.

She knocked again, and kept knocking until her knuckles began to ache. Realizing it was useless, Alex strode toward the rear of the house, her heels sinking into the soft sand. Mentally cursing Ernie Galloway, she reached the back patio just in time to see Garrett drawing curtains across the sliding glass door. Her last glimpse of him was a dazzling smile—smug, self-satisfied and completely in control.

She rapped smartly on the glass. "Mr. Garrett, this is really very silly. I just want to talk to you."

No answer.

"You can't stay in there forever," she called.

The curtains moved a little, but again there was no reply.

"I'm a very patient woman, Mr. Garrett. I can stay out here longer than you can stay in there."

"Lady, for all I care, you can stay out there until you turn into lawn furniture," she heard him say.

Now we're getting someplace, Alex thought. At least she had him talking to her. "I'm not going away."

"I could call the police," he threatened. "You're trespassing."

There were sounds of muffled conversation and movement. Then the biologist's voice came through the glass again, hard and flat. "I have a dog. Don't make me turn him loose on you."

Alex jerked back, debating her next move. Irritating the man was one thing, annoying his dog was another. Then she smiled when she realized that not once had she heard a bark or a growl. If he had one, it wasn't much protection. He had to be bluffing.

The sun warmed the top of her head unpleasantly and bounced off the glass so that she had to squint against the glare. Running out of patience, she scoffed in a brisk, no-nonsense tone, "Stop being ridiculous. You don't have a dog."

A moment later, she jumped back as deep-throated barking suddenly came from within. Loud. Like a Baskerville hound eager for fresh blood. Oh, yes. He had a dog. And a big one, from the sound of it. She stepped back.

"Look, lady," Hunter Garrett called over the dog's vocalization. "I'm hanging on to the biggest Doberman you've ever seen. Killer's attack-trained. I got him for people just like you. If you're smart, you'll get the hell out of here."

It was, Alex decided, an excellent idea.

THE TWO MEN WATCHED the reporter march through the weedy front yard and drive away. With a satisfied chuckle, Hunter turned from the window. High in one hand he held a T-bone steak, and Buster, Riley's bloodhound, made another leap for it.

"Good boy, Buster," Hunter praised. "I knew this would get you moving." Ushering the dog outside, he tossed the steak after him. "Enjoy it, fella. You earned it."

He turned back to his friend. Riley leaned against the end of the couch, arms crossed. From the look on Riley's face, Hunter could tell the man knew a miracle when he saw one. Buster seldom got excited over anything.

Riley shook his head. "That was...interesting. And weird."

Hunter shrugged. "It worked, didn't it?"

He reopened the curtains over the sliding glass door, and together they watched Buster wolf down the last of the steak.

"Well," Riley said with a sigh. "There goes dinner. Looks like we hit the steak house in town."

Hunter pulled open the refrigerator door. "I'll defrost something else. How about burgers?"

Riley moved to the breakfast bar, resting his elbows on the counter. He gave his friend a sharp look. "How 'bout telling me what the hell's going on? Who was she?"

Hunter kept his eyes on the inside of the freezer on the pretense of surveying its contents. "I told you. A news hound. Some reporter from a Miami rag looking for a story."

"So why not just give it to her? Send her away happy."

Withdrawing a package of hamburger, Hunter slipped it onto a plate. "Because the man she's looking for doesn't exist anymore."

"You sure about that?" Riley asked quietly.

"Watch it, Kincaid."

Their gazes collided at last, and Hunter's was the first to skitter away. The reporter's arrival had annoyed him, even worried him a little. Did she know anything about Braddock's visit yesterday? The Mark I kit with its six autoinjectors that sat on his desk in the study?

Ah, hell, he'd thought he was done with the past, but this woman's appearance meant there were still people out there who wanted a piece of him.

His grip tightened on the edge of the sink. Realizing Riley was still watching him, Hunter concentrated on the two cold beer bottles perspiring on the counter. "The beer's getting warm and we're missing the game."

Riley took one of the bottles Hunt offered, but made no move toward the living room. Instead, he said, "You going to tell me who that guy was who came to the shop yesterday?"

Four years ago, when everything had gone to hell, Riley had been in Tenerife, managing a marina for a high-class resort. He'd never seen Ken Braddock take the stand, never seen the man swear to tell the whole truth. Never seen the man lie to Congressman Westover and the rest of his cronies on Capitol Hill. It should have been easy to manufacture a small lie for his friend's benefit. But he couldn't do it. Not with Riley, who knew him so well. "You don't believe he was a fisherman?"

"Yeah, and I'm the Queen Mother." They both smiled at that, then Riley gave him a worried look. "We've been friends too many years to beat around the bush, Hunt. Just how long are you going to hide out here?"

Absently, Hunter ran his finger down the side of the beer bottle, slicking off beads of cold moisture. He'd known Riley Kincaid since high school, but there were demons from the past he couldn't share with him. Not yet. Maybe not ever.

"I'm not hiding out."

"The Hunt Garrett I knew wouldn't have been afraid to go into town for a lousy steak dinner."

He flashed Riley a warning scowl. "Leave it alone, Rile."

Before Riley could reply, Hunter retreated to the living room and flipped on the television. Settling into one of the overstuffed chairs, he took a healthy swallow of beer and parked his feet up on the coffee table. From the corner of his eye he saw Riley follow his example and hoped he would take the hint that the previous topic of conversation was closed.

Ten minutes later, the baseball game went to a commercial.

"She was good-looking," Riley remarked suddenly. "Did you notice?"

Yeah, he'd noticed. Reporters were supposed to wear baggy, lived-in clothes and fedoras. They had fingers stained yellow from chain-smoking and possessed names like Scoop and Ace, not a ridiculously old-fashioned name like Alexandria. And with all that wavy, dark hair and those long legs, she'd made him want to forget just who she was and what she might want from him.

"I said—"

"I noticed," Hunter grudgingly acknowledged.

Riley huffed out a wistful sigh. "Yep. Lois Lane with a set of great legs. I wouldn't mind giving her *my* story."

Annoyance surged through Hunter. He squinted into the dark glass of the beer bottle. "Too bad you're boring as hell."

Riley laughed. "If she ever shows up again—"

"She won't."

"If she does, what are you going to do?" He glanced out the sliding glass door. Buster lay dog-dreaming in the sand. "I don't think Buster's got another bark in him."

"Then I'll get a real Doberman," Hunter Garrett growled.

CHAPTER TWO

YOU'D THINK a biologist would have an interest in keeping his yard nice, Alex thought sourly.

Garrett's lawn had more sand than grass, and a good amount of it had gotten trapped in her new pumps as she'd beaten a hasty retreat. She sat on the hotel bed and knocked a tiny sand dune from her shoes into the trash can, dissecting this first sorry contact with Hunter Garrett.

She hated to think of the amusement her family would have derived from today's pitiful attempt. It had always been a big source of family pride that *nothing* stood between a Sutton and the story they went after.

The threat of an attack dog? They would have laughed themselves sick.

She blew the last particles of sand from her shoe, tossed it across the room, then settled back on the bed.

I should have checked out the dog. It could have been a poodle. No, she amended that thought with a frown. Those barks hadn't come from anything that small, and Garrett didn't look the poodle type.

In fact, the man didn't look anything like she'd expected. In spite of his credentials as a scientist, she had thought he'd resemble something of a loser, a naive idiot who'd taken on big government and been foolish enough to think he could win.

Or a kook. After he'd been discredited, he'd carried the banner for enough weird environmental causes to get him branded as one. But once you got past the cynical twist of his mouth and the mistrust in his eyes, Hunter Garrett looked almost . . . normal.

No, better than normal, Alex admitted. That wide chest emphasized by the snug T-shirt he wore. The outline of powerful, athletic thighs so obvious in those well-worn jeans. When he wasn't telling her to get lost, that rich, baritone voice had made the nerves under her skin dance.

He had also made her angry. Ernie expected a story. But more than that, *she* needed it, if only to prove to herself she had what it took to be a hard-boiled reporter.

Since graduating from college eight years ago, she'd tried hard to fit the pattern of the life mapped out for her from birth. She'd started at the bottom at her father's newspaper, doing her best to become a journalist worthy of the Sutton name. She'd even become engaged to the city editor, a man of her parents' choosing.

But the newspaper ink that flowed so strongly through their veins had evidently diluted to anemic proportions in hers. She didn't care about scooping the competition. She didn't want to be hard-hitting or ruthlessly ambitious. As a result, her pieces had lacked punch, her interviews had revealed no surprises and her articles had been relegated to that wasteland every reporter dreaded, the inside pages of the local section.

Convinced that the Suttons' badgering had played an important part in her inability to focus, she'd quit her job, broken her engagement and taken a position with the Miami paper. She needed to prove to herself she could succeed without her family's interference or help. And maybe, once she garnered a reputation here, she'd feel better about turning her back on the profession and pursue the career she'd always dreamed of.

After college, the hopes she'd had for a full-time writing career had gotten sidetracked somehow, lost in the crush of meeting newspaper deadlines and chasing leads. Oh, she still dabbled with hazy, convoluted plots that might shape up into the "great American novel" someday. And she continued to fill her notebook with snatches of verse, character sketches, ideas for short stories. But she'd never actually submitted something to a publisher, and as time passed she wondered if she would ever find the courage to do so.

Her family had warned her years ago—the writing game was for dreamers. Tough to break into, hard to make a living at and not nearly as honorable a profession as honest, hard-hitting journalism.

Someday I'll find out. Someday I'll take that leap of faith and see if I've got what it takes.

But not today, Alex thought with a resigned sigh as she rolled to pull the file on Hunter Garrett off the nightstand. Today she had to figure out some way to get one surly ex-biologist to talk to her.

She flipped through the sequence of pictures again. The biologist receiving an award. A still taken on the

courthouse steps after he'd testified against Cavanaugh Laboratories. A photograph of Garrett being
led away in handcuffs after an environmental protest
had apparently gotten out of hand. Within a short
time, the man had gone from serious-minded scientist to flamboyant activist to surly recluse.

One particular shot caught her interest: Hunter
Garrett and his wife standing arm-in-arm at some
company banquet. In a classy black dress and up-
swept hairstyle, Julie Garrett had the kind of cover
model looks that any woman would envy—tall, blond
and beautiful. And brainy, too, Alex mentally added,
remembering reading how the two scientists had
worked as a team.

In the picture, Julie Garrett's eyes were full of love
for her husband, and their hands were entwined. Alex
frowned down at the image. Why had this woman de-
fected when the going got tough? She didn't look the
type.

And yet she must have, because in all that had happened four years ago and since, she'd never appeared
at Hunter Garrett's side again. She was Norwegian by
birth, coming to the United States to attend college
and meeting Garrett shortly after her arrival. According to the information Alex had pulled off the computer, it had been widely rumored that she'd returned
to her home country in embarrassment over her husband's behavior. But when questioned, Garrett would
neither confirm nor deny that story.

Alex studied one of the close-ups. There was little
resemblance between this man and the one she'd met
today. The camera had been kinder to him four years

ago. His hair still looked as though fingers of liquid sunshine had been raked through it, but it was too long now. He was leaner, too. And in those brief moments before he'd shut the door in her face, she'd sensed a tightly coiled tension and iron control.

It was the eyes that had suffered the most, she decided. In the photograph, there'd been indications of ready humor in laugh lines around those pale blue eyes, but they weren't there anymore. Today, the granite hardness of the man's jaw had mocked their existence. Wariness and a piercing mistrust were all that remained.

Ernie was right. Hunter Garrett was an enigma waiting to be solved. There had to be a story here.

To her brothers, Garrett's attitude would have trumpeted a challenge they couldn't resist. They would have dogged his steps and invaded his world until he had no choice but to acknowledge their presence. By now, they would have gathered enough information to fill a book.

Alex plumped the pillows under her head. Follow their example, that's what she had to do. Get in his face. Drive him crazy. Sooner or later, he'd have to give her *something*.

If only to get her out of his life.

PLAGUED BY restlessness, Hunter couldn't sleep that night. He rose with a resigned sigh, made himself a cup of coffee and drifted into the study. Slouched in the chair behind the cherry-wood desk, he scrubbed his face with one hand, massaging eyelids that felt grainy and swollen. A lock of hair slipped across his forehead and he shoved it back in annoyance. To-morrow—no, today—he'd have to make a stop at the barbershop.

In front of him, the Mark I autoinjector kit sat squarely in the middle of his desk blotter. Unflinch-ing illumination poured down on it from the goose-neck lamp.

He shouldn't have brought it home, didn't even want the damned thing in the house. Not that it mat-tered much. He'd already made up his mind. Brad-dock would have to find someone else willing to help him cleanse his soul and take on the Cavanaughs.

He cocked his head, examining the kit from vari-ous directions without actually touching it. They'd changed the catch. And this model was sleeker, smaller than the one he'd worked on at the lab. What else had been altered? he wondered.

With one finger he popped off the top.

The injector barrels had been streamlined, too. It was obvious someone had decided that the units needed to be more compact if they were actually go-ing to be carried by soldiers out in the field.

Funny what a little thing like a war could do for re-search money. Let a desert despot threaten to use "the poor man's atom bomb" on U.S. soldiers, and sud-denly the sky was the limit. This kit, and its six life-saving hypos, was about as efficiently put together as the government could manage.

It might be what was *inside* the injectors that wasn't so perfect.

Hunter snapped down the lid. That wasn't his problem anymore. He was tired. He'd given up playing defender of the faith, champion of lost causes. All his energy for that sort of fight had gone out of him like the flames of a neglected bonfire. If he had salvaged one lesson from the whole sorry episode years ago, it was that he'd finally learned the art of going with the flow.

Such knowledge hadn't come easy. In his naiveté he'd thought the Whistle Blower's Act would protect him. But when he'd filed suit against his own company, accusing them of diluting their nerve gas vaccine, Charlie Cavanaugh had struck back, and struck back *hard*.

The smear campaign against Hunter had been swift, ruthless and effective. So effective that afterward he'd been left with little of his former life intact. No family. No career. No respect.

All of it gone.

Forever.

Abruptly, he stood and snapped off the light, plunging the room into total darkness. He wasn't going to put himself through any of that again. Not for Ken Braddock or Leo Isaacson or the great and mighty United States of America.

Nothing in his life was worth that kind of risk anymore.

HE SPOTTED Alexandria Sutton the moment he came out of the barbershop.

She wasn't the kind of woman a man easily forgot. With that halo of chestnut hair surrounding her face like the softest silk, and those wonderfully long legs, there was a certain endearing prettiness about the woman that made her stand out in a crowd.

She lounged against the rental car he'd seen yesterday. As he approached, she uncrossed her arms and pushed away from it. The movement pulled at her blouse, making him very aware of her femininity.

He didn't like that awareness. His interest shouldn't be captured by someone who posed such a threat to the calm, peaceful existence he wanted so badly.

Hunter's hands balled into fists as he expelled a harsh sound of disbelief. His features formed a hard, unrelenting mask meant to intimidate her and yank his own wandering interest back in line.

She responded with an unperturbed smile that irritated the hell out of him.

When only a few inches separated them, Alex Sutton moved to circle him as though viewing a piece of sculpture in an art gallery. Her expressive brown eyes sparkled. "I like it," she stated, seeming to give his haircut serious consideration. "Definitely an improvement."

"Miss Sutton—"

"Call me Alex."

"I don't intend to get to know you well enough to call you Alex. Miss Sutton, I thought I made myself pretty clear yesterday."

"You did. Where's Killer?"

"Who?"

One silky eyebrow tugged upward. "You know, your big, bad Doberman."

Two could play this game. He dug up a smile full of malevolent pleasure and predatory menace. "I left him home studying a picture of you. For the next time you trespass.''

She laughed, and he discovered he liked the rich, full-throated sound of it. He also liked the crisp inflections of her New England accent. Nothing girlish or artificial about her voice. He frowned, suddenly remembering that he shouldn't find anything about this woman enjoyable or entertaining.

''What are you doing here?'' he asked.

''I want a story, Mr. Garrett. A few opinions. That's all.''

With a weary sigh, he shook his head. His truck was parked beside her car, and he moved past her to grasp the door handle. Before he got inside, he favored her with a disgusted look over the hood. ''You're wasting your time. And mine.''

A wayward summer breeze lifted a lock of her hair and she swiped it back from her face with one hand. ''I don't think so.''

He shrugged. ''Suit yourself.''

Seconds later, he pulled out of the parking lot and drove away.

He ran into her again when he stopped at the sporting goods store. It surprised him to turn up an aisle and find her planted firmly in front of the fishing tackle. She offered a vague smile and asked if he was ready to talk yet. With a glare, he paid for his purchase and left, so aggravated that he forgot the bait box.

The next day, he wheeled his shopping cart through the grocery store and discovered her standing in front of a beer display. His irritation threatened to rev into overdrive.

He didn't like being followed, and he wouldn't be forced into altering his life just to avoid one pesky reporter. With the trip to Eric's Island planned for first light, there were still a dozen errands to run. He was determined to finish them whether Alex Sutton accompanied him or not.

With an attitude of nonchalance, he rested his arms on the cart's handlebar. She held a plastic basket and turned that same innocent smile on him he'd seen in front of the barbershop and in amongst the fishing tackle at the sporting goods store.

He tried to give her a look that said these sudden appearances in his life didn't throw him off stride. "Well, well, Miss Sutton. Fancy meeting you here."

"A girl's got to eat, Mr. Garrett."

He threw a look at the empty basket dangling from the crook of her arm. "But not much, from the looks of it."

"I'm just getting started."

"Shop here often?"

"Do you?" she retorted.

"Almost never."

She shrugged. "Then I doubt if I will, either."

Her gaze slid down to the contents of his shopping cart, settling on a package of cheese balls. "You shouldn't eat those," she advised. "High in cholesterol."

"I like to live dangerously."

Her dark eyes skipped back to his, full of a reporter's inquisitiveness. "Really? How dangerously?"

"If you've done your homework," he answered in a gruff tone, "you'll know everything that's been printed about me."

"It's the things that haven't been printed about you that I want to know."

"Sorry. Like I said, you're wasting your time."

He wheeled the cart into the next aisle, pulling items off the shelf without much thought. It was no surprise when he turned to find the Sutton woman standing right behind him.

"Are you planning a trip, Mr. Garrett?" Alex asked suddenly.

He kept his expression unfathomable, but the question threw him. How could she know he planned to spend a week on Eric's Island? No one but Riley knew, and his friend wouldn't have said a word about Hunter's private retreat. In a carefully neutral voice, he said, "Why do you ask?"

She retrieved two items from his cart. "Travel-size deodorant and toothpaste, a dead giveaway."

Irritated by how easily she was on to him, he reached beyond her to whisk a huge package of condoms from the shelf. "You're absolutely right, Miss Sutton. I've got one heck of a weekend planned." He held up the package for her to see, giving her a leering grin. "And I'm hoping to get lucky, if you know what I mean."

If he had hoped to shock her, he was disappointed. She only stared at him mildly and cocked her head to one side. "I talked to the manager of the sporting goods store. Seems he's known you a long time, and you only buy new lures when you're going to do some fishing.''

He met the quizzical entreaty in her eyes with flat disinterest. "Looks to me like you're on your own fishing expedition.''

Her mouth lifted. "A simple yes or no will suffice."

Forcing his hands to loosen their death grip on the shopping-cart handle, he moved past her. He caught the clean, flowery scent of the perfume she wore as he concentrated on rearranging the items in his cart.

"Am I making you nervous?" she asked.

He shook his head. "This isn't going to work, you know."

"What's that?"

"You can't follow me around forever."

"Not forever. Just until I get what I want."

He faced her then, his mouth set in harsh lines that were replayed by the look in his eyes. "Lady, do you even *know* what you want?"

"A story, Mr. Garrett."

"There isn't one to give you."

"I think there is." Determination made her voice hard.

He had to give her credit. She had the tenacity of a bulldog. If he hadn't been so annoyed, he might have been more impressed. Instead, he gave her one last cold look, wheeled the cart around and headed for the check-out stand.

She followed him to the bank and to the cleaners. She wasn't sneaky about it, and, refusing to give her the pleasure of knowing she was getting to him,

Hunter didn't try to lose her with evasive driving maneuvers. If she wanted to waste her time by watching him take care of the most mundane errands imaginable, that was her prerogative. Soon enough she'd get bored with this game and give up.

He thought she'd done just that when he stopped at Riley's marina to check on the boat. No little white car pulled in behind his. No long-legged female blocked his path.

He found Riley down at one of the dry-storage barns, pulling the *Lady Jewel* off the rack in preparation for tomorrow's trip. All around him were floating docks where sleek yachts and trim sailboats dipped and curtsied in their berths. Hunter's own boat fit somewhere in between, not showy or fast, just practical.

The breeze ruffled his hair and brought with it the familiar odors of boat oil and fish. The huge, aluminum barns held at least a hundred vessels, stacked into slots three high, like books on a bookshelf.

He thought back to the day he and Julie had picked out the cruiser. He had insisted it be christened after his nickname for her and vividly remembered how she'd blushed and protested, embarrassed by such an obvious expression of his love. But he'd known her well enough to know she was secretly pleased, as well.

He had to swallow around a lump of discomfort at the memory. Tomorrow would be the first time in nine months he'd put the *Lady Jewel* in water. The last time he'd used it had been disastrous. He'd nearly lost the boat *and* his life.

Riley grinned a welcome. "She's all set, Hunt."

"Looks good," Hunter replied, his eyes surveying the boat, stopping briefly on the patch job where nine months ago a fair-size hole had been punched in the fiberglass hull. "You can hardly tell where the damage was."

"I hope you learned your lesson. Don't mess with shrimp-boat captains with attitude. A few inches either way and all the gel-coating in the world wouldn't have helped her. You were lucky."

"Yeah," Hunter muttered, remembering that night. "Lucky."

"Why don't you think about selling her? You've gotten your money's worth."

"No." Afraid the rejection had sounded too abrupt, Hunter changed the subject. "Are you ready for the weekend?"

"Just about. I've still got to make arrangements for someone to baby-sit Buster. But I should get over to the island Saturday afternoon at the latest. Think you can manage a few days without me?"

Hunter grinned. "I'll try not to catch all the snook."

"Man, my first weekend off in six months. I'm looking forward to it."

"I am, too, Rile." After a short pause, Hunter added, "It's been too long."

Riley vaulted to the floating dock to stand in front of his friend. "It sure has."

"The fishing ought to be—" Hunter broke off with a low curse, his gaze drawn past Riley. "I don't believe it!"

"What's the matter?"

With a vehement shake of his head, he muttered, "I've had it with you, lady."

Riley turned. "Well, if it isn't Lois Lane."

"Stay here," Hunter commanded. "I'm going to put an end to this, once and for all."

THE LOOK IN HIS EYES made Alex more nervous than she already was.

She didn't like being around this much water. Her fear of it only reminded her of another glaring difference between herself and the rest of her family. The Suttons had always owned big, beautiful boats and considered yachting second nature. She, on the other hand, couldn't swim a stroke and sickness threatened every time she boarded even the most seaworthy vessel.

She had stopped midway down the dock, letting Hunter come to her. He probably thought she'd done so simply to be perverse, but the truth was, she didn't think she had the courage to walk that narrow strip that ran across the water.

He surprised her. Instead of stopping, he moved past, latching his fingers around her wrist at the last minute with just enough force to make resistance foolish. Pulling her along so that she had to hurry to keep up with his long-legged stride, he didn't halt until they'd reached the shady inside of one of the storage barns, where he pinioned her against the aluminum wall, one arm on either side of her body.

The building was deserted and the water lapped too close, but the only thing Alex was aware of was Hunter

Garrett's blue eyes. They sparkled with cold, piercing lights.

"Enough is enough," he said tightly. "What do I have to do to get you out of my hair?"

"I think you know the answer to that."

The grim line of his mouth tightened. "No."

She shrugged and with forced nonchalance said, "Then it looks like we'll be playing me and my shadow for quite some time."

"I don't play games, lady." He expelled a disgusted breath, dropped his head and remained silent for a long moment. When he lifted his eyes again, the fire in them had banked a little, replaced by an emptiness she suspected he'd deliberately called into play. "Why are you doing this?"

This calm, chilling query with its underlying trace of bewilderment slipped past Alex's defenses and shook her far more than his anger. Despite her best efforts to the contrary, guilt seared her. "It's nothing personal, Mr. Garrett. It's my job. People want to know—"

"Your readers?" He swore in disbelief. "No one's interested in my opinion anymore."

"My editor thinks differently."

"Your editor thinks wrong."

"I wouldn't expect you to agree with him."

His eyes searched hers, and she witnessed the lacerating contempt in his gaze. "What is it that you want? Are you so low on the assignment totem pole that all they'll give you is a story about a washed-up biologist who once was stupid enough to think he could make a difference? What's next for you? A story about Elvis working in a New Jersey doughnut shop?''

Remembering that one of her brothers had once stared down an angry Texas senator with a loaded shotgun, her chin lifted in defiance. ''You don't know anything at all about my ability.''

''You're no different than the rest. You want to make a name for yourself, and you've decided I can help you do that.''

''That's not true!'' she objected, but the accusation was a twisted truth, close enough that she slid her eyes away from his, settling her gaze on a nearby cruiser.

''Isn't it? So how come you're having such trouble meeting my eyes, Alexandria Sutton?'' He laughed without humor, and her gaze swung back to his. For the briefest moment, she thought she saw the warm glow of sympathy in his eyes. ''Thank God,'' he said. ''There must be *some* glimmer of conscience left in you, if the truth can still make you look so uncomfortable.''

She resented his attitude, and her awareness of the harsh, angular cut of his features. ''I'm uncomfortable because I'm not used to having men strong-arm me in broad daylight.''

''Isn't this what you want, Miss Sutton?'' The words held a ring of ancient bitterness. He cocked his head to one side, assessing her idly. ''Wouldn't you like to see the raving maniac you've read so much about? Maybe a little foaming-at-the-mouth routine left over from my activist days?'' One of his hands suddenly pounded the wall beside her head, making the aluminum respond with a hollow echo. She flinched, and ripples of uneasiness spread through her. With a wild-eyed grin, he said, "Think of the papers you could sell."

He was trying to frighten her. Foolish pride forced her voice to remain steady. "With Dr. Isaacson's pending lawsuit and death such a mystery right now, my only interest is in writing a truthful follow-up to what you claimed years ago."

His mouth thinned and hardened. "You can't be that naive. An editor wouldn't accept that."

"My editor isn't after sensationalism, and neither am I."

"A purist in search of truth? No ulterior motives for following me?"

"None."

Hunter grinned. "You're a lousy liar, lady." He tilted his head back, searching the cavernous barn as though answers were written on the exposed steel beams. Almost to himself, he said, "Hell, maybe you're not even a reporter."

She started to speak, but his gaze raked hers again. The sudden, nasty gleam in his eyes roamed her features until it threatened to shatter Alex's hard-won courage.

"What are you? An environmentalist looking for help? If you're in the market for a champion, princess, I'm fresh out of lances to tilt at windmills."

"I'm not—"

"Money," he accused, his hard tone relentless. "Do you think there's some way I can be blackmailed? I'm afraid my life was too much of an open book to give you much hope there.''

"That's ridiculous,'' she said, thoroughly disgusted and beginning to lose patience.

"Okay. So maybe you're looking for sex. Has all this harassment been some sort of weird come-on? You want a little fun in the sack with someone who used to be famous?''

Astonishment made her momentarily speechless. She glared at him. "Don't flatter yourself, Mr. Garrett. You weren't *that* famous.''

"There've been women who wanted to drop into my bed just for the chance to get their names in the paper.''

"I hope they've found a good psychiatrist by now.''

His smile widened, a provocative, wicked grin of dazzling whiteness. "You don't find me attractive?''

"Your sex appeal ranks even lower than your manners.''

"Maybe we should give it a try.'' His eyes had shaded to sapphire. "We might discover something we both like.''

Alex shoved at one of his arms, finding it frustratingly solid. Beginning to lose her temper, she snapped, "The only thing I'd like is for you to let me out of here. I've had enough—''

"So have I.'' His eyes fell to her bottom lip as though mesmerized. "I don't know who you are,'' he said in a hoarse, ragged whisper, "but you have the sweetest-looking mouth, Alex Sutton.''

Her chaotic, rambling thoughts recognized that he intended to kiss her. Grasping the tattered edges of sanity, she turned her head aside quickly. Desperate for any conversation to keep him from fulfilling the promise in his eyes, she said, "I thought you weren't going to get to know me well enough to use my first name."

A subtle play of emotions crossed his features, then the strong arms that held her dropped away suddenly as Hunter stepped back. In the next moment, the cold, unyielding light returned to his eyes.

"You're right," he said in brittle agreement. "And you'll have to do better than kisses if you want a story."

She felt a flush of angry humiliation stain her cheeks. "If you're implying that I'd be willing to trade sex for an interview—"

"It wouldn't be the first time I've had an offer like that."

Alex's hair had tumbled forward, soft filaments of chestnut escaping the colorful scarf she'd tied at the base of her neck. Hunter's fingers reached out to tuck a wayward curl behind her ear, but she batted his hand away. "Touch me again, and your next interview will be from a hospital bed."

Sweeping past him, Alex strode out of the shadowy barn and down the concrete docks. Angry and embarrassed, she forgot to be fearful of the water lapping gently against the ribbons of concrete.

Hunter watched her go, listening to the sound of her footsteps echo off the water as she hurried down the dock. She fumbled for her car keys, then jammed one into the lock of the white sedan as though she were a fencer thrusting a rapier into an opponent's heart. A moment later, Alex had slammed the car door behind her and spun out of the lot.

She didn't look back.

He didn't expect her to.

"So long, Lois Lane," he muttered.

Mission accomplished, he thought, and wondered why the idea of getting Alexandria Sutton out of his hair for good didn't have a better feel to it. Maybe it was that tempting, soft mouth of hers. And those lively, trusting brown eyes.

His jaw clenched. It annoyed him that a woman he'd met only a handful of times could imprint so clear a memory.

He realized suddenly that Riley was standing beside him. He turned toward his friend, frowning. "Did you say something?"

"Yeah. About five minutes ago," Riley replied with a grin. "I said, what did you do to have her hightailing it out of here like that?"

Hunter shrugged, as though what had passed between them was of the smallest importance. "We had a talk. I think that's the last I'll see of her."

"A talk! She was moving faster than a fox being chased by a pack of hunting dogs."

"I think she got more than she bargained for." His chuckle carried traces of smug triumph as he waggled his eyebrows and growled in mock menace. "I gave her a glimpse of the madman she came to find."

Riley's own eyebrows lifted. "So what's your problem?"

"What do you mean?" Hunter asked with a scowl.

"Well," Riley replied, flashing a superior smile, "if you're the winner of that little confrontation, how come you're the one who looks like a beaver with a sore tooth?"

CHAPTER THREE

SOMEWHERE BETWEEN the marina parking lot and the second traffic light, Alex realized she'd been had—manipulated by an expert.

Hunter Garrett wanted her to leave him alone, and he'd found the perfect way to ensure that. By using her own emotions and uncertainty against her, he'd driven her off, so rattled she'd almost forgotten why she wanted to talk to him in the first place. She'd played right into his hands.

By the time she reached her hotel room, she was furious. The cheap Monet reproductions on the wall behind the bed canted out of alignment as she slammed the door. Kicking off her shoes, she threw herself on the bed, and sifted through the contents of her oversize purse until she found her pad and pencil.

The problem still remained: how to get Hunter Garrett to talk.

She spent the morning scribbling notes as she reevaluated his actions the last two days. For a man who shunned the public, the biologist had made a lot of trips into town lately. Alex felt certain her guess in the supermarket had been correct. A trip was in the offing. But where? And when? Someone must know. Who would Garrett trust with that information?

She went through her notes and pictures again. In most of the photographs, he appeared to be accompanied only by his attorney. But she did spot a familiar face in a picture of him taken a year ago. After a botched attempt to free a captive dolphin from a pond in back of a real-estate office, Garrett had spent the night behind bars. As the activist reached the bottom steps of the county jail, the photographer had snapped his picture.

Standing right beside Hunter, obviously angry and concerned, referred to as a "longtime friend," was the man who had posted bail.

Riley Kincaid.

SINCE HIS BROTHER'S death, Richie Cavanaugh had worked for Cavanaugh Laboratories as his father's right-hand man. He was a vice president of the company, had a corner office all to himself and a secretary who'd been chosen for her great legs rather than her typing ability. His father introduced him to business associates as his company "troubleshooter," but that was just to save face. Richie knew his place in the company and in Charles Cavanaugh's life. When it came right down to it—he was nothing more than a toadie to the old man.

That was all right. He'd learned to live with that distinction a long time ago. What he could not accept was the idea that this latest mess might get him pegged as a murderer. Which he wasn't. No way. A victim, maybe. Or a slave to his father's greed and ambition. But certainly not a cold-blooded killer.

Isaacson had been an accident. A horrible miscalculation that should never have happened.

He'd tried desperately to explain that to his father, but Charles Cavanaugh wasn't a man partial to long explanations. In the end, Richie had stood in front of the old man, sobbing like a damned baby and sweatdamp with fear that the D.C. police would be pounding on his door at any moment, ready to cart him off to jail.

They hadn't, but Richie didn't fool himself that it was because he'd been particularly clever in making Isaacson's death look like suicide. The truth was, after the biochemist tumbled out the window, the note Richie had left in the typewriter in the man's office had been a pitifully flimsy attempt to cover his tracks.

Now this latest development meant that people were beginning to ask questions. Standing in front of a bank of telephones in the hotel lobby, Richie Cavanaugh had to take a couple of fortifying breaths before he could drum up the courage to make the call to his father.

The old man would have a coronary about the arrival of this Sutton woman. There'd be a lot of swearing involved, blistering criticism, then the inevitable mention of his older brother, Lyle—Richie suffering by comparison, of course, because the only thing patriotic, idealistic Lyle had ever done wrong in his whole life was be stupid enough to enlist in the service and get himself killed.

When his father's fury finally wound down, he'd give Richie orders, and Richie would do his best to carry them out, because that was what he always did, hoping that his father would someday realize that he still had one son left. That life hadn't ended on the dreary, black day the army had come to tell him about Lyle.

Richie punched in the number, dread building in the pit of his stomach. He winced as the phone rang once and then was snatched up, as though his father had been sitting beside the telephone, waiting.

"Where are you?" the old man demanded.

"The Winddrift Hotel, north end of Fort Myers Beach."

"What are you doing there? You're supposed to be watching Garrett. If Ken's got that S.O.B. worked up again and he's going to make trouble, I told you I want to know about it."

The desk clerk Richie had just bribed for information glanced his way, and Richie turned his back into the phone. "He's not doing anything but running a bunch of errands. But I think you should know, Pop, I'm not the only one tailing him. There's a woman reporter in town from Miami."

"Jesus, Joseph and Mary. Have they met?"

"Yes, but they don't seem on friendly terms."

"That doesn't mean he won't spill his guts to her."

"What do you want me to do?"

Charlie Cavanaugh let loose a string of vicious curses. "Do I have to do all the thinking in this family? How could you have made this latest mess, Richard? You never cease to disappoint me."

Richie hardly reacted to that kind of debasement anymore, for this was the basis of their relationship now. He'd made up his mind he wasn't going to humiliate himself with any further pursuit of Charlie Cavanaugh's approval. And yet, when he spoke, he still had to tame the anxious tremor in his voice. "I swear, there wasn't anything I could do to stop Isaacson from going out that window. I just thought I could scare him into dropping the idea of a lawsuit. We were struggling and he fell . . ."

"You couldn't fend off an old man with a history of heart problems? Lyle would have found a way to control the situation."

"I did the best I could to make it look like suicide." The words stumbled lamely from his tongue. "The cops may stick with that."

"Richard, the cops in D.C. aren't *all* stupid. The fact that this woman reporter is trying to get a story out of Garrett may mean someone's already made the connection between his claim four years ago and Isaacson's press announcement that he intended to file suit against a government contractor. Add to that your dear brother-in-law's visit to Garrett, and we've got a lot of exposure here." He heaved an exasperated sigh, and after a long moment, added, "I've had Isaacson's place here turned upside down. Have you searched Garrett's house like I told you?"

"I haven't found a way in yet."

"Holy Mother, what are you waiting for—an invitation! You get in there and see if Isaacson or Ken gave him anything concrete that Garrett can show the authorities. He's not going to take up where Isaacson left off. We can't afford another investigation like the last one."

"And if I find anything?"

There was a silence from the old man's end of the conversation. Richie had a feeling now that was very much like panic, something to be held down for fear it might make a fool of him in front of his father.

"Then we'll deal with the problem—once and for all."

Fear flowered in Richie's gut. He didn't know what his father meant by "dealing" with the problem, but he had a healthy imagination and he didn't like the sound of it. "Pop, maybe it's time to rethink this. I could hop a plane out of the country. Lie low—"

"And leave your father to face a senate investigation." The words cracked across Richie's proposal like a whiplash. "I would expect that from you. What's happened to this family? I have a traitor for a son-in-law and a spineless jellyfish for a son. Lyle would—"

"Lyle's dead," Richie dared to state.

"Do you think I don't remember that every day of my life, Richard?" Charles said with quiet force. "The army took Lyle away from me forever. But I've made them pay for that, haven't I?"

Before fear could get him firmly by the throat, Richie said, "Nothing's going to bring him back. Why can't you accept that?"

"I'll never accept what the army did. Never. And Lyle would never have questioned my judgment."

"I'm not questioning—"

"Then find out what Garrett and that reporter are up to. And I'd better not read about it in the morning papers."

"But, Pop—"

"I want them stopped," Charlie Cavanaugh's voice hissed across the telephone line. There was a short, pungent silence. "Do you understand me, Richard?"

Ripples of uneasiness cramped his innards. Yes, he thought he did understand what his father wanted from him. He understood far too well.

IT PROVED to be a great day to start a fishing trip. In the marina, sea gulls sat on rocking-chair waves as a gentle breeze ruffled the water. The early-morning air felt fresh and sharp. It was the kind of day Julie would have loved, Hunter thought.

"You're sure you've got everything?" Riley asked for the third time. He shifted the weight of the cooler so he could maneuver down the steps to the *Lady Jewel*.

Hunter inclined his head toward the enormous box of groceries he toted in front of him. "Doesn't it look like it?"

"Beer?"

"Yeah."

"Tackle box?"

"Yeah."

"Our special cheese balls?"

"They're high in cholesterol, you know."

"Since when do you care?"

"I don't," Hunter replied with a shrug, but he couldn't help smiling a little, remembering who'd furnished that information. He wondered if Alex Sutton had returned to Miami yet, and just how she'd explain to her editor that all she'd learned about

Hunter Garrett was his predilection for junk food. "A lady just pointed that out to me recently."

Riley threw him a worried look. "Did you bring them or not?"

"Relax. They're in here."

The *Lady Jewel* bobbed placidly against pilings decked out in barnacle stockings. Hunter jumped aboard, then began stowing away the last of the supplies. His hand stumbled over the box of condoms that he'd forgotten to take out of the grocery bags.

Spotting the package, Riley frowned at him. "What are you going to do with those?"

"Jeez, Rile, how long has it been since you've had a date?"

"Not nearly as long as it's been for you," his friend retorted. "So what are you doing with them?"

Hunter grimaced. "They must have gotten in my bag by mistake. Okay? Anything else you're worried about, Mom?"

"Nope. Oh, did you pick up the new lures?"

"Got 'em. If I've forgotten anything, I'll call you on the radio. You can bring it over on Saturday."

"I just want to make sure we've got everything."

"It's an island, not the moon."

"Might as well be, since we'll be the only two people on it."

"You're going to love the quiet."

Riley removed the bowline from the anchor cleat, looped it several times in his hands, then tossed it to Hunter. "I just remember the last time I stayed at the stilt house. No running water, no electricity, and the mosquitoes nearly ate me alive. It was like being at scout camp and watching it rain all week. I'd have come back early except Julie and Eric would never have let me live it down.''

''Yeah,'' Hunter said with a light laugh. ''They gave you a pretty hard time.''

Eric's imitation of Riley slapping away mosquitoes had been particularly on target, and for the sake of friendship, Hunter had been forced to play the stern parent and order his son to have more respect for his elders.

He frowned down at the coil of nylon rope in his hands. All that seemed so long ago. Yet the memory of him and Julie and Eric seated around the dining-room table, the sound of their laughter mingling like harmonious chords, remained clearly etched in his mind.

He was aware of Riley watching him, waiting for him to cast off. To cover the awkward silence, he said, ''I've put in a generator since you were there last.''

''Ah. All the comforts of home.''

''It suits me just fine, and you'll manage.''

Riley suddenly bent down, catching the side of the cruiser to keep it from drifting farther away. His eyes were filled with an unexpected intensity. ''Listen, Hunt, if you change your mind and decide you'd rather have the whole week to yourself, I'll understand. Call me on the radio.''

The offer caught Hunter by surprise. What had generated this suggestion? ''Are you trying to weasel out of coming over?''

''No. I'm just saying it won't upset me if you want the privacy.'' He looked oddly uncomfortable.

"Friends just want to do what's best for one another. That's all."

Hunter felt completely at a loss to understand Riley's sudden, uncharacteristic behavior. He shook his head, and switched on the cruiser's motor. When the noise from the outboard died down, he said, "Don't go getting weird on me, Kincaid. I'll see you Saturday."

ALEX STIFLED a sleepy yawn, then slid closer to the inside edge of the captain's chair. Though her family would have considered the wide swells of the Gulf too puny to be called waves, her stomach lurched every time she glanced over the side into the blue-green water.

She decided even her brothers would have been impressed by her determination to get this interview.

Yesterday's meeting with Riley Kincaid had been tough, and for a while she'd feared nothing would come of it. She'd had to call into play every one of her brothers' techniques, but after endless badgering and the use of a fair share of feminine wiles, she had finally convinced Kincaid she meant Hunter Garrett no harm.

The marina owner's concern for his friend was touchingly genuine, and Alex quickly realized that Kincaid was more concerned about the man's future than his past. When she explained that her contact with Garrett thus far had been more confrontational than communicative, Kincaid seemed to find that fact extremely interesting and even positive.

With dire predictions that he would pay dearly for giving away the information, he had told Alex about the week Hunter planned to spend on Eric's Island, and even offered to rent her a boat to get there. Though the thought of being out on the water made her mouth go dry, she'd reluctantly accepted. After a half-hour lesson in yachtsmanship, she had promised to return to the marina first thing in the morning, far ahead of Garrett's departure time.

Now, tired and uncomfortable, she waited in a sheltered inlet up the coastline from the marina. Her shorts and halter top were too thin for the fresh morning breeze. The rental boat bobbed wildly on the waves. And if Garrett took another route to his island home than the one Riley had given her, she might miss him. All hopes for an interview would slip through her fingers.

What had seemed like such a good idea yesterday now had the ring of pure insanity.

AS SOON AS Hunter idled out of the no-wake area of the marina basin, he threw the throttle into full power.

Once he passed under the bridge, he'd be in Pine Island Sound, where small, uninhabited islands abounded. But there were also larger tracts of land, lush, primitive Edens with no link to the real world.

Thirteen years ago, Hunter had scrounged enough cash to buy one of these postage-stamp pieces of paradise. He'd never regretted it. The stilt house had been a vacation home and a research base for projects. Lately, it had also been a fortress of protection from the outside world. He loved it more than any-place in the world.

Some sixth sense told him this week would be a turning point. The five days before Riley came over would help clear his mind and rejuvenate his spirit. But it was also time to make a few decisions that he'd been putting off for far too long.

Crusading might be personally rewarding, but it didn't pay very well. Savings and investment divi-dends had provided a modest income the past few years, but they couldn't last forever. If the scientific community still regarded him as a pariah and since he'd been out of the picture too long to be much help to the environmental groups he'd been associated with, then maybe a career adjustment was in order.

Maybe he'd take Riley up on his offer. Go into partnership with him on the marina. Or start that charter service they'd always talked about.

His eyes rested on the duffel bag that slouched on the seat next to him. He knew what he *wasn't* going to do, and that was get involved in anything remotely connected with Cavanaugh Laboratories.

It had been stupid to bring the hypo kit along, but he hadn't wanted to leave it at home, sitting on the desk in the study. It would be easy enough to get rid of it, bury it somewhere on the island this week. What-ever secrets the kit held would remain undisclosed, just as Isaacson's intentions would never be revealed.

He felt a niggling regret over Isaacson's death. They had once worked on the same project for NASA, and while they'd never been close friends, the biochemist had been supportive during Hunter's fight four years ago. Isaacson had been plainspoken and eccentric and definitely *not* the kind of man to suddenly take a nosedive off a twenty-story building.

Hunter grunted and swiped a distracted hand across his face. It didn't make any sense. But then, nothing made much sense anymore.

A trio of dolphins caught his attention by breaking the water off the starboard bow and offering a playful escort. The morning sun arrowed into the bay, creating splashes of silver and turquoise.

He smiled and slicked the faint taste of salt off his lips with his tongue. He wasn't going to think about Cavanaugh or Braddock or Isaacson this week. That was all part of the past, a past he had no intention of revisiting. If there *was* something fishy about the biochemist's death, the authorities wouldn't need his help to find out what it was.

There weren't many other boats in sight. It was early, and until the weekend sailors showed up, the bay would be quiet.

A hundred yards off, a lone Bowrider drifted in the current. The woman at the helm waved as he passed. He waved back, recognizing one of the runabouts Riley rented out to tourists. The sun bounced brightly off the woman's hair, turning it to burnished copper. With a shock, Hunter realized who the boater was, even before she revved the motor into full throttle and swung into his wake.

He couldn't believe it. Alexandria Sutton was back on his tail, and his best friend have given her the means to stay there! Through the white spray of the boat's wake, he glared over his shoulder to find her closer than he liked. Riley, damn him, must have given her the fastest craft he had.

He shook his head at her. The witch smiled.

There wasn't a chance in hell he'd let her follow him to the island. Time to put a stop to this, once and for all. And wait until he saw Riley on Saturday, he thought.

He veered back the way he'd come, past the lighthouse at Sanibel. For the next half hour, Hunter tried to shake her off, but every time he turned back to look, she was there. The woman was either a lucky fool or the most daring sailor he'd ever seen. She took chances even he wouldn't have attempted.

Inspiration sizzled into his brain. He maneuvered the boat in a sweeping arc that brought him around to face her, then idled the motor. She did the same. The two boats drifted closer together.

She stood up, one hand still on the wheel, the other swiping wind-sifted locks away from her face. She looked pale and edgy, but the sparkle off the water gave her eyes a nice luminous brilliance, and those smooth-as-satin legs, gloriously exposed in shorts, soaked up sunlight like a kiss.

In a tightly controlled voice, he said, "I don't know what you said to Riley to get him to help you, but it's not going to work. Go home, Miss Sutton."

Her sigh was unexpectedly quick and frightened. "Believe me, Mr. Garrett, right now I wish I could."

"Look, you've given this your best shot. Following me now only makes you irrationally stubborn and foolish."

She shrugged. "The same could be said about running away."

His hand tangled in his hair as he squinted toward the sun. Then, as though he'd come to some decision, he met her gaze across the distance of the waves. "Okay. You win."

She looked as though she didn't dare believe his words. "Really? I mean—I think that's a wise decision, Mr. Garrett."

"The sooner I get you off my back, the sooner I can resume a peaceful existence. But first we set some ground rules."

"What kind of ground rules?" she asked with sudden suspicion.

"Let's talk." He jerked his head to indicate a hazy speck of land in the distance. "Do you see that sandbar with the scrub bushes that look like a camel?"

"Yes."

"Meet me over there."

"I thought you have some sort of cottage on an island nearby. Couldn't we just go there?"

"Not until we get a few things straight."

"You're not going to roar off when I'm not looking?"

"Lady, you got me. You might not like what you end up with, but that's your problem."

"I'll manage."

"Fine. Stay out of my wake. The sandbar extends quite a ways, so trim up your motor or you'll drag the prop."

He could tell she thought this idea of an impromptu meeting in the Gulf of Mexico was unorthodox, but an acceptable compromise. "Whatever you say."

"If only that were true," he muttered. He powered up the motor, and the boat swung away.

Alex's hands threatened to crumble the steering wheel, they were clasped so tightly. Hunter's water games had left her stomach quivering with each pitch and bounce of the waves. There had been no skill in her reckless maneuvering, and she suspected that she was lucky she hadn't capsized herself. She felt so relieved the man had finally decided to be sensible she could have wept for joy.

The sandbar was a half-moon-shaped refuge for crabs, dotted with palmettos and mangroves. They switched off the motors, then let the boats glide against the sand. The beach was narrow, marred with the hieroglyphic-like tracks of birds.

Garrett took away Alex's worry of what she should do next by dropping his anchor over the side, then hopping into the water to grab her bowline. "Sit tight a moment," he directed. Barefoot, he jogged with it to a nearby bush and tied it off.

He returned to his boat and retrieved a beach towel from a box of supplies. She was a little surprised when he came to extend his hand and help her out. "Let's sit a while."

The look in his eyes told her he half expected a refusal. Snatching her carryall off the opposite seat, Alex placed her hand in his. The boat dipped as the weight shifted. Hunter's fingers were hard and steady on hers, disappearing the moment she found her footing.

He trudged up the beach and spread the towel near the place her bowline had been tethered. He sat down and crossed his legs, motioning her to do the same.

She hadn't forgotten how appealingly handsome he was, but she wasn't prepared for the force of his presence sitting so close to her in the bright sunlight. The azure depths of his eyes glowed with an odd interest and intensity.

"Now what?" she asked, to cover a sudden discomfort.

"The shelling's good here."

"Your ground rules, Mr. Garrett."

He ignored her prompting. "What do you think of the view, Miss Sutton?"

She scanned the panorama of the coastline, sensing he'd take his own time getting to the point. "It's lovely."

"It's a mess." He pointed along a line of high-rise hotels that hugged the coast. "When I was a kid, you could have walked the beach from Fort Myers to Naples without running into another soul. All the building, the dredging..." He lifted a handful of sand, holding it out for her to see, then let it sift through his fingers. "Look at this. It isn't sand anymore, it's waste by-products." He rattled off the names of a half-dozen minerals she remembered from her college days. Brushing his hands together, he said, "Do you know, Sanibel used to be the second-best shelling beach in the world? Now you're lucky if you can find a decent queen's crown."

She didn't know what a queen's crown looked like, but she tried to look suitably distressed. Cautiously, she said, "Progress sometimes calls for hard sacrifices."

He looked at her as if she'd just sprouted horns. "That's not a philosophy I subscribe to, or believe we have to accept." He locked his elbows behind him, then closed his eyes as he lifted his face to the sun. She noticed that his body looked extremely fit and tan in the cutoff denims and shirt he wore. "Wait until I see Riley again," he remarked with a smile that was little more than a grimace. "He's going to pay for this."

"He's a good friend."

He didn't open his eyes, but the smile widened. She realized with surprise that Hunter Garrett had dimples. "Yes, but is he yours or mine?"

"He was only trying to help."

"Right." He sat up and looked her straight in the eyes. "I'm sorry to tell you this, but I don't have any intention of giving you that interview."

She unconsciously mimicked his position, her back going ramrod straight. "What! Then what's the purpose of this? I assure you, you're wrong if you think I'm going to change my mind and disappear quietly."

"I realize that. That's why I brought you over here."

Alex's heart hammered as she watched his gaze shift, playing over her face with an intimacy that brought color to her cheeks. She stammered out, "I—I won't be intimidated that way again."

"No. You've forced me to consider sterner measures."

Her throat tightened. He moved closer, so near she could see the sunlight filtering through his blue gaze and feel his breath whispering against her cheek. "Miss Sutton," he said with a soft, rueful smile. "You've brought this on yourself."

He would kiss her now, she thought, and she wasn't at all sure she minded. But she should, shouldn't she? "Stop!" She offered the weak protest. "Don't come any closer."

He shook his head. "I don't want to kiss you, Alex. I just want to stop you."

One of his hands lifted. At first, she thought he meant to touch her, but with shocked horror she saw that his fingers held a pocketknife. The sun flashed off the blade.

She closed her eyes in shock, wondering if he planned to kill her now. Hide her body under the sparse scrub on the island. Her parents would never know what happened—

The gruesome scenarios halted suddenly when she opened her eyes. He wasn't beside her on the towel any longer, but almost to the water. While she watched in stunned surprise, he tossed his anchor into his boat, shoved the craft away from the sand, then vaulted over the side.

"What are you doing!" She jumped up, but it was already too late. Her own vessel was sliding backward, as well, pulled along by the severed bowline now resting in Garrett's hands.

She ran to the water's edge. Panic seized her. "Where are you going?"

"I'm leaving you here," he replied mildly.

"You can't!"

"I just did."

His gaze scanned her dispassionately. Alex's boat continued to drift backward, lured by the beckoning current in the channel.

"Wait!"

The flare of terror in her voice made him almost reconsider. If it was possible, she looked even more pale than she had before, and the way she churned through the water, then quickly retreated to shore as the sand dropped off, suggested the movements of a true landlubber.

He clamped down on the impulse to modify the lesson he planned to teach her. She was a reporter. He couldn't afford to care. Besides, she'd be back at her hotel before sundown.

"Now listen to me carefully. Do you see that large island?" He pointed to a low-lying oasis of blue-green that looked impossibly far away. "Low tide is six or seven hours away. Between here and there it'll be no more than waist-deep water. Head in a straight line for the spot between those two palms that form a V. There's a run-down fish camp at the base of it called Crazy Joe's. You'll be able to call Riley from there. He'll pick you up."

"You're out of your mind!" she yelled at him. Through fading hope, anger was the only thing left to her.

He appeared unperturbed. "By the time you get back to the mainland, I'll be grilling my afternoon catch for supper. Don't think you can talk Riley into bringing you to Eric's Island. When I get there, I'm going to raise hell with him. I guarantee, he'll think twice about helping you again."

He wasn't joking—he was really going to leave her here. Alone on a nearly barren sandbar. Surrounded by water.

There were probably half a dozen brilliant and scathing retorts her brothers would have come up with to fit this occasion. She stretched her mind to think of an appropriate one, and came up with, "Mr. Garrett—Hunter—please don't do this." Her anger had quickly been replaced by desperation.

"I warned you, lady," he said, shaking his head as though she had only herself to blame. "You should have listened. You'll be fine if you do what I told you." He gave her a rakish salute. "You can keep the towel as a souvenir."

CHAPTER FOUR

"YOU DID WHAT!"

Riley's voice boomed over the radio waves, the only link between the mainland and the stilt house.

Calmly, Hunter tabbed the microphone button. "I said, I left her cooling her heels on a sandbar. Remember the little one that popped up after—"

"Who cares *which* one?" his friend replied impatiently. "How could you do it, Hunt?"

"She'll be fine. Madder than hell by the time she calls you, but fine."

"You just cut the bowline and took off? Are you nuts?"

"Don't worry. I'll replace the line."

"You know that's not what I mean."

While Riley ranted on, Hunter glanced around the cluttered living room. Overflowing bookcases. Eric's dusty collection of shells. Behind the Formica dinette hung the macramé sunburst Julie had labored over early in their marriage. There probably weren't many people who'd find this assortment of attic rejects and personal memorabilia pleasing, but this place represented a haven he hadn't found anywhere else. His gut flipped as he imagined a stranger touching these things. Worse, a nosy reporter, prying into memories he couldn't bear to share with anyone.

Shaking loose from the past, he thumbed the mike again. "No one comes to this island that I don't want here," he said sternly. "Least of all, reporters. You should have known that, Kincaid."

"She's a nice person."

"She's the press."

"Who are you really running from, Hunt? Alex Sutton or yourself?"

The question caught him off guard, and in irritation, he nearly flipped the switch to end the discussion. Damn that woman. She must have done quite a number on Riley to make him willing to trespass into forbidden territory neither of them ever explored.

Wearily, he said, "I've told Crazy Joe to expect her at low tide. Pick her up and send her home. And if she gets one more piece of information about me, you can start looking for a new friend." He let go of the radio's transmitting button, then, remembering Alex Sutton's attractiveness, he pressed it again. "I mean it, Rile. Not one more word."

To ALEX, the distance between Crazy Joe's and this miserable stretch of nothing looked insurmountable.

She spent most of the torpid, overheated hours of the afternoon walking an endless path around the island, trying to reason a way out of her predicament other than the one Hunter had suggested.

She watched sea gulls squabble over a meal of fish while her stomach growled an envious complaint. Shading her eyes, she gazed longingly at sailboats on the horizon. The sun began to feel uncomfortable on her shoulders, back and nose. Mostly, she sat on the sand, writing in her notebook all the terrible things she'd do to that man if she ever saw him again.

By the time low tide ruffled the water, Alex seriously considered taking Hunter's advice. The two palm trees marking the site of Crazy Joe's beckoned like a desert oasis.

She told herself that trudging through waist-deep water should be nothing more than uncomfortable and tiring. When the tide looked its shallowest, she set out, placing each foot carefully to avoid any sea creatures basking in low pools. At first, the mucky bottom promised to keep her firmly anchored in place. But the moment the sand dropped off and rippling waves rose past her hips, she broke out in a sweat.

She panicked and retreated to the island.

The sandbar might be a wasteland, but it was solid.

She tried using logic. In some places out there, she could see short-legged birds walking across sand barely covered by water. But, her frightened brain argued, there were just as many spots that still looked dark, a sure sign of deeper pools.

All right, so there were. So what? They weren't life-threatening. In all honesty, she didn't think Hunter had deliberately left her out here to die. He couldn't have known about her fear.

In the end, she sat and watched the day slide toward extinction. The tide began its laborious crawl back into place. She thought wistfully how much she would have enjoyed the sunset from her hotel balcony. Sand gnats came out to play with her skin. She pulled the towel around her shoulders, eager for its protection. Bringing up her legs, she rested her head against her knees, willing away the headache that pounded.

Dusk would settle soon. It was going to be a grim evening.

FOR HUNTER, the day was long and satisfying.

Settling into his favorite fishing spot at the tip of the island, he waited for a bite and thought about Alex Sutton.

He'd played a pretty rotten trick on the woman, but he absolutely refused to recall the solitary, crestfallen figure she'd made as he'd pulled away from the sandbar. She had, after all, said she could handle anything he threw her way. So maybe she hadn't planned on being stranded, but a reporter couldn't afford to be a delicate flower. Maybe this would toughen her up. She might even thank him one day.

He glanced toward the sun, a hot, wavering ball of heat in the cloudless sky, and suspected her thanks wouldn't come anytime soon.

By now, she'd be back at her hotel, tired, cranky and probably sunburned. He could imagine her furiously hurling clothes into a suitcase, each item accompanied by an invective meant just for him.

She'd go back to Miami and write a scathing article and cherish the slim hope that her words would bring him out to retaliate in person. They wouldn't. He'd been crucified in the papers before. One more time wouldn't matter.

For reasons he didn't fully understand, Hunter realized he was going to miss her. Just a little. He had to admit, these past few days had brought a stimulating change to his normal routine.

The memory of her mouth, and how badly he'd wanted to kiss her, still bothered him. That desire intruded on the detachment he'd carefully cultivated. Thank God he'd come to his senses in time.

Reeling in his line, he discovered that a fish had stolen his bait. He shook his head in disgust and determinedly thrust Alexandria Sutton from his thoughts.

WITH LESS EXPERTISE and more noise than he would have liked, Richie was finally able to break into Garrett's house in Fort Myers.

He found nothing.

His father might think that was a good sign, but, determined to have something more substantial to report, Richie put off making the call and returned to the marina instead, where the man seemed to spend so much of his time. His momentary delight at seeing Garrett's truck in the parking lot dissolved when he saw the empty boat slip.

The man he was supposed to be watching had slipped away from him.

For one awful moment, Richie envisioned calling his father to tell him he'd blown the surveillance. It was a phone call he was determined not to make.

Instead, he surveyed the activity on the docks. Local kids made extra money as boat jockeys and, spotting a derelict-looking teenager pumping gas, Richie checked his available cash.

"Got a second?" he asked the boy, wondering if he should try to pass himself off as a cop. He hated the idea of losing money to a bribe.

The kid stopped pumping long enough to give Richie his full attention. With his dark tan, sunglasses and white teeth, the boy looked like a low-rent version of Tom Cruise.

"What happened to the boat in slip twenty-six? I heard it might be for sale."

"Left this morning. Probably be gone about a week."

"Gone where?"

"Where do you think, man?" Tom Cruise gestured toward open water with the gasoline nozzle. The smell of diesel fuel drifted across the hot, summer air. "Out there."

"Do you have any idea where exactly?"

"Let me get the boss. Riley will know."

"No," Richie said quickly. "I think your boss may be looking to buy the boat, too, and I'd rather have first crack at the owner. You understand?" He punctuated the question by peeling off a few bills from his wallet.

The kid slid his sunglasses down to the end of his nose for a closer look. He had good eyes. Bright blue and greedy. "No problem. I think I can get ya' within spitting distance."

A short time later, Richie idled out of the marina in a rental boat. Armed with a good map and a stash of supplies he'd hastily purchased at a nearby minimart, he felt extremely pleased with himself. Even his brother Lyle couldn't have managed such resource-fulness.

AS SUNSET BEGAN a spectacular light show over the water, Hunter headed back to the stilt house, rod and reel in one hand and enough fish for that night's supper in the other.

He took the stairs to the upper deck two at a time, then flipped the panel of switches beside the front door that worked the lights. The generator had been Julie's idea, a concession to civilization he hadn't wanted to make. Now he was glad he'd lost that argument.

Inside, he rummaged through a kitchen drawer for his favorite cleaning knife. On the desk in the living room, the ham radio suddenly crackled his call sign. He discovered Crazy Joe hailing him, probably unable to resist a little good-natured teasing. He could imagine Alex Sutton waiting for Riley in the grubby bait shop, cursing him to hell and back with every breath.

"Just thought you'd like to know," Joe informed him, "your little friend didn't show up at low tide."

It took him a full second to absorb that information. "Are you sure?"

"I been looking at smelly fishermen all day, so I think I'd notice if a good-looking brunette walked in."

Hunter frowned, trying to control new frustration. Where the hell was she? "She couldn't have gotten lost."

"You want me to take a quick run around the bay before I head home?"

"No. I'll go. She probably got picked up by someone before low tide. Thanks, Joe."

THE HOT, STICKY NIGHT pressed against Hunter's skin until perspiration beaded his upper lip. The sandbar was only five minutes away, but he'd never had to find it in the dark before. Overhead, uncooperative clouds hid the moon, cloaking the landscape in varying degrees of darkness. He switched on the boat's running lights and churned through the sound slowly, playing a flashlight over the dark water.

Everything seemed different at night. So many small islands. The beam of his flashlight gave the golden eyes of raccoons a supernatural glow, and ghost crabs skittered away from the light like retreating armies eager to escape capture.

Somewhere between here and the neon sparkle of the mainland lay the sandbar and Alexandria Sutton.

If she was still on it.

He refused to believe something bad had happened. She'd probably hailed a passing boat. Or missed Crazy Joe's and walked ashore farther up the island. Instead of racing into the night, he should have contacted Riley to see if she'd called him. That would have been the next logical step.

Except that guilt made a powerful motivator. *He* was the one responsible. If anything happened to her, he'd be at fault. And he had enough on his conscience already without adding Alex Sutton to the list.

He had to find her. And when he did, she'd better be healthy and in one piece.

And then, as though his thoughts had somehow materialized her, his flashlight caught the coppery gleam of her hair. She was sitting on the beach, her face buried in her arms. He splashed ashore even before the boat slid against the sand, his heart thundering.

He crouched beside her. "Miss Sutton?"

When she heard her name, Alex figured it had to be the wind again, fooling her with its merciless, taunting song. She had spent the last hour trying to keep warm. The towel's sandy dampness clung to her skin and chafed unbearably.

"Miss Sutton?" the wind whispered again, and this time she felt its touch against her shoulder.

She turned her head slowly, blinking into the bobbing brightness. Momentarily her universe pitched, then righted itself.

"Are you all right, Miss Sutton?"

Her sluggish mind registered the fact that she'd never heard him use such a gentle tone with her before. Ill-functioning logic told her she ought to be angry, but frankly, she was too glad to be rescued.

She stared at him. "Why don't you like my first name?"

He touched the icy wing of her cheek. "I do. It's a very pretty name."

"I'm named after the city, you know."

"In Egypt?"

"Of course not. Virginia."

He scanned her face, realizing her hazy comprehension and stiff, unnatural movements indicated a mild case of sunstroke. "Alex," he murmured, "what are you still doing here? You could have been back at your hotel by now if you'd done as I said."

"Couldn't."

"Why not?"

"Can't...swim."

"You didn't need to swim. All you had to do was walk across the water."

"Can't," she replied. "I tried. But I'm only mortal."

She laid her head against her knees, as though her neck would no longer support the weight. A barrage of shivers went through her and Hunter muttered a string of dark curses as he peeled off his windbreaker, draping it over her shoulders. "Of all the foolish, nitwitted—"

"If you've come back to gloat," she said, "I can live without it."

"Come on, I'll take you home."

"Sure you wouldn't rather stake me out here? Let the crabs feast on my body?"

"I could, but I doubt they'd find you to their liking. Can you walk?"

"Of course I can walk."

She made a clumsy effort to get to her feet, but before she could even attempt a step, he scooped her into his arms.

He settled her on the bench seat at the stern of the boat, wedging his windbreaker under her for protection from the wind. Her breath escaped in a velvety sigh. "Hunter?"

"Yes, Alex?"

"Do you have any food?"

He shook his head. "No, but I'll fix you something when we get to my cottage."

She seemed satisfied. Then her lashes drifted down and she was asleep in moments.

It was another few seconds before he turned to start the motor. He rocked back on his heels, savoring the sight of her. Her cheekbones resembled flawless marble, so much so that he couldn't resist tracing the soft line of her features with his fingertips.

A new and unwelcome yearning settled low in his belly. He was suddenly aware of Alex as he'd never been before. And more importantly, he recognized that years of a careful, orchestrated immunity were perilously close to giving way to doubt.

His smile faded and he pivoted quickly, not liking the direction of his thoughts and this uninvited tenderness. It was just relief, he told himself. All that adrenaline settling.

His attention snared on movement from the beach. It was Alex's notebook, the pages fluttering in the breeze. She'd probably never forgive him if he left it behind.

He hopped from the boat and retrieved the notebook, along with the towel and her carryall. He flashed the light over the strong handwriting, and his mouth curved into a grin as he read a few choice words describing his less admirable characteristics. He closed the book with a snap, wondering what the woman's attitude would be once she fully recovered. Not good, he'd wager.

They reached Eric's Island in a matter of minutes. Hunter tied the boat off at the dock under the house, then lifted Alex once more. The woman in his arms stirred and blinked in dazed confusion.

"Where are we?" she asked sleepily.

"My island."

Once inside, Hunter proceeded to the small bathroom. He sat Alex on the shower floor. Twisting the knobs, he adjusted the water temperature, then pulled the shower curtain across the opening. He heard Alex gasp as the first spray of water hit her. "Hey, I still have my clothes on," she shouted.

"Throw them in the corner of the shower," he called over the sound of the water. "There's shampoo in the hanging tray. I'll be back in a minute."

She had to admit the shower felt wonderful. Sliding against her chilled flesh, the warm water revived her and washed away the salt stiffened on her skin. She wiggled out of her shorts and peeled the halter top off her shoulders.

She still had a killer headache, but at least the fuzziness in her brain had started to recede. It occurred to her she should be furious with Hunter, but at the moment, she couldn't drum up much energy or enthusiasm for it. Instead, she inched up the shower wall and squirted shampoo into her palm.

When she stepped out of the shower, she found a pair of cotton shorts and an overlong T-shirt lying on the counter. Placed on top was a tube of sunburn cream and two aspirin. She slathered lotion over her body. Her shoulders had benefited from the towel's protection but her back stung. Unable to reach most of it, she left it alone.

Swiping beads of moisture from the mirror over the sink, Alex regarded her reflection. She groaned.

She looked like a boiled lobster. Lipstick had kept her lips from getting burned, but the rest of her features were slightly swollen. Hunter was bound to find her unappealing.

Her head jerked up to meet her eyes in the mirror. Did she *want* to be appealing to the man? And what did that have to do with getting the story? She'd already come off as foolishly inept. She mustn't make it any worse by indulging in inane fantasies.

Besides, she wasn't sexy and she couldn't pretend to be. Growing up around two protective older brothers, she'd soon been relegated to one-of-the-gang status with their friends. Even her relationship with her fiancé in Boston had become a comfortable, sensible alliance that demanded very little from either of them.

But Hunter had a complex nature, one she hadn't counted on. He had the ability to be cold and distant one moment, compassionate and tender the next.

Her mind and body had been dulled by fatigue on that horrible sandbar, but not so much that she hadn't noticed. His tone hadn't been as devoid of feeling as he might have wished, and it was that memory that unexpectedly brought a flush of pleasure racing through her veins. The dark side she'd glimpsed behind his eyes, the secrets of his past piqued her interest, but it was the man himself who rocked her balance and did fascinating things to her biochemistry.

She jumped as a knock sounded on the door. "You all right in there?" Hunter called.

"Yes. I'll be out in a second."

Raking a hand through her damp hair, Alex opened the door to find Hunter leaning against the opposite doorframe. He straightened, his eyes traveling up and down her body. Every feminine instinct she possessed told her he wasn't displeased by what he saw.

"The shirt's a little big, but the shorts seem to fit all right," he remarked with casual interest.

His frank perusal left her feeling distinctly uncomfortable.

"They're fine," she said curtly. "Who do they belong to?"

"They've been in a drawer for a few years. Clothes don't get dragged back and forth from the mainland much."

The fact registered that he hadn't given her a direct answer. Maybe he'd decided to reerect the barriers now that she was coherent again.

"How do you feel?"

"Sleepy. Hungry." She touched her nose gently and grimaced. "Fried."

He motioned toward the tube of sunburn cream she held in one hand. "That ought to take away the sting in no time. Did you have enough?"

"Too bad you don't have the institutional size," she said. "I think I got everywhere but the middle of my back."

"We'll take care of that," he said, then turned to enter the room behind him with an indication she should follow.

The bedroom was small and sparsely furnished, which probably accounted for the way the double bed drew her eyes like a magnet. Hunter had moved beside it and thumped his hand against the mattress. "Lie down on your stomach. I'll do your back."

"That's really not necessary," she replied stiffly.

"Come on. I guess I owe you. Although you have to admit you did ask for it."

Further objections vanished as she caught the look in his eyes. Challenging. Intimidating. He expected her unwillingness. With a defiant gaze, Alex went wordlessly to the bed and lay facedown, her head buried in a pillow.

A few moments later, the mattress shifted under Hunter's weight. She drew a deep, fortifying breath as his fingers gingerly lifted the hem of the T-shirt up to her neck. It wasn't sudden exposure to the air that made her shiver. Self-consciously, she brought her arms down to tuck them against the sides of her breasts.

Hunter whistled softly. "Ouch. This is gonna hurt tomorrow."

"It hurts today," she muttered, then gasped as the cold sunburn cream touched the center of her spine.

Like liquid silk, his hand slid along her back, blending the medicated lotion into her heated skin— flesh against flesh, hot against cold. His fingertips held magic, finding irritated nerve endings with the deftness of a therapist.

It should have felt odd, having a man who was almost a stranger touch her so intimately. But the gift his hands carried felt so good. Her eyes closed and her lips parted with pleasure.

"Feels...wonderful," she murmured. When Hunter made no response, she added, "Is this really your private island?"

"Yes."

"I didn't expect you to bring me here."

"Where did you think I'd take you?"

"I thought you'd dump me off in the parking lot of Riley's marina."

His fingers stopped a moment, then slid onward. "You really think I'm a heartless bastard, don't you?"

It took her a moment to respond. "I don't know what to think anymore."

She wasn't the only one. Hunter tried to concentrate on the task at hand, but he couldn't. The pungent fragrance of the sunburn medication drifted into his nostrils, but woven into the coldness of the cream, he felt Alex Sutton's warm flesh beneath his fingers. The shallow cleft of her spine gleamed; the gentle arch near her waist invited exploration.

With a low groan of delight, Alex lifted her arms, placing her hands under her head. His gaze shifted to the meager glimpse of her breasts, pressed against the mattress.

He jerked his hands away and pulled down the T-shirt to cover her back and anything else remotely tempting. "All done," he said with crisp, impersonal efficiency.

She rose to sit beside him, and when their glances met he saw with a kind of resounding surprise that he wasn't the only one indulging in fantasies. Her eyes regarded him with heavy-lidded yearning. A tight, audible sigh marred the rhythm of her breath.

Acutely conscious of how close she was, how easily the situation could get out of hand, Hunter found ridiculous importance in replacing the cap to the sunburn cream. He needed a moment to regain his composure, and he hoped to God she had the sense to get up and move away from him. Because he couldn't.

After a long hesitation, she broke the silence.

"Thank you," she said, and Hunter thought he'd never been so glad to hear those two words.

He looked at her again, sensing her confusion. "I'm sorry about today, Alex. I don't want to hurt you." He spoke in a low, sensible tone, and from the way her eyes widened, he knew she understood how much more those words were meant to convey.

"I don't want to hurt you, either," she replied.

He gave a short, painful laugh, and said briskly, "Finally, we seem to be in agreement."

He stood, before that simple act became impossible. "Rest while I fix us something to eat. What will it be?"

She settled on a cheese sandwich, and watched him leave the room as though he couldn't wait to quit her presence. She curled on her side, pillowing her head with one arm. Beyond the room, she heard Hunter opening cupboards, the clatter of utensils. She wanted to join him, but would he welcome her company?

She couldn't be sure.

IN THE KITCHEN, Hunter slapped mayonnaise across a piece of bread, glad for the distraction of preparing a meal. He was irritated by his inability to do just what she had expected him to do—dump her off in Riley's parking lot. Far better to be pegged a bastard than a fool.

It had been a long time since he'd had a woman. A long time since he'd wanted one. Ambivalence toward the opposite sex came easy enough if you worked at it. So why were his insides twisting at the mere thought of how close Alex lay?

He finished fixing the sandwich. He'd brought milk and soda over on the boat, and he wondered which one she'd like. He dreaded approaching her again. Then, with a flash of annoyance that the woman should have this effect on him, he turned and headed for the bedroom.

He stopped in the doorway. She was asleep. Her hair, still damp from the shower, fanned like ribbons of dark chocolate across the pillow. The lamplight cast golden shadows. She looked endearingly sexy in spite of the redness.

His eyes took in her body, traveling lower. Under the freedom of the T-shirt, her breasts rose and fell with a gentle rhythm, the nipples outlined by the material every few seconds, teasing the imagination. *His* imagination.

He willed away that awareness. A feeling of resentment crept into his system, as though Alex Sutton had managed somehow to isolate him from this final refuge, the one place he felt secure.

With a half-spoken curse, he slid his pillow off the bed and scooped up a blanket. The second bedroom had been Eric's and he still couldn't bring himself to enter it. Tonight, the couch would have to do, and tomorrow she'd be gone.

Morning, however, promised to be a long time coming.

CHAPTER FIVE

AWARENESS SLID into her subconscious like layers of receding mist. With a sigh of contentment, Alex opened her eyes, drawing in the mingled summer scents of salt air and oleander, sunlight and cedar. The morning, golden in its glory, streamed through the bedroom window.

After a moment of confusion, she remembered where she was. Behind her eyes, yesterday's headache throbbed a subdued beat, but the fuzziness had disappeared. She sat up and stretched, then frowned as the movement made her sunburned shoulders flare a warning. She was still dressed in the T-shirt and shorts she'd been given, and sometime during the night the quilt from the end of the bed had been drawn up over her. Hunter, she supposed.

Rising, Alex ran a hand through her tumbled hair and padded out of the room. At the entrance to the living room, she hesitated, calling Hunter's name softly. She had no idea what time it was, but if he was asleep on the couch, she didn't want to add waking him to her list of sins.

She needn't have worried. The living room was vacant, a pillow and blanket folded neatly on one end of the couch. She took the opportunity to let her gaze wander.

The decor was an interesting mix of the whimsical and utilitarian. A playful sea-gull mobile turned gently in a corner, a detailed nautical map of the area affixed on the wall behind it. A collection of home-made palm-frond hats, each one more fanciful than the next, adorned the wall behind a functional desk that held a ham radio and an array of impressive-looking textbooks.

The cottage itself had been designed to take advantage of the view. From large windows and sliding glass doors Alex could see sparkling blue water in several directions, and a wide deck appeared to run completely around the house.

Fresh air wafted across her skin, and Alex realized that the door to the patio stood open. She spotted Hunter out there, leaning over the railing, a coffee cup in one hand as he stared out at the wide expanse of water.

This morning, he was barefoot, and he wore shorts and a blue T-shirt she knew instinctively would match his eyes. The morning sun bounced brilliantly off those fingers of gold in his hair. His expression wasn't visible from where she stood, but he appeared relaxed, reflective.

After another moment, she walked out to the deck. "Good morning."

He turned at the sound of her voice, offering a remote, cool look. Too remote to put her at ease. "Good morning. How do you feel?"

"Much better, thank you."

His eyes trailed over her briefly, leaving her acutely conscious of her fiery red nose and cheeks. And the fact that she wasn't wearing a bra. "A little over-done, I'd say, but it'll fade."

She took a few steps in his direction, then realized that this part of the house had been built on pylons over the water. Slipping quickly into a deck chair, she tried to ignore the shadowed movement beneath the floorboard cracks, the gentle slap of the tide as it washed against the pilings below.

She looked up to find him watching her, his eyes speculative.

"You ought to work on that," he said with quiet conviction.

"I beg your pardon?"

"Your fear of water. Anyone who lives in Florida should know how to swim."

"I didn't come to Florida to play water games."

He tilted back to rest the weight of his body on his elbows. One eyebrow rose speculatively as he studied her. "What kind of games *did* you come to play?"

She decided to ignore his cryptic question. "Not knowing how to swim has never been a problem before."

"Yesterday wouldn't have happened," he refuted.

"And we'd have missed this opportunity to get to know each other better, now, wouldn't we?"

She realized immediately that her comment had been a mistake. He frowned and remained silent for a long moment, as though he had to think hard about how much pleasure getting to know her better had brought him. Then, seeming to lose interest in the conversation, he pushed himself away from the railing. "Would you like a cup of coffee?"

She nodded. "Black, please."

He stopped as he passed her chair. In an expressionless voice that brooked no argument, he said, "After breakfast, I'll take you back to Riley's."

Swallowing despair, she squinted into the sunshine. The cottage's only neighbors, herons nesting in nearby mangrove trees, were engaged in a noisy battle over breakfast, but she was hardly aware of their antics.

All hope of an interview faded, but her greater disappointment came from the fact that Hunter clearly wanted her out of his life as soon as possible. Last night's moments of intimacy and tentative friendship might never have been. He had returned to the distant, cautious man she'd met that first day.

His ill-tempered manner did nothing to dampen her determination to solve the mystery of Isaacson's death. In fact, his attitude only strengthened her resolve to return to Miami with something wonderful to show Ernie.

There had to be some way to keep him from getting her into that boat...

Her stomach tightened into knots as sudden inspiration took hold. The insanity of the idea scared her, but she was fresh out of ways to deal with this man. Would the opportunity even present itself? Alex wondered. And if it did, what would Garrett's response be?

HUNTER FIXED BREAKFAST. They sat opposite each other at the kitchen table. Though her hunger had surfaced, she could hardly swallow for the nervousness churning in her stomach. Under lowered lashes, she watched her companion. He seemed no more interested in the food than she was. He pushed the eggs around on his plate and remained silent, as though lost in thought. She would have cut out her tongue before breaking the oppressive stillness in the room.

When the eggs had congealed and it became ridiculous to remain at the table any longer, she scraped back her chair and rose, carrying her dishes to the kitchen sink.

"Leave them," he commanded. "I'll wash them later."

After I'm gone is what you mean, isn't it? The oblique message was there in his tone, and she conquered volatile emotions that made her want to reach out and slap him for his indifference. Any misgivings she might have had about what she was about to do evaporated in the face of his dismissal of her. "I insist," she replied, letting her mouth lift in a cool smile. "It's the least I can do after you've shown me such generous hospitality."

She busied herself at the sink, aware that he sat at the table and watched her. When he swung out of the chair and disappeared toward the bathroom, she felt absurdly relieved. But he returned moments later and tossed several scraps of material over one of the kitchen chairs. She realized they were the clothes she'd worn yesterday.

"I rinsed these out last night. They're not quite dry, but you should be able to wear them."

Her eyes traveled over the silky splash of lavender peeking from beneath the wrinkled blouse and shorts—her bra and panties. She'd never considered herself an overly modest woman, but the idea that Hunter had handled her underwear, had performed this task on her behalf, seemed uncomfortably intimate.

She dipped her head, certain that her reddened cheeks had gone an even deeper crimson. Her pulse was jumping. It seemed an eternity before she could look at him again.

"Th-thank you," she managed to stammer.

He shrugged. "No need to thank me. It was the least I could do, since I'm the one who stranded you in the first place. Remember?"

"Oh, I remember. I spent the better part of yesterday thinking some very unpleasant things about you."

His mouth quirked in a smile. "And today?"

"You have *some* redeeming qualities."

"Don't give me too much credit."

She eyed him curiously. "Why don't you want me to think you're capable of doing nice things?"

The smile dropped and disappeared, leaving his eyes flat and blank. "You don't know what I'm capable of." He swung away, heading toward the bathroom once more. "I'm going to take a shower. Be ready to leave in fifteen minutes."

IN JUST LESS than that, he entered the living room from the bathroom in a swirl of escaping mist. His hair, still wet from the shower, curled against his neck.

Alex sat primly on the couch, her few belongings gathered around her. Her heart hammered in her chest and her hands were clasped tightly together to keep them from shaking visibly. With more bravado than she felt, she mustered a sweet, hopeful smile. "I don't suppose you'd reconsider? About the interview, I mean?"

"Nope."

"Well, then," she replied with a resigned sigh, "I refuse to go."

One eyebrow crested, and he shook his head as though he was sure she'd taken leave of her senses. "You can refuse all you want. But you're still going back, even if I have to carry you down to the boat and stuff you under a seat cushion."

"I don't think so."

He spun on his heel, grabbed keys from a wooden peg by the front door, then faced her with a calmness that only added to her irritation. "I'm going to start the motor. You have about one minute to rethink this decision."

He swept out the door. The windows shook in their casings as he pounded down the porch stairs. Reality hit her with a jolt. Oh, God. What had she done? She'd be fish bait when he found out. Calm. Remain calm. Her brothers wouldn't have been intimidated by a little frowning obstinance. Why should she?

Except her brothers weren't here. And Hunter was—

She jumped as the front door flew open and banged against the wall. He stood in the doorway, his hands on his hips. Alex watched him approach her slowly, her insides somersaulting.

"You scheming little witch. What do you think you just accomplished by cutting the fuel lines to the boats?"

From between the couch cushions, she removed the paring knife she'd found earlier in the kitchen. She extended it toward him. In her steadiest voice, she said, "You know, these are sharper than they look. Not as sharp as the one you used yesterday on *my* boat, but it managed to slice through those rubber hoses pretty well, don't you think?"

He snatched the knife away and flung it toward the kitchen table. It skittered across the Formica and landed on the linoleum with a clatter. The flesh across his cheekbones had gone white and taut. "You think you're very clever, don't you?"

Alex wet her lips, thinking *clever* was not the word she would have used to describe herself at that moment. She knew her family would have scoffed at the notion that what she'd just done was underhanded, but she couldn't help feeling like a low-life sneak all the same. She had to keep reminding herself that, even if she hadn't desperately wanted to impress Ernie with her ability, there was still a good reason behind her actions.

To assuage some of her guilt, Alex tossed back at Hunter, "You were Leo Isaacson's friend. If his death wasn't a suicide, don't you want to help find the people responsible? The story my paper runs might help—"

"It won't help anything," he snapped. "And don't pretend to have noble aspirations about any of this. I'm not buying it."

His eyes, full of hawklike scrutiny, bored into hers. With a kind of hypnotic fascination, she saw that their blueness had darkened with the fury of a summer storm. She steeled herself against her own feelings of remorse and the power of his anger, trying to remember that, in spite of his actions yesterday, he was still a decent human being. He'd still come back for her.

"I'm sorry," she said at last in a quiet voice. "I didn't feel you left me with any alternative."

"Cutting those lines was foolish. You've only delayed the inevitable."

As she'd anticipated, he moved toward the desk where the ham radio sat. Her apprehension nudged upward a notch. In about three seconds—the time it took for Hunter to realize the plug-in microphone was missing—all hell was going to break loose.

Instead, he remained still, his back to her, but his head lowered as though entranced by the sight of the now-useless radio. She watched his hands ball into fists. The silence spun out to a small eternity. The only sound in the room was their hurried, uneven breathing competing for the same oxygen.

Suddenly, he swung to face her again. The cold gleam in his eyes made her feel like a mouse trapped beneath a cat's paw. She found herself the object of a careful, assessing scrutiny, as if he hadn't expected her to be shrewd enough to guess he'd use the ham radio. That willingness to dismiss her as an adversary gave her the courage she needed to meet his withering gaze.

"Where is it?" he demanded, the whisper of steel in his voice slicing like a rapier leaving its sheath.

No use pretending she didn't understand. She answered matter-of-factly, "I've hidden it. I considered taking something out of the back of that thing, but I don't know very much about hams. I figured taking the microphone would be enough."

He tilted his head in her direction. "I acknowledge your resourcefulness. Now... *go get it.*"

"No."

"I'm not interested in playing any more games with you, Alex. I want that microphone."

Crossing her arms, she turned her head away from him. "No. Tear the place apart if you like. You won't find it."

She was aware of sudden movement as he lowered himself beside her, so close she felt the heat emanating from his body. Subduing the impulse to move farther down the couch, she faced him. "One hour of your time. That's all it would have taken. Instead, you have to be stubborn. So now we're stuck here, just the two of us."

"You're making a mistake, Alex. I'm not going to give you an interview. Riley comes on Saturday. You'll go back with him."

"That's four days from now. I can wait."

"Four years wouldn't be enough time."

His overbearing certainty of right made her arch a superior smile his way. "We'll see, won't we?"

Fury kindled in his eyes, and he plucked the tote bag off her lap. Ignoring her gasp of surprise, he dumped the contents onto the cushion between them, his fingers sifting through the items.

She laughed, feigning a bravado she didn't feel. "You won't find it there. I wouldn't be so obvious."

When he looked up, she sensed he'd reached the limit to his patience. Contempt flashed in his eyes. "Do you honestly think if we're forced to keep each other company I'll start reminiscing for that rag of yours?"

"Something like that."

After a moment of weighty silence, he said, "Lady, you'd have had more company if I'd left you on that sandbar last night."

HUNTER SPENT the day away from the cottage, presumably to go fishing since he'd snatched up his rod and reel before striding out without a word.

After that, the hours plodded by as Alex filled her notebook with observations about her surroundings, her situation and the obstinate man who refused to talk to her. She read and played solitaire at the kitchen table. Finally, to keep from considering the day a total failure, she found a can of furniture polish and methodically set about putting the cottage to rights. The place was full of old dreams and spent history, most of it dusty and disorganized. Surely Hunter wouldn't mind a little tidying up.

She had just finished polishing the boomerang-shaped coffee table, when she glanced out the window and saw him making his way toward the cottage.

RICHIE HAD HAD a few false starts—all these damned sandbars looked alike. The kid at the marina hadn't known which small spit of land Garrett owned, just that it was somewhere between Pine Island and Estero Beach.

Fortunately, dumb luck intervened.

While he sat in the bay and tried to keep his map from being snatched out of his hands by a snapping breeze, he spotted movement on the next island up the sound. Unable to resist a closer look, he let the boat drift nearer.

The stilt house, poised over the water like a fat spider wading out to take a bath, was unremarkable, but the woman pacing behind the wide picture window sure wasn't. Richie nearly swallowed his gum when he saw the reporter. Garrett was nowhere in sight, but Richie recognized one of the boats bobbing at the dock under the house, so it was a sure bet the guy was there with her.

On the opposite side of the island he pulled the powerboat into a tangle of red mangroves and trudged ashore, feeling smugly confident for the first time.

A few unlucky ghost crabs crunched beneath his booted feet. He grimaced. A city boy all his life, he considered getaway spots like this good for only two things—getting stoned or getting laid. Since he could do neither, he wanted to discover Hunter Garrett's intentions as quickly as possible and get the hell back to Fort Myers.

All he had to do was watch and wait for an opportunity. His stomach growled, and he swung his backpack onto his lap, searching for the bag of cookies and the binoculars he'd brought. His hand passed over the holstered gun, sliding down the grip, but he resisted the temptation to pull it out. He supposed he might have to sooner or later, but not yet.

Settling into a more comfortable position, Richie pressed the binoculars to his face and wheeled the focus dial. The large cottage windows made surveillance easy. He smiled when he found the soft swell of Alex Sutton's breasts hidden beneath a modest blouse. She had an uncomplicated, pretty profile and the silkiest-looking hair.

He watched her and wondered if, when the time came, he would have the stomach to kill her.

ALEX DIDN'T SEE any fish; evidently they hadn't been biting. She hoped that was the reason Hunter's features were as harsh and unyielding as they had been earlier.

He didn't come up the stairs, but instead headed under the cottage toward the boat dock. It would be dark soon. Her stomach protested, demanding attention, but she wasn't anxious to rummage through the box of supplies on the kitchen counter without his approval. There were already enough strikes against her.

With a determined sigh, she went quietly down the stairs. The dock area lay in deep shadows. Hunter's boat, with Riley's rental tied behind it, barely moved in the sluggish current. At the end of the dock, two gulls fought over a handout thrown to them by Hunter. Self-consciously, she waited to be noticed.

He turned around, and instantly his eyebrows dropped dangerously low. She manufactured a vague smile and tried for a conciliatory tone. "I take it the fish weren't biting today."

"No."

That cold, curt response nearly made her reconsider the wisdom of approaching him. Clearing her throat she said, "I—uh—was wondering about dinner."

He stopped in front of a waist-high table a few feet away from her, a work area of sorts where his tackle box lay open. He rummaged through lures and hooks and sinkers for several moments. Then, without looking her way, he asked, "What about it?"

"I noticed a box of supplies in the kitchen. I don't mind fixing something, but I thought I should probably check with you first."

He slanted her a look of narrow-eyed skepticism. "Asking permission? That's a novel idea, coming from you."

She'd forgotten how easily he could unbalance her. The blood came up in her cheeks, but grimly she hung on to her temper, sensing it would not serve her well in this. "I make a pretty good hamburger."

He went back to rooting through the tackle box. "Suit yourself," he replied with a shrug.

Not exactly enthusiasm, but it was a start. He couldn't stay mad at her forever, could he? Ready to put her theory to a subtle test, she said, "Will you join me?"

He shook his head. "I'll grab one later."

"They'll get cold."

"Then I'll make myself a sandwich."

"Hunter—"

He turned to face her. In the departing light, his features were no more than shadowed planes and angles. "What do you want from me? You want me to come up there and chitchat with you? Pretend we're on a blind date, maybe, trying to get to know each other?"

"No, of course not—"

"Then leave well enough alone. I'll come up when I feel like it."

His rejection stung, but she wouldn't let him guess how much. She bit her lip against the flood of words that threatened to spill out. Without a backward glance, she went up the stairs.

A MOSQUITO LANDED on the back of Hunter's neck. He slapped it away absently, trying to concentrate on threading a lead weight onto his fishing line. Damned bugs!

He *could* go upstairs and join Alex. Problem was, he didn't think he should.

In spite of the tenacity she'd shown in the past, he hadn't expected that stunt with the fuel lines. She'd disappointed him. Turning out to be no more than what he'd suspected all along—a nosy reporter hungry for a story. If he had briefly thought she was different somehow, he'd quickly discovered the error in that judgment this morning.

For the better part of the day, he had maintained the barricading anger that came so easily when he thought of what she had done. He'd been so tense that when he'd snagged his best tackle on a rock in the lagoon, he'd snapped the line rather than work it loose with a patience he didn't have. He wanted to keep that animosity, nurture it, make it last the four days until Riley got here.

And he could do it, too, if she'd stop looking at him with those hurt-filled eyes of hers, all lost and forlorn. As if *he* was the one who'd left her stranded here. There were limits to a man's endurance, and Alex Sutton was out to torture him.

The smell of frying hamburgers drifted into his nostrils and his stomach reacted a second later with a noisy complaint.

Damn! Was he going to let a little healthy male interest scare him away from his own domain? He had a right to be upstairs eating the food he'd brought over. This was his territory. *She* was the one who should feel out of place.

WHILE THE BURGERS sizzled, Alex sat at the kitchen table and scribbled a few last-minute notes in her notebook.

Nothing she'd written so far would make much of a story, but that wasn't surprising. Her notes were rarely a compilation of facts, but rather, a outlet for her feelings and frustrations. Personal observations about her surroundings, free-flowing poetry, sensory perceptions, all of it went into her notebook. Given Hunter's lack of communication, her journal had taken on more importance than ever.

When he strode into the cottage, she glanced up in surprise, feeling ridiculously pleased. With a tentative smile, she stood, closing the notebook. His eyes drifted to where her hand rested protectively against the cover. She knew he thought she'd been writing about him, but she wouldn't say anything to confirm his suspicions. Let him think she'd compiled reams of notes. "You're just in time," she said. "The burgers are almost ready."

His expression shifted into a frown as his eyes roamed the living room. His response, however, was less hostile than she expected. "I'll wash up and be out in a minute."

He rejoined her a few minutes later, and they sat at right angles to each other at the table. She didn't have to worry about meeting Hunter's eyes; he seemed content to stare into space, apparently absorbed with his own thoughts. Disappointed, she nibbled potato chips, her mouth so dry she could hardly get them down.

"The burger's good," he said so suddenly that Alex nearly jumped in her seat.

"Thank you."

Another few minutes of silence. Then, "The place looks different. What have you done in here?"

"I cleaned up a little."

"I don't want things moved around."

"I didn't move anything," she protested, resisting the temptation to stir uncomfortably beneath his gaze. "I just cleaned under them. There was an inch of dust—"

"I don't want you touching my things. I like them the way they are." He gave her a sudden, probing stare. "What did you think you'd discover by poking through my stuff?"

"I wasn't trying to discover anything. I was just trying to make your life easier."

The look he gave her was dangerously mild. "If that was true, you'd have gone back to the mainland this morning like you were supposed to."

She tossed him a frown. "Look, couldn't we agree to make the best of a bad situation? I'd really like to try and get along with you for the next few days."

"Try to get along, or try to get what you want?"

The accusation brought a peculiar tightness to her throat. "I think we could be . . . friends, if we'd both put forth a little effort."

"I don't want to be your friend."

Her eyes snapped to his. "Why? If I weren't a reporter, could we be friends?"

The twist to his mouth held a sardonic edge. "But you are a reporter, Alexandria," he said in a soft voice. "And I know you can't possibly be that naive."

Beneath his fierce scrutiny she felt strangely unsettled, and because she didn't know how to deal with him, Alex pushed back from the table. Her appetite was suddenly gone.

She dropped her paper plate into a plastic bag, leaving him to polish off another burger. Unnerved, and desperate for a topic that seemed less volatile, she scooped up the net bag of oranges that lay on the counter. "Would you mind if I juiced a few of these?" she asked. "It might be nice to have with tomorrow's breakfast."

"Be my guest. There's a hand juicer in that far drawer."

Locating a knife and the cutting board, she spent an inordinate amount of time preparing the oranges. She was aware of Hunter behind her, watching her as he munched his burger. She wished he'd polish it off and go into the living room. Her earlier wish that he would return to the cottage seemed foolish now; the loneliness was far more desirable than his scrutiny of her every move.

She sliced the oranges. Their sweet, citrusy aroma escaped upward. Focusing on the task, she ground half an orange against the ridges of the juicer, then another. The liquid pooled in the plastic well, before she siphoned it off into a pitcher.

"You're supposed to juice them, not mash them," Hunter said, and Alex jumped, turning her head to find him right behind her.

She swung her attention back to the oranges, not liking the way her breathing reacted to his nearness. Imperceptively, she tilted her head away. "You're an expert, I suppose?"

He laughed, and the hair against her bare shoulder stirred. "I'm a Floridian. I grew up with orange trees in my backyard. You're trapping more juice in the pulp than you're getting."

She twisted the orange half against the juicer. A trickle of golden liquid dribbled into the cup, and inwardly she cursed the blasted fruit for refusing to cooperate. She wanted to run, which seemed like a very silly response to a man's advice on how to juice oranges.

"Here, let me show you." His right hand was suddenly on top of hers, pressing against her fingers. "Push it down on the point, then twist in one direction, not both. It isn't a washing machine."

She studied the subtle flex of bone and muscle as he guided her hand with his. Through the orange rind, the ridges of the juicer rubbed against her palm, a slow, jolting stimulant. The liquid slipped out to coat the tips of their interlaced fingers with its golden nectar.

"Now, squeeze as you turn," Hunter continued, his voice soft and detached, as though he were a teacher lecturing a student. "Gently. You can almost feel the juice sliding out of each membrane, can't you, Alex? That's it."

She nodded. She *could* feel the fruit giving up its treasure. She could feel that and a lot more. She was afraid to move. Afraid to breathe. It seemed the only thing holding her up was the mesmerizing, erotic tether of Hunter's hand, the cool juice that slid between their fingers melding them together with its sticky sweetness. Her senses flared, leaving her lightheaded.

He sensed it, too, she thought, because a silence came between them as he continued to guide her hand and each orange onto the juicer. Wandering strands of her hair, loose and curling, sifted back and forth against her neck as his breath warmed her throat, then caressed her cheek.

Her peripheral vision caught the movement of his head. He was so close now. The fragrance of him drifted into her senses to mix with the piquant per-

fume of the oranges: the clean smell of soap, the slight
tang of sea spice, intermingling with the solid, appealing scent of the man himself. She stood utterly
still. He would kiss her now. She was sure of it. And
oh, she wanted him to.

Instead, his warm breath brushed against her ear as
he spoke. Softly he asked, "Still think we can be
friends, Alex?"

CHAPTER SIX

THE NEXT MORNING, Alex rose to find Hunter already gone. In the kitchen sink a rinsed-out juice glass bore the remnants of orange pulp, a jarring reminder of the intensely charged attraction that had surfaced between them the night before.

Foolish perhaps, but because of that brief interlude, she'd spent a sleepless night in the spare bedroom. It had been a long time before her racing heartbeat returned to normal. And one thought had circled her brain for hours—she'd found far too much pleasure in Hunter's touch.

Her eyes gritty from lack of sleep, she wandered around the empty cottage. It was early, but already bright swatches of golden sunlight bathed the living room.

Another day in paradise.

To be spent alone again?

WITH THE EXCEPTION of the time he'd done in jail for drunk driving as a teenager, Richie Cavanaugh had never spent a more miserable night.

Mosquitoes the size of half dollars had feasted on him. Sand as sharp as ground glass had worked its way

into his underwear, and his legs were in spasm from so
many hours spent crouching in the bushes.

He was tired of this Peeping Tom routine. Tired of
trying to lip-read the few conversations—if they could
be called that—between Garrett and the Sutton
woman. He'd come to the conclusion that hostility
was the only thing between these two. Last night's
dinner had passed in silence, and they held themselves stiffly, as though they were no more than two
strangers who happened to be stuck in the same guest
quarters. From what Richie could see, body language
and a few revealing facial expressions said it all.

Of course, there *had* been that meeting in the
kitchen. Whatever they'd been doing carried an odd
intimacy about it and the promise of a little excitement to relieve the boredom. The voyeur in him
wouldn't have minded witnessing a little hot sex. But
the confrontation had ultimately proven disappoint-
ing. So he'd been forced to settle back and be content
with the stale crackers and warm beer he'd brought
from the mainland.

By now, a call to his father was long overdue.
Charles would chew him up for not checking in
sooner. He didn't like it when circumstances felt out
of his control. Of course, if Richie returned to Fort
Myers empty-handed...

No. Better to let the old man stew a little longer.
Maybe Garrett and the reporter would call a halt to the
hostilities long enough to leave the cottage for a while
so that he could search it.

What happened to the two of them after that de-
pended on what he found.

BY NOON, ALEX WAS almost ready to concede defeat.
Hunter hadn't shown up for lunch. She'd made a long
entry in her journal, cleaned everything in sight,
worked a jigsaw puzzle and sunbathed on the deck.
Who could have guessed that paradise could be so
boring?

Her brothers might have come up with a dozen different solutions to grasp victory from the jaws of defeat; she couldn't think of a single way to *make* Hunter
cooperate. And she might as well have been invisible,
for all the attention he paid her. *When* he bothered to
stick around.

Absently, her fingers ran along the books in the pine
bookcase. She'd dusted them yesterday, straightened
them this morning. Maybe she ought to alphabetize
them. Oh, Alex, she thought, how desperate you've
become.

She tilted her head to read the titles and her glance
caught on a photograph album. Her interest piqued,
she settled on the couch with it.

The pages were all blank and almost completely
stuck together, but in between each page lay three or
four pictures and small strips of paper obviously
meant to headline the snapshots. There were memen-
toes too, a blue ribbon from a science fair, a ticket stub
from Walt Disney World, a computerized report card.

The life chronicled here was that of a sweet-faced
young boy with hair like summer hay. Chatty, hand-
written headers made it easy to follow the years. Eric's
first birthday. The first day of kindergarten. Christmas, age seven. Evidently, the organizer of Eric's life
had run out of time or enthusiasm. Alex could sym-

pathize. She had dozens of pictures at home just waiting to be pasted into albums.

She smiled down at a photo of the boy holding a fish nearly as big as he was. Eric's Big Catch, the header proclaimed. He stood on the steps of this very cottage, and with a suddenness that made her straighten, Alex knew this child had to be the son mentioned in the computer bio she'd pulled on Hunter. The resemblance was startling. Same vivid blue eyes. Same mouth.

That helped explain the decor in the spare bedroom. But retrieving her notes, she found no further mention of the boy. If Hunter and his wife were divorced, who had custody of the child?

Frowning, she ran her fingers over the pictures, as though by touching them the answers would be revealed. Was this part of the reason for Hunter's unwillingness to open up? He might not want to share this part of his life with outsiders. If he had been with his son these past nine months, that would explain a lot. And if he hadn't, that might explain even more.

She had to think of some way to approach this topic with him. Hoping an answer would come to her, she began pressing the pictures against the adhesive pages.

Hunter returned early in the afternoon, looking exhausted. Bits of vegetation clung to his arms and neck, but Alex couldn't help noticing that the sweaty T-shirt molded to his chest admirably. She rose from the table, tossing him a speculative glance.

"I got hungry," was all he said.

He headed toward the bathroom and she heard water run into the basin. When he returned, his face was free of dirt, and his hair sparkled with water droplets.

"I can make you a sandwich," she offered.

He shrugged. "I take it you're not much of a cook?"

She paused on her way to the kitchen, favoring him with a cross look. "I'm not here to slave over a hot stove."

He smiled. "Yes, I know." He spotted the photograph album and picked it up. "Where did this come from?"

"I found it wedged between some books."

The softening of his mouth faded. "I told you, I don't want you disturbing my things. You have no right."

"I only put the pictures in the album the way they were intended to be placed. They'd already been sorted. All they needed was someone with time to stick them in there." In a discontented mutter, she added, "Lord knows, I've had plenty of that."

"That's your own fault."

"Have you heard me complaining?"

"Don't touch this again," he ordered, each word a slow, careful enunciation.

Since clearly her actions had already destroyed any chance for congeniality, she decided to jump in with both feet. "That boy in the photographs is your son, isn't he?"

For an instant, his eyes lost their focus. Then he looked down at the album. His hands moved over the cover, as though he were imprinting the contents in his mind. "There's no story in here, so don't look for one. I'm putting up with you, but if you continue to pry into my things I'll lock you out of the cottage. You can sleep in the boat and keep the mosquitoes company until Riley gets here." His eyes snapped back to hers. "Understand?"

"Perfectly," she replied in a frigid tone. "And it wouldn't surprise me if the mosquitoes could make better small talk."

"You're welcome to find out," he retorted.

He ate a sandwich in silence, and afterward Alex ran a cloth over the table, expecting him to disappear down the stairs at any moment. Instead, she turned and found him blocking her path to the kitchen. He lifted her hand and slapped a bottle of suntan cream into her palm.

"Put on some lotion," he told her.

"Why?"

"I've changed my mind. You're coming with me."

"Where?" she asked warily.

"If you're going to bulldoze your way into my life, then you're going to have to take the bad with the good."

"So far, there hasn't been any good," she muttered. When he continued to stare at her, she sighed heavily and said, "All right. So what's the bad?"

"I didn't come over here just to fish and soak up the sun. I've got work to do, and you're going to help me. If I can't trust you to stay out of my things, then I want you where I can see you."

He thrust a large plastic garbage bag into her hands, and she followed him out the door a moment later. At the bottom of the steps, he lifted a huge, wicked-looking machete.

He ran one finger carefully along the edge of the implement, picked up some sort of sharpening stone that sat on the bottom step, then began running it along the blade.

Alex blinked and glanced at him uneasily.

"What's the matter?" he asked.

"Nothing."

"You're uncharacteristically quiet."

"I make it a point never to argue with a man carrying a machete. Especially one who doesn't like me."

"Good idea," he said with a lazy grin.

Now that her heart rhythm had begun to readjust, she cleared her throat and held out the garbage bag. "However, I think I should tell you that if you're planning to chop me up in little pieces with that thing, I'll be darned if I'll tote the bag you plan to stuff me into."

"God, you've got a morbid imagination. Relax. I don't plan to use this on you." When she smiled sheepishly at him and looked relieved, he added, "Too much work."

Then he turned and headed toward the curve of the beach.

About a hundred feet away from the cottage he stopped and swung toward her. Pointing at a clump of undergrowth, he said, "I'm going to clean out those mangroves. While I do that, I'd like you to clear the beach of everything that doesn't belong here. Any problem with that?"

She could tell he expected an argument, but she
wasn't going to let him get to her. She could tolerate
whatever petty revenge he decided to indulge in. Besides, he still had that darned machete.

"None at all," she replied mildly and immediately
bent to retrieve a crushed cola can from the sand. She
tilted her head quizzically at him. "Do you recycle?"

With one last glowering look, he strode off to the
underbrush. From the way he viciously began attack-
ing the tangled growth, Alex would have bet Hunter
had found a suitable outlet for his displeasure with
her.

They worked within a few feet of each other for a
long time, barely talking and seldom taking a break.
Hunter began to make progress—a noticeable clear-
ance began to appear in the mangroves, and Alex filled
three bags with trash, everything from empty wine
bottles, to miles of knotted fishing line, to one well-
worn sneaker. Her back ached from bending over so
much, but she would have cut out her tongue before
voicing a complaint.

She came upon a gold mine of trash buried in a
clump of seaweed and had to laugh as she discovered
what it was.

Hunter stopped hacking at the mangroves and
turned her way. "What's so funny?"

"Ah, young love," she said, holding up her latest
treasure for him to see—a soggy, sandy mess of glass,
a red cardboard candy box and plastic. "Cheap chocolate and beer sipped out of plastic champagne
glasses. It has a certain whimsy, don't you think?"

"I don't know why mainland Romeos with raging hormones can't find somewhere else to stage a love-fest."

"Oh, come on. This would be the perfect place for it. Didn't you ever have a secret rendezvous for you and your best girl?"

"No."

That one syllable came with such a lack of enthusiasm that Alex found herself saying tersely, "Are all scientists fuddy-duddies, or just you?"

She had never met anyone so unconcerned about silences. Hunter stared at her for an uncomfortably long time. Then, with an irritation in his voice that he took no trouble to conceal, he said, "I'd like to finish this stretch of beach by the end of the afternoon."

He returned to swinging his machete, and Alex sharply saluted his bare back. Under her breath, she groused, "Right away, warden."

She combed the shore with new vigor, telling herself she'd simply ignore the man's unsociable attitude. Unfortunately, she discovered her plan was harder to follow because of the fact that his hostility was packaged in the most virile form imaginable.

More than once she'd found her glance wandering. Hunter, all hard lean muscle, and his body detailed by the sun's confetti flecks of gold shining through the trees, was capable of making her brain burn like brimstone and her heart turn somersaults. She entertained the passing thought that she might once again be suffering from a touch of sunstroke, and rather hoped she was.

"Do you want to take a break?" he interrupted her thoughts suddenly.

"I'm fine," she responded lightly. "Wouldn't want to upset your schedule." She was aware of him standing a few feet away, watching her, and wondered what complaint he'd have against her next. Moving down the ribbon of beach, she scooped up another beer can, shaking her head disgustedly. "Why did you buy this place? Was the city offering a good deal on the county dumping grounds?"

"It's always worse after I've been away for a while. It's a popular spot for picnics."

"Among other things," she added as she held up an object for his perusal. A skimpy, red bikini top dangled from one finger. "Anyone you know?"

He crossed the distance that separated them in a few slow strides. "Hmm," he said as he pretended to examine the bathing suit seriously, though all Alex was aware of was how sexy he still managed to look, even sweaty and covered with bits of clinging vine. "No one I can remember right offhand," he concluded. He passed the top back to her. "You're welcome to keep anything you find."

"Gee, thanks," she grumbled and tossed the bikini into the garbage bag.

"I like privacy."

She swung back to face him. "What?"

"You wanted to know why I bought this place. I like privacy." He plucked a runner of twisted vine off the machete's blade and tossed it away. As though it was an absentminded afterthought, he added, "I knew it would make a good vacation home. A place we could come to when the pressure at work got to be too much to handle."

She straightened, realizing that this was the first information Hunter had volunteered about his past.

"Everyone needs a place like that," she said. "My parents had a cottage on Martha's Vineyard. A really spooky old place that creaked when the wind blew hard. My brothers used to tell me it was the footsteps of dead sea captains." She twisted the bag closed. "Do all little boys like to scare little girls?"

"Well, they all like to scare their sisters."

"Are you speaking from personal experience?"

"I don't have any brothers or sisters," he said in a bland voice.

Alex bent to retrieve a sandy pair of sunglasses with one lens missing. "What about your wife...and son? Didn't they find being out here alone a little frightening?"

"Julie loved it here. And my—" He stopped. Then suddenly he was coming closer, and although there was nothing threatening in his movement, Alex took a hesitant step back.

He stood directly in front of her, so near she could see the sunlight dancing in his eyes. "You know, if you're wanting a good story, you ought to consider doing a little research on this area. This entire chain of small islands is supposed to be haunted."

The change of subject disappointed her, but she refused to give up. Keeping her tone lighthearted, she said, "Really?"

"Some two-bit pirate used this very island for a white-slavery camp. He kidnapped women from the mainland and brought them here, then shipped them off to Arab sheikhs.''

"Nice guy."

He stuck the machete blade-down in the sand. His glance wandered over her, then rested on her face with the intimacy of a caressing hand. In a graceful, seemingly unpremeditated gesture, he let his fingers trail down her bare arm. "I'm told the man had an excellent eye for the ladies," he said slowly. "Always found the most beautiful women for his buyers.''

"Ah. A pirate with good taste," Alex said with some desperation, finding herself in a state of wholesale confusion now that all those lovely chest muscles were so darned close.

"Supposedly, the ghosts of his captives still walk the beach at night, carrying lanterns to signal for help."

"And have you ever seen any of these unfortunate women?"

"No." Hunter gave her a wry smile. "All I ever get are nosy reporters."

"Very funny," she retorted. In an effort to break the link between them, she moved to lift the trash bag.

Hunter's hands caught her upper arms. She tilted her face up and discovered that the oddly enticing warmth of his eyes left her feeling shivery inside.

"Alex, you're wasting your time," he said without rancor. "You'd be better off writing about our white slavers than trying to trick information out of me."

"Hunter—"

His vivid blue gaze held a smile. "Yes?"

She felt a telltale blush stain her cheeks. Whether it was from embarrassed guilt or the realization that the fine-boned elegance of his features had a decided effect on her nervous system, she couldn't have said. She stammered out, "Y-you're too suspicious. I wasn't...I wasn't trying to trick you into anything."

"Weren't you?" he refuted. "Did your parents really have a place on Martha's Vineyard?" Something in her face made his grin widen. "That's all right. I wasn't telling the truth about the pirate, either."

His hands stroked idly, slowly, up and down her arms, and though her flesh was already warm from the sun, Alex felt her skin begin to tingle. The hard planes and angles of Hunter's face seemed to become softer. He cocked his head to one side, as though he'd suddenly found something strange within his grasp and wasn't sure what to do with it.

Alex brought a hand up to still the movement of Hunter's fingers on her arm. She knew she must seem visibly ruffled, but any more of his gentle touching and there was no telling how she would disgrace herself.

She lifted her eyes to his. "You don't play fair, Hunter."

"I told you I didn't want to 'play' at all, Alex. You're the one who keeps pushing."

"It would take so little to get me out of your hair and off this island," she said in a low, determined voice.

His grip tightened ever so slightly as he shook his head. "I don't believe you. Nothing's ever that easy where the press is involved."

"It can be. Give me *something*. *Anything*."

With a grim look, he said, "I can't resist a request like that."

She felt the heat of his uncovered chest as he drew her toward him and his mouth suddenly connected with hers. Her surprised gasp had left her open-mouthed, and he took quick advantage of that fact. His kiss was hot, arousing and thorough. It burned like brandy on her lips and tasted twice as potent. Unfortunately, it was also over nearly as quickly as it began.

He released her swiftly. She had to take a stumbling half step backward just to keep her footing in the soft sand.

"See what you can make of that, Lois Lane," he said, and walked away.

DINNER WAS another quiet meal. She supposed that examining that photo album had placed an irrevocable black mark against her. And truthfully, she didn't want to examine Hunter's silence too closely for fear it might have more to do with this afternoon's folly than any effort on her part to pry into his past.

When he wasn't looking, she allowed herself to study his profile.

Formidable, but completely unreadable. Illogically, the very lack of emotion on his features made Alex want to reach out to him. She couldn't, of course. Suddenly the lack of trust between them was something she regretted more than anything.

Hunter washed the dishes. Alex wondered how they'd get through the evening with no television to pretend an interest in and no chance of conversation.

She'd just finished sponging off the table when the cottage lights flickered, then died.

His voice reached out to her in the darkness. "Don't move. There should be a flashlight in one of these drawers."

She listened to him grope around the kitchen. Utensils clattered, and once he muttered a soft curse.

"What's the matter?" she asked.

"I just speared my hand on the ice pick."

She couldn't help laughing. "Should have paid that electric bill."

"It's the generator. It's touchy sometimes. Ah-hah!"

The flashlight beam stabbed through the darkness, swinging in her direction. "What are you going to do now?" she asked.

"Fix it, of course. It shouldn't take long."

"I'll come with you."

"Why? Do you know anything about generators?"

"I know how to hold a flashlight."

"I can manage on my own."

"Stop being difficult. I can help, and I'm not going to sit here in the dark by myself."

"Fine. Wait here," he ordered, then left her standing in the dark room while he disappeared toward the master bedroom. A few minutes later, he reemerged. "This is the best I could do," he said, tossing her a yellow slicker several sizes too large. "If the mosquitoes are bad, you're going to want as much covered as possible."

The garment hung past her knees and fingertips. She felt ridiculous, like a tramp in found clothing.

Hunter zipped into his jacket while she fumbled with the too-long sleeves, trying to close the top button on the slicker. Tossing her an exasperated look, he slid the flashlight under one arm and pushed her fingers away. "Here, let me."

He tugged the two ends of the slicker together, his knuckles brushing warmly against her throat. She couldn't make out his eyes in the darkness, but some sixth sense told her he was watching her closely.

"Turn up the collar so your neck will be protected," he said.

The collar stood so high—nearly touching her forehead—that she couldn't see over the edge of it. Hearing his laugh, she snapped it back down into place. "You're doing this on purpose, aren't you?"

"I'm just trying to keep you from becoming dinner for the mosquitoes." His voice was suspiciously innocent. He shook a can of insect repellent. "Stick out your legs."

She lifted first one, then the other, and Hunter bent to cover every bit of exposed skin. "I feel like a school bus in this thing," she complained.

He straightened and sprayed some of it directly into his hand. "Hold still and close your eyes," he said. His fingers were suddenly against her skin as he coated her face. She closed her eyes and coughed at the unpleasant odor, but she was more aware of the intimacy of his hand.

The moment Hunter touched her, he wished he hadn't.

Be careful, you fool. This is a mistake. Can't you see what a mistake it is to touch her?

His breath caught as he gently glided the liquid against her flesh. Beneath his fingers, her high cheekbones, her nose, even her chin seemed perfectly molded, sculpted by a divine hand. She might have been an angel awaiting the benevolent hand of God.

Or a woman eager to receive a lover's kiss.

Desire crackled along his nerve endings and sent a swift kicking sensation to his gut. The only thought that penetrated was how much he wanted to pull her into his arms again, taste her lips in the warm, quiet intimacy of the darkened cottage...and explore. Just explore...

"Alex—"

She twisted her face away. "Enough! That stuff smells horrible," she said with a light laugh, but her voice was shaky enough that he knew she'd felt something, too. "I'd rather take my chances with the mosquitoes."

He turned and she followed him out the front door. On the deck he halted momentarily, playing the light down the staircase. Beyond the cottage the island waited in utter silence, suddenly foreign and intimidating.

"Give me your hand," he directed.

"Why?"

"Because there are a dozen things between here and the generator that could trip you up."

"That's very thoughtful, but—"

"Give me your hand," he said more firmly. "I have no intention of being sued just because you were clumsy enough to fall over a tree root and break your leg."

He scooped up her hand and she let him take it, too disappointed to object further. So much for his concern about her safety. What an annoying man he was. She could not think of a single reason why his hand encompassing hers should be such a delightful stimulus.

He picked his way across the cottage grounds to a small shed. Hunter thrust the flashlight into her hands, then popped the lock with a key. The door creaked open, and the unpleasant smell of fuel drifted out to meet the balmy night air.

The building was hardly big enough to allow both her and Hunter in the room at the same time. Inside, an oily, green monster of a motor sat in the middle of the floor. With vague interest Alex bobbled the light over the walls, creating menacing shadows.

"Stop sight-seeing and bring the light over here," Hunter ordered.

She joined him at the generator and waited while he flipped switches and checked dials. When he pushed the Reset button, the machinery growled like a dying beast, but refused to start. He moved to its side and began removing the cables from a large battery.

"Is that like a car battery?"

"Uh-huh."

For the next few minutes, she watched while he cleaned corrosion from the cable connectors with his penknife.

"Try the Reset," he said. "Maybe it'll turn over."

It didn't.

"Now what?" she asked.

"Process of elimination. If it's not the battery, we'll go on to the next thing it could be."

"Maybe it's out of gas."

"It runs on diesel." He shook his head as though such knowledge should have occurred to her already. Poor man, forced to explain how a motor worked to a mere woman.

Refusing to lose patience, she replied, "Okay, so maybe it's out of diesel."

"Shouldn't be. I checked the tank the last time I came."

"Maybe it's the spark plugs."

She caught the glint of his hair and knew he'd shaken his head again. "Diesel generators don't have spark plugs."

"I'm just trying to think of all the possibilities."

"Just hold the flashlight," he said with an exasperated sigh. "And stop whispering. No one's going to hear you."

She subsided into mutinous silence. Fine. Let *him* figure out what was wrong with the thing.

He tried different approaches and eventually discovered that the fuel line needed to be bled of water. It would take some time. Her job, he instructed, would be to give him enough light to work by and press the Reset button when he told her to. Hardly a taxing assignment.

He shed his jacket and retrieved the pump from a corner of the shed. Disconnecting hoses, he began forcing air through the system. Determined not to give him any further cause for complaint, Alex focused the flashlight on his hands.

Absently, she listened to the steady hiss of air as Hunter plunged the handle. He had wonderful hands. Long and elegant, but with a masculine bluntness at the tips. They curled around the handle with brisk, determined power. Last night they had been gentle. Playfully seductive. This afternoon they'd been hard and demanding.

She ought to stop such fanciful thoughts right now. To punish herself, she forced her eyes upward—and ran right into the sight of Hunter's arm and shoulder muscles bunching and stretching with each stroke. Sinewy strength coupled with fluid efficiency.

Up...down.

Up...down.

There was a hypnotic perfection in the rhythm. It made her blood pound faster and faster, until it seemed to keep pace with Hunter's movements.

Being alone with him in this cozy intimacy held a certain unreality, as though they were the last two people on the rim of the universe. He'd find that notion laughable, of course. He just wanted the generator fixed. Which was the only thing she wanted, too, she reminded herself sharply.

Twice, Hunter stopped pumping and instructed her to try the Reset button. Both times the motor sputtered, then subsided into rolling grunts. Disgusted, Hunter muttered a curse. He'd been at this nearly an hour now. If he couldn't get the generator started...

He shot a glance in Alex's direction. She stood only a handful of steps away, and Hunter thought that if she didn't stop looking so sweetly sexy in that ridiculous raincoat, he might have to close the distance between them and show her he wasn't *totally* incompetent. No matter how inept the generator was making him out to be, there were still some things he knew how to do.

Her gaze remained fixed outside the shed. "What's the matter?" he asked.

The flashlight jumped as she faced him. "Nothing. Why?"

He jerked his head toward the doorway. "What's so fascinating out there?"

"I thought I saw something move in the bushes."

"Probably raccoons."

"Oh. It's just . . . so dark."

He laughed as he folded his arms against his chest. "No wonder you're a reporter. Nothing gets past you."

He caught her frown of displeasure. "I'm not used to such total darkness. In the city there's always *some* kind of light."

"Ah, yes. A neon wonderland."

"At least you don't feel so isolated . . . so alone."

Was she trying to make him feel guilty about all the hours he'd left her by herself, the times he'd been intentionally rude and hostile? He'd been so sure she'd give up and go home.

But she hadn't. She'd been more determined than he expected. Tougher. But looking at her right now, maybe she wasn't as tough as she pretended to be. Maybe she wasn't tough at all.

Damn her. The thick, undefended note in her voice made his heart twist in all directions. She had the uncanny ability to jumble every emotion he possessed. Control threatened to evaporate, but somehow he found the strength to make his words light and mocking. "I thought that's what you wanted. You and me." He lowered his voice until it was no more than a warm, intimate rumble. "Alone."

She must have been aware of a change between them because she turned to focus on the generator. He let her find distraction there, glad she'd forced the unexpected tension to die a quick death. "Do you really know what you're doing with this thing?" she asked.

Yes, this is better, Alex. Much better. There's no danger in a conversation about this damned generator. "I'm open to suggestions."

"I don't think I like your island much."

"Cough up that microphone. I'll have you back in Miami before you can say, 'I accept defeat.'" She shook her head and he shrugged. "Better get used to the dark then, because if I can't fix this we could be back to candle power. No showers, no drinking water except what's already in the plumbing—"

"No showers?"

"The generator runs the water pump."

"Oh." She tossed him a look filled with sudden suspicion. "Is this a trick to get the microphone back?"

"No. Would it have worked?"

"No."

"I didn't think so," he remarked with a shadowy grin and went back to plunging the pump handle.

A few minutes later, he sent her back to the front of the generator. She whispered a silent prayer and leaned hard on the Reset button. The motor settled into its monotonous, whining refusal.

"Come on, you miserable hunk of junk!" Hunter shouted over the noise. "Turn over, dammit."

Feeling as frustrated as he sounded, Alex added her own encouragement, a well-aimed kick of her sneakered foot. Amazingly, the motor revved into life.

Stunned, Hunter and Alex stared at the machine, then each other. They burst into laughter. Tossing down the pump, he came to her, catching her arms. "You lied to me," he yelled over the noise. "You *do* know how to fix a generator!"

Flushed with breathless merriment, she stuck out her foot and wiggled it. "All it takes is the right equipment!"

They laughed together again, and she realized this was the first time she'd heard genuine amusement in his voice. No mocking derision. Nothing held back. Enjoyment that struck a deep, answering chord within her.

She met his eyes. For just a moment, in that shadowy, too-warm shed, their thoughts connected. Their unguarded emotions intertwined in response to a delicate shift in the mood. Their laughter wound down. Hunter's lips tucked into an odd, quizzical smile, as though he understood even less than she why this sudden, potent bond arced between them. His eyes, bright and searching, examined her features, trying to find a reason and a way around it.

Alex didn't care about answers. She liked the quick, excited leap her pulse indulged in. She leaned closer, and just when she thought the need to touch might finally outweigh the need for caution, his hands dropped to his sides and he turned away.

CHAPTER SEVEN

HUNTER SETTLED on the couch, tilted his head against the cushions and waited his turn to take a shower. Lord, he was tired. He didn't have an ounce of strength left after a day spent cleaning out the mangroves, babying the generator back into operation and wrestling a few baser instincts into submission out there in the dark. He still felt jumpy and irritated by how close he'd come to acting on impulse with Alex.

What was wrong with him? Why couldn't he keep his thoughts from drifting into all kinds of silly, misguided fantasies about a woman he ought to be avoiding like the plague? He hated the fact that she had this effect on him. And that he couldn't seem to control it.

He combed his fingers through his hair in annoyance. How many more days before Riley showed up and carted the woman off the island and out of his life? Too many. Way too many.

He turned his head...and his gaze fell on Alex's notebook lying on the far end of the couch.

He never intended to pick it up. Yet it was suddenly lying in his hands, all its dark secrets hidden behind a nondescript imitation-leather cover. What notes had she made about him? What conclusions had she drawn?

He told himself he didn't need to know. No matter what she decided to write, she couldn't do him any more harm then he'd already done to himself. But even as he hugged that knowledge close, his fingers were plucking apart the pages. Any small twinges of guilt dissolved with the reminder of how shamelessly she'd invaded his privacy.

ALEX EMERGED from the shower feeling pleasantly relaxed. The hot water had washed away the day's frustrations and revived her spirits. Maybe tomorrow she'd think of some way to bridge the gap between Hunter and her. A foolish idea, perhaps, for nothing had really changed.

And yet, that moment of sharing in the generator shed had given her hope.

She entered the living room, only to find it empty. The sliding glass door stood open, and beyond it the porch light bathed everything in a golden glow. In the lazy breeze, wind chimes tapped out a haphazard melody. She walked quietly onto the deck in her bare feet.

It took her a moment to spot Hunter, seated in one of the far lounge chairs, out of the lamplight. She started toward him, then halted, suddenly unsure. Maybe he'd chosen the shadows because he wanted to be alone. "The shower's all yours," she stated. "I tried not to use all the hot water."

He gave her an abrupt nod of acknowledgment.

No, he wasn't looking for company. She swiveled to return inside.

"Alex?"

She paused, drawn by the unexpected softness in his voice. "Yes?"

"The breeze keeps the mosquitoes away and it's still early. Maybe you'd like to sit out here a while."

The invitation was so unexpected that she found it suspect. She tilted her head to one side, trying to see through the shadows to determine the truth. "Are you asking the woman, or the reporter?"

His light laugh sifted through the hush of night. "I'm asking the lady who knows how to fix generators."

She experienced a momentary thrill, then swatted it down ruthlessly. He was probably just tired, looking for diversion before heading off to bed. Even a conversation with her would be better than nothing.

She settled into the lounge chair next to him, lifting her face toward a sky that was saturated with stars. The night breeze winnowed through her hair. Beneath the deck the tide gurgled against the pilings, a steady, hiccuping rhythm that she tried to ignore.

She turned her head to look at him. "What would you like to talk about?"

Her eyes were drawn to his lap, and she realized the photo album lay open across it. The light glinted off the plastic overlay of the pages. She frowned, watching his fingers trace blindly down the edge of the book.

"I'd forgotten this album was even here," he remarked in a quiet, distracted voice. "My wife brought it over to organize the pictures, and I suppose she never got around to finishing it.''

"It's one of those things you always mean to get to and just never seem to find the time.''

"You did a nice job.''

"It was easy. All they needed was to be put in place.''

"I was angry that you were prying through my things but I was probably rougher on you than I needed to be. Seeing the book took me by surprise.''

The explanation—was it an apology?—stunned her even more than the invitation to talk. Uncertain, she shook her head. "Hunter—''

In the poor light their eyes made sudden, troubled contact. His words came out hurried, impassioned. "You were right. This is my son, Eric.''

"The mouth and chin is a dead giveaway. Same stubborn lines.'' Ripples of uneasiness tripped through her. She wasn't sure why this conversation was happening. Why was he suddenly prepared to discuss personal things with her? What had changed his mind? "Do you see him much?''

"No.''

"I'm sorry. I'm sure that must be very difficult.''

After an extended pause, he said quietly, "My wife and son are dead.''

His words, too terrible to hear, sent the air rushing from her lungs. A chill of shock settled within her as remorse knotted her throat. She felt a sudden, fierce need to protect him from his sorrows, and an overwhelming regret that she had no idea how to do so. "I'm sorry. I didn't know.''

With a brisk movement, he rose. "We should go in."

He had almost reached the circle of light when she found her voice. "Hunter, please," she murmured in a soft entreaty. "Please don't leave."

He halted, but didn't turn around, and she knew he was debating the wisdom of remaining. She suspected he'd long ago decided to shelve the bleaker emotions of the past, but putting them away and keeping them there, all neat and tidy and resolved, were two different things.

Quietly she went to his side. His face was no more than a moonlit profile that threatened to blend into the darkness.

After a very long time, his voice, soft and lonely, reached out, breaking the stillness. "I was about to file suit against Cavanaugh Labs and didn't want my family to be hurt by the publicity, so Julie took Eric back to Norway to visit her parents. They live in a little backwater town that's not even on the map. I thought they'd be protected there."

Chilly fingers of guilt and despair curled around his words. She knew in that moment that whatever else had transpired since the death of his wife and child, the painful process of recovery was not over yet.

She placed her hand along his arm, feeling the muscles bunch and twitch. "How did it happen?"

"Julie wanted Eric to know more about his roots. She was showing him the sights. Their car ran head-on into another and tumbled off the side of a mountain." His lips and jaw molded in taut, hard lines. "Her parents phoned with the news."

"Is it possible that it wasn't an accident?"

He turned his head, giving her a small smile that carried no humor. "You mean Charles Cavanaugh? Believe me, I was seeing bogeymen behind every tree back then, and I was ready to think the worst of him. But Julie's father assured me that it couldn't have been. A couple of German tourists overshot one of the curves and just plowed into her. It happens all the time on those mountain roads."

"The wire service never picked up the news."

"Julie was staying there under her maiden name, and the town's small—they look after their own. Her parents are prominent and well-liked. They didn't want a media circus, and neither did I, so the news got buried. It was easier to let the press think she'd left me. Over here, Riley's the only one who knows." He shook his head slightly. "Ironic, isn't it? If they'd stayed here to weather the publicity, in spite of how bad it got, they'd probably both still be alive."

"You couldn't have known it would happen."

"Realistically, I know that's true. But some-times—" he denied her logic with a quick, negative shake "—it just doesn't work."

"Hunter..." She didn't know how to respond. All the words that came to her seemed horribly inade-quate. "I want to help you, but I'm not sure I know how. Tell me what to do."

"There's no easy answer. Right now I'm trying to take one day at a time, until—" The rest died abruptly as he swung his head to gaze out across the water.

"Until it doesn't hurt so much anymore?"

"Until I can look in the mirror and not see a man who killed his own wife and child."

She gasped at the vileness of that self-accusation. He couldn't be serious! And yet, she knew he was, because the tension in his features had jerked every muscle even tauter. "You *can't* think that. Why would you blame yourself?"

"*I* sent them over there. Julie didn't want to go."

Such pain in his voice. But when his eyes found hers, they were more expressionless than she had ever seen them.

"We argued. I was so angry about the way our research had been misused, I don't think I listened to a word she said. I just wanted to handle things my own way."

"You did the right thing. What you believed in, whether the investigating committee sided with you or not."

"Don't you see? If I'd been less stubborn and idealistic, Julie and Eric might never—"

She felt him withdrawing, and cut across his words quickly. "What good does it do to torture yourself this way? They loved you. They wouldn't want to see you hurting for something so totally beyond your control."

He frowned momentarily, then his mouth reshaped into a small smile that was no more than a mockery of humor. With his forefinger he tilted her chin up so that her features found the moonlight. "Sweet Alex. You've got too tender a heart for the career you've chosen. You shouldn't be finding excuses for me. You should be looking for an angle your paper can use."

She blinked and listened to the sound of her own uneven breathing. "I can't hurt you, Hunter."

His gaze roamed her face, lingering on her mouth. "In some ways... you already have," he said softly, as though the words had been dragged from him against his will.

She shook her head. "I don't understand."

"Don't you?"

Hunter's hand slipped to the back of her head, drawing her closer, and when his lips brushed hers, it seemed the most natural thing in the world. With a sudden greed to experience more, she sagged against him, eager to fill the warm space that separated their bodies.

His touch came delicately, delving with the lightest exploration. Beneath his gentle appeal her lips quivered, then opened to receive his long, beguiling kiss. When he lifted his head from her at last, she felt immediately bereft. The cool night air chilled the moisture on her lips, but could not extinguish the fire that burned within her breast.

"You taste so good," he whispered against her ear. "Like warmed honey. When I kiss you, I start to believe anything is possible..."

The flare of passion was in his eyes, but so was some inner disquiet. She watched the battle wage between his heart and his mind, and knew the moment when his mind won.

His hands cupped her shoulders, gently pushing her away. He shook his head. "Go to bed, Alex. This isn't right for either of us. I don't need any more sins added to my conscience."

HIDDEN IN THE UNDERGROWTH the next morning, Richie emitted a wavering sigh. Another bug-infested night had passed, and he'd devoured the last of his food this morning. His senses were completely dulled by heat and monotony and frustration.

He would have to call it quits. Confess to his father that he hadn't found out a thing, hadn't even been able to search Garrett's cottage. *That* was sure to make the old man happy.

He sat up straighter as the cottage door opened and Hunter Garrett came out on the deck, tackle box in hand.

Oh, great. Another day spent observing the man pretending to be after the big one that got away. The guy was terrible! If there was anything worse than fishing and catching nothing, it was watching someone else fish and catch nothing.

But just then, the Sutton woman came out, too, looking sleek and sporty in a white swimsuit that showed off those magnificent legs...well...magnificently. And she and Garrett actually smiled at each other as they headed toward the lagoon.

He held his breath as they went right past the palmettos where he was hiding. Exhilaration hammered through Richie's body. Finally, after hours—days—of watching the two, his opportunity had come.

Waiting a few tedious minutes for safety's sake, he worked life back into legs that had gone rubbery from disuse. Then he sprinted across the ground, taking the cottage stairs two at a time. His momentary fear that he would find the house locked subsided as the doorknob turned under his hand.

ALEX LAY on her stomach on the beach blanket and watched Hunter fish.

The sport itself didn't generate much excitement, but she had to admit, he made an awfully attractive fisherman. With the morning sun bouncing off his hair and that deep tan getting richer every day, he was movie-star handsome. He'd waded into the lagoon, and the turquoise water lapped at his powerful thighs. The sight made her wish he'd taken off his shirt, as well, just to see if his chest compared well with those muscular legs. If she remembered correctly, it did.

She was still stunned and delighted that he'd asked her to join him this morning. He'd been waiting for her to rise, and his invitation had taken her completely by surprise, so unexpected that she hadn't thought to wonder why. She'd just grabbed her tote bag, and hadn't even objected to his insistence that she make use of one of the spare bathing suits left behind in the cottage.

She watched him recast his line.

Why had he invited her? Loneliness? Was he ready to concede defeat and grant her a real interview?

Or was it guilt over last night's kiss?

A sudden splash broke through her thoughts and she shaded her eyes against the sun's glare. Hunter had caught something. A small, silver fish that flopped once or twice, then settled into its fate without further objection. He held it up for her to see, his smile reminding her eerily of the picture of his son in front of the cottage. She applauded his expertise.

"I've got *my* dinner," he boasted. "Now all I have to do is catch yours."

"I don't suppose you could catch a nice green salad with blue cheese dressing. Maybe some croutons?"

"I thought you said you liked fish."

She made a face as he attached the poor creature to the stringer. "Just remember," she reminded him, "you clean anything you catch."

He laughed and rebaited his hook.

Alex sighed and went back to scribbling in her notebook. Whatever attraction he'd felt toward her last night, he seemed able enough to ignore today.

SOMEONE WAS SHAKING her shoulder gently.

"Turn over, Alex. Before your back burns again."

She groaned and her eyelashes fluttered open. Turning her head, she squinted up into the haloed silhouette created by Hunter's body against the sun. In her half conscious, half dream state, she thought she felt his hand stroke along her cheek, but she couldn't be sure. "What's the matter?" she mumbled.

"I guess watching me fish put you to sleep."

Setting aside his pole, he sank cross-legged onto the blanket. She sat up, making adjustments to the top of the white maillot bathing suit.

Hunter had told her that guests to the island often left items behind accidently, but she had the nagging suspicion that this suit had belonged to Julie Garrett. It had just the kind of sophisticated simplicity that would be very flattering on a Scandinavian beauty like Julie, and it reminded Alex how different she must be from Hunter's late wife.

She felt daringly exposed by the deep neckline and high-cut legs. Self-consciously, she wrapped her arms around her calves and settled her chin on her knees.

"Am I making you nervous?"

Her eyes flashed up to meet his. Was she really that transparent? "No," she denied. "Of course not."

"Then it must be that Yankee upbringing of yours."

"I beg your pardon?"

He smiled at her defensive tone. "If it's not me, then it must be the suit. You're shy about it."

She straightened in indignation. One of the suit straps slid down her arm, but she refused to give in to the temptation to slip it back into place. "I most certainly am not!"

"Yes, you are. Is that why you never learned to swim? So you wouldn't have to wear a bathing suit?"

Discussing her body didn't seem like a good idea. She tried a diversionary tactic. "No, that's not why. When I was five, my father threw me into the pool and it was sink or swim."

The laughter left his eyes. "You're joking."

She gazed out across the lagoon in order to give herself time to formulate an answer. "My parents never had much patience with us as kids, and they didn't believe in pandering to our fears. So I learned, but I never liked it."

"Kind of hard on a kid, don't you think?"

She shifted uncomfortably on the blanket. By now she should have come to terms with a family that never did anything in half measures. "They've always led adventuresome, exciting lives," she answered carefully. "My brothers were older, following in their footsteps. My parents weren't about to put up with any foolishness from me just because I was a girl. I learned early what was expected of a Sutton.''

He scooped up a handful of sand, then watched it as it drifted through his fingers into a tiny dune. ''So did they expect you to become a journalist?''

Expect? That career might as well have been engraved on her birth certificate. ''I come from a long line of journalists. My father is William Sutton.''

''*The* William Sutton? The Boston publisher?''

''That's the one.''

He whistled softly and shook his head. ''No wonder you're so willing to drive me crazy for a story. You go back empty-handed to Mom and Dad and those two killer sharks they have for sons and they'll eat you alive.''

''I'm not doing it for them,'' she replied quickly. Was it a lifetime of trying to measure up that made her response sound so intense? Hunter's gaze was unwavering on hers. She licked her lips and tried to keep her voice unperturbed. ''Initially, my editor in Miami wanted this story, but now, so do I.''

''Why?''

How could she confess that he was one of the most fascinating men she'd ever met? That she'd come here expecting to find an erratic, wild-eyed lunatic worthy of the reputation he'd created with the press, and instead, found a sexy, enigmatic loner who still carried the scars of blame for the loss of his family. No. She couldn't tell him any of that. ''Maybe I just like a challenge,'' she hedged at last.

His grin told her he didn't believe that for one moment. "Do you? Then I've got one for you. I'll answer three of the questions you've been dying to ask since the moment you got here."

"And what feat of magic would I have to perform in return?" she asked skeptically.

"In return, you let me teach you to swim."

"I told you, I already know."

"No kid should learn that way. I can teach you to enjoy it."

Enticement pulled at her. Did he mean it? And if he did, could she make such a bargain? She stared out across the turquoise water, where hardly a ripple disturbed the surface. She imagined Hunter leading her into its cool depths. Imagined the bottom dropping away from her feet. Her stomach flipped unpleasantly. "No."

"Alex, you can't spend the rest of your life being afraid of the water."

"Why not? I've gotten this far—"

"Three questions. Any three you want answers to."

"You're horrible to bait me like this."

"It's the opportunity you've been waiting for. If you phrase them right, you can build a whole story." He waited, letting the idea sink in. "What do you say?"

"I say no."

"You'll never get a better offer."

"Hunter, I can't—" She broke off and looked away, ashamed because her fear was so obvious, even in her voice.

In the next moment, she felt his hand along her arm, oddly cool against her sun-warmed skin. She turned back and watched as he carefully slid the wayward bathing-suit strap into place. "I won't let anything happen to you, Alex," he said gently. "Did you know I put myself through college by lifeguarding at one of the resorts near here? Bet that's not in your notebook."

He continued to stroke along her arm slowly. The reassurance of his touch began to feel mesmerizing. His mouth formed an easy smile made to make a woman melt, and bright sunlight danced in his eyes, turning them into blue diamonds. Trust me, they said, and Alex realized how easily she could give in to such tender temptation. "That isn't the kind of information I can make much use of."

His hand dropped. "Ah, yes. Hard-hitting, Lois Lane–type questions." With a deep sigh he suddenly caught the tail of his shirt and pulled it over his head. He moved so that they sat face-to-face. "So how about this?" he asked softly.

At first she thought he meant his chest, and as chests went, she had to admit it was pretty magnificent. Tanned and contoured by muscles, lightly furred with crisp, dark hair that whorled and patterned down to the waistband of his swim trunks and beyond. Oh, yes, she remembered this chest, and there was nothing wrong here.

And then she realized that something *was* wrong, because tucked in amongst all that fine hair matting his left pectoral was a long, arcing scar that she hadn't noticed before. It lay almost directly over his heart, marring his bronzed flesh in a thin, red line. In spite of its wicked-looking length, it was clearly surgical, for tiny suture scars lay on either side.

Hunter's fingers ran along its ridged length. "It's a souvenir from my days as a radical activist," he said in a quiet voice.

She couldn't take her eyes off the scar. "What happened?"

"You can make that one of your three questions."

He was baiting her again. She read the determination in his eyes that told her she'd never get the answer any other way. And something else. He was willing to meet her halfway, to share a part of his life he'd kept hidden for too long.

His eyes remained intent on hers. "I won't lie. I won't hedge. I'll trust you with my past. You trust me with your future."

She looked toward the water again, a lifetime of caution fracturing bit by bit. With Hunter beside her, what could she have to fear? Memory danced across the hot coals of suspicion. This was, after all, the same man who had left her stranded on a sandbar. She angled a narrowed glance his way. "How come you're suddenly so agreeable? Yesterday you threatened to make me sleep in the boat."

He smiled. "Maybe you've worn me down."

"Don't," she said with a harsh shake of her head. "Don't make fun of me."

"I apologize." His glance flickered down to her journal, then back again. "Maybe I like a challenge, too. Figuring out exactly who Alexandria Sutton really is."

"What's that supposed to mean?"

"Let's just say I'm learning to like the woman," he replied with a shrug. "Well enough that I'm willing to overlook the unfortunate choice of profession." She would have liked to give that remark more thought. But he rose in one quick, graceful movement and held out his hand. "What do you say?"

Alex swallowed hard and sent up a prayer that she wasn't making a big mistake. This was her golden opportunity. With cold dread settling in the pit of her stomach, she placed her hand in Hunter's and let him pull her to her feet.

He led her to the water's edge, and with their hands still linked, they waded out to knee-deep depths.

"Sit down," he instructed.

Given the shaky condition of her legs, she was more than willing to comply. Sitting, the water was only waist-high, the pull of the tide such a minor influence that she might have been relaxing in her bathtub back home.

"This isn't so bad, is it?" he asked.

She shook her head, her throat so dry that words would have been an impossibility. They sat together and Hunter began to talk of inconsequential things—commenting on the temperature of the gulf, lifting tiny shells off the sandy bottom and holding them out for her inspection, pointing out the courtship voices of herons perched in nearby trees. In between their conversation he dribbled water against his chest and over her shoulders.

Fifteen minutes later he had her lower her face into the water. All the while he reassured her with soothing words, encouraging her to accustom herself to the feel of water flowing against her face. She felt silly, but followed his directions. The reward of answers to her questions dangled temptingly in the recesses of her mind.

Hunter gave her a satisfied grin. "That's step one. Getting used to the water against your face. Now I want you to put—"

"Wait a minute," she cut in. She hadn't forgotten just why she was putting up with this swimming nonsense. "When do I get answers to my three questions?"

"When I'm through with you."

"That sounds ominous."

He tugged on her hand, pulling her toward deeper water. "Trust me."

She definitely didn't like the sound of that.

CHAPTER EIGHT

HUNTER LED her farther into the gulf, until the rippling waves reached just beneath her breasts. In spite of the fact that her feet were still solidly planted against the lagoon's sandy bottom, apprehension sent a cold shiver down her spine. He held both her hands, and much as she wanted to loosen her grip just a little to show she wasn't afraid, her brain wasn't translating the message to her fingers.

"It's all right," he encouraged. "I'm right here and I won't let anything happen to you. Dig your toes in. You can feel the bottom, can't you? You don't have to be nervous."

"I'm not nervous." The smile she offered him was too stage-managed to be convincing.

He grinned back with a look full of understanding. "Good."

"I don't lie very well."

"I know," he replied kindly.

"Now what?"

"Now jump."

"What?"

"Jump. Straight up. I'm holding you, and the bottom's right there. If you can, let the buoyancy of your body settle you back in the water. Try to wait until the last minute to get your feet under you.''

At first Alex was reluctant, but she did as he instructed. This silly jumping maneuver wasn't really swimming at all. The water frothed around them like a small typhoon. She wondered if she looked half as ridiculous as she felt. Hunter's eyes followed her, his smile broadening with every jump.

''Are you sure this is going to help?'' she asked in midair.

''Don't you trust me yet?''

''No. And you could stop looking so darned amused.''

''I can't help it. You ought to see the view I have.''

''What?'' She stopped. Following the direction of his glance, she discovered that her suit, skimpy enough to stuff into a mouse hole—with plenty of room left over for the mouse—didn't hide much. Horrified by the imminent exposure of her breasts, Alex felt her sun-brushed cheeks go a darker red. ''You letch. I should have known this was just one of your tricks—''

''It isn't, I swear,'' he protested with a laugh.

She stepped back a few paces toward shore, crossed her arms over her chest and shot him a determined look. ''Question number one—''

''*Step* number three,'' he countered. ''Wrap your fingers around my arm.''

He extended his forearm as though she hadn't spoken. Suspicion flared within her. Was he just playing with her, not intending to give her answers to her questions?

Some of her skepticism must have shown on her face, because he shook his head and with an ill-suppressed chuckle said, "I don't break my promises, Alex. Three questions. Three answers. But *my* way." He dragged his fingers through the water in a wide arc, creating a small wave between them. "Take my arm and stretch out. I'm going to pull you slowly. Try to keep your head under, but don't wait until your lungs feel ready to burst. When you want to come up for air, tap me on the arm and I'll stop. Just don't raise your head or you'll get a noseful of water. Okay?"

No, it was not okay. Sure, she wanted answers to her questions, but was this really the way she had to get them? Would either one of her brothers have agreed to such blackmail? It seemed doubtful. But then, Rio and Mel could swim like fishes.

Don't think about the water, she chided herself. Her eyes flickered down to Hunter's dripping forearm where droplets sparkled amid the dark hair. How easy it should have been to find distraction in the irresistible lure of his masculine nearness. But the slight rocking motion of the waves made a lump of cold nausea gurgle at the back of her throat. It was absurd, really. A moment ago she'd been playfully jumping up and down in this depth, willing to humor Hunter for the sake of her story.

But a moment ago he hadn't tried to lead her out to deeper water, tried to make her keep her face submerged . . .

No. She wouldn't do it. She couldn't.

She stepped back, digging her toes into the sand as though the shifting bottom could ground her somehow. "Hunter—"

He must have sensed the resurgence of her fear. He took a step toward her. "I'll be right beside you. You'll do fine."

She shook her head, a slow, helpless gesture. "Hunter, please. I can't." For a moment, her vision blurred as her courage folded up like a magician's trick box. Her entire body was thumping now, in sympathy with the panic soaring in her heart.

"Yes, you can. I'll help you."

His forehead was harshly furrowed; concern shaded his eyes. He meant well, he meant well, but didn't he know?

"No. You don't understand."

Now Alex was certain that she was about to do something incredibly foolish and immature. She drew a deep breath as adrenaline jittered along her nerves. She couldn't. She just couldn't. She wanted out: back on shore where the sand was hard and dry against her feet, where the water could still seem as pretty and inviting as a picture postcard.

She staggered back blindly, tripped over her own feet and went under.

Panic became full-blown terror as she inhaled seawater. Her nose and mouth was full of it—choking, fiery pain. She scrambled to get her feet under her, dimly realizing that Hunter's arm had come around her, and he was already scooping her upward.

He drew her toward shore while coughing spasms shook her. She was unharmed, she knew, and yet she was still clinging to Hunter like a baby spider monkey, all arms and legs and wretched embarrassment.

She felt herself being shifted onto Hunter's lap as he sat in water no more than a few inches deep. She was shaking with reaction and humiliation. Her hair hung in a wet curtain down her face, and she felt his hands tunneling through it, pushing it away as he tried to coax her out of terror. "It's all right, Alex. You're safe now."

She opened her eyes. He was so close she could see the water droplets that starred his lashes. The look in his eyes was direct and apologetic. He tipped her face up, letting his thumbs find the soft understructure of her cheekbones. "Your parents were damned fools to throw you into that pool," he said savagely.

For a moment, she was ashamed and filled with the old self-disgust. The past came tumbling down on her. It wasn't her parents' fault. They'd had certain expectations. They'd given her every advantage, every opportunity. But in so many ways, she just wasn't Sutton material.

"Are you all right?" Hunter asked gently.

She nodded, suddenly aware that his hands still held her face. It was a nice feeling. "I'm sorry. You must think I'm such an idiot."

"No," he replied. "I don't. I think maybe I'm the idiot here."

She stared at him, meeting the painstakingly slow survey of his gaze as best she could. All her verbal skills deserted her. Forbidden fantasies materialized into life, touched by lightning currents of arousal. Her blood felt laced with excitement, the drive of her pulse as strong as if she'd been running hard.

"Alex..."

He felt it, too, she could tell. His voice had turned so seductive it seemed to enfold her. A stillness had come over him. The hard wall of his chest was pressed against her, as close as anatomy allowed; her slightest movement rubbed against the fine hair matting his upper torso, bringing the perception of his different textures and tickling her flesh. Her eyes lifted to his again, not exactly eager, but pulled by a longing she couldn't explain.

His gaze continued to touch her everywhere, beautiful in its intensity. The moment lay between them, awaiting instructions, a moment when their closeness seemed to demand something more.

"Alex, I want to kiss you so much," he said, his voice no more than a husky, exotic whisper. "Knowing I shouldn't, and wanting to anyway—I don't know how to make you understand what that does to me."

A warning stirred within her, the fleeting knowledge that maybe Hunter was right to be so cautious. He had the ability to crumble all her good sense. She mustn't allow it. This was just the chemistry of physical fever, she told herself sternly, but oh, her body was alive for him, her pulse racing to keep pace with her breath, and didn't it feel wonderful to be this close?

His mouth hovered over hers, lifting in a diffuse, blurred smile. "Too late..." His breath bathed her lips. "Ah, Alex, it's just too late for both of us, isn't it..."

The first sweet contact seemed inevitable. He flexed against her gently, gently, as though trying to learn the shape and contour of her mouth. The tip of his tongue stole forward, playing at the corners until she opened for him. He tasted like salt and sunshine, and she was lost in the spinning sensations he created.

And then that quick, nourishing touch was gone. He pulled away, leaving her a little breathless, a little flushed and more than a little confused. Her unsettled emotions made her daring. "Why did you stop?"

His mouth had found its favorite shape, the mocking slant she was used to from him, so much more familiar to her than passion. "Do you want to make that one of your three questions?"

Doubts and vague suspicion fanned the last wisps of desire from her brain. Was he merely trying to romance his way out of answering her questions? She felt suddenly foolish and unprofessional for allowing herself to be sidetracked.

She straightened. Clearing her throat uneasily, she said in a carefully neutral voice, "Question number one. You and Dr. Isaacson once worked on the same project together. He publicly supported you. Is there a connection between his death, which the police already find suspicious, and the accusations you made back then?"

He settled beside her, slapping water against his shoulders. She resented how effortlessly he seemed able to move from passion to business. "There's a possibility."

"You said you wouldn't hedge."

His eyebrow rose. "Throwing my words back at me, Lois Lane? If you're going to use such tactics, I'll have to be on my guard." After a moment, he said matter-of-factly, "I haven't spoken to Isaacson in over a year. The first I knew about his intention to file suit was when I turned on the news and caught his press conference. I don't know the names of the two companies he was about to expose."

"But you have your suspicions?"

"Should I count that as one of your three questions?"

"It's part of number one. Sort of a follow-up."

"Isaacson was seen at the corporate office of Cavanaugh Labs shortly before he died."

"That won't make much of a case," she replied almost to herself. After a thoughtful moment, she asked, "Assuming Cavanaugh Labs is one of the companies, and assuming his death wasn't suicide, who at the lab would kill him? Charles Cavanaugh?"

"Charlie's ruthless. But I can't imagine he'd be stupid enough to wait so long."

She sat up straighter, the sudden movement sending little ripples through the water. "Who told you Isaacson was at the corporate office?"

He tipped his head to look at her closely, and she suspected he was debating whether or not to answer. After a long moment, he replied in a quiet tone, "Ken Braddock, Charlie Cavanaugh's son-in-law and a vice president of the company."

"Why would he come to you?"

"You'll have to ask him."

"You know something, don't you?" she asked, trying to keep excitement out of her voice. "You're holding out on me."

Hunter's features were an expressionless mask. "Sorry, Lois. You've had your three questions and we've both had enough lessons for today. It's time to go in."

She began an automatic protest, but he was on his feet immediately, gathering their things. Without looking back, he crunched his way down the shelly path. Disappointed, but intrigued, Alex was left to follow in his wake.

It was much later, soaping the dried saltwater off her body in the shower, that she realized she'd forgotten to ask about the scar.

RESTLESSLY, Alex rolled over in bed to steal another glance at the Mickey Mouse bedside clock. Five-fifteen. Only an hour since the last time she'd looked and another two hours before sunrise. Such a miserable time of day.

"Birds and bad women," she muttered into her pillow. "Those are the only things up at this hour."

And one sleepless reporter who couldn't force her mind to shut down and stop thinking about a silly little kiss.

Abruptly, Alex tossed back the bed covers and walked to the window. Like everything else in this room, the curtains, stamped with pictures of some comic book hero, brought a reminder of the son Hunter had lost. Matchbox cars ready to race along the top of a dresser, the slick sheen bouncing off posters of rock stars, a mobile of the planets spinning an impossible orbit in the breeze produced by the ceiling fan. The typical trappings of a little boy's life, she thought.

Why hadn't Hunter put away his son's things? Had he simply not had the time or the inclination? Or was this room a shrine to Eric?

She took a deep breath, fighting off the urge to succumb to sadness. Would knowing the answer to any of those questions help her better understand why Hunter was so determined to hold her at arm's length—even when he obviously didn't want to? No. None of that seemed to matter now.

Not now... when she'd made the decision to leave.

She didn't think for one minute that she had enough information to make a decent article, but some things just weren't worth the cost. Somewhere along the line her heart had raced well ahead of her common sense. She'd lost all objectivity, let herself become too vulnerable. If she remained, her relationship with Hunter was going to take an inadvisable turn, a turn she wasn't sure she could handle.

For the past couple of hours, she'd mentally rehearsed what she would say, the excuses she would offer. Her brothers would have been able to pull it off, but to her own ears the reasons sounded weak, almost defensive. That didn't matter. The truth was, she felt she'd already exposed much more of herself than she could bear.

She left the bedroom, moving quietly past Hunter's closed door and around the living-room furniture. Moonlight streaming through the curtainless win-

dows provided enough illumination by which to maneuver. Her fingers inched along the underside of the
desk until they were over the microphone, still
strapped snugly into place with the electrical tape she'd
found in one of the drawers.

She tugged it loose, remembering how resourceful
she'd thought she'd been in hiding it so close to
Hunter's grasp. But these past few days hadn't been
the clever adventure she'd expected. They'd brought
nothing but a curious ache in her heart and the certain knowledge that she lacked the will to test her
courage any further.

She set the microphone in the center of the kitchen
table where Hunter was sure to spot it come morning.
He'd know immediately what its return meant. No
need to leave a note, even if she could have thought of
anything remotely appropriate to say.

How long after Hunter found it would he call Riley
Kincaid to come get her?

WHEN SHE AWOKE AGAIN it was midmorning and the
cottage was quiet. She fumbled into the same clothes
she'd worn the day Hunter had stranded her on the
sandbar and slowly stuffed her few belongings into her
beach tote. Stifling a yawn, she headed for the living
room. She needed to be ready to go when Riley came.
The last thing she wanted was for Hunter to have to
tell her to pack.

She came to a halt in the doorway, surprised to find
him seated at the table, working on what looked like
some sort of fishing gear.

He looked up at her and smiled, a cheerful grin that brought a good hard lump to her throat. "Good morning. I was beginning to think you were going to sleep the whole day away."

Her glance flickered to the center of the table where she'd left the ham microphone. It wasn't there, and another quick look to the desk revealed it was back where it belonged. Riley was probably already on his way to the island with new fuel lines. Her heart sank a little to realize she could be back in her hotel room by lunchtime.

"Do you like crab?" he cut into her thoughts.

She responded with a vague nod, puzzled by the disinterest he showed in discussing the reappearance of the microphone.

"It's a little past season, but there are bound to be a few stone crabs still out there. Have you ever hunted?"

Was he talking about lunch? One last meal together before sending her on her way? Confused, she replied, "I went skeet shooting once with my family. I'm afraid I'm not very good with a gun."

He laughed at that. "If we use a gun, there's not going to be much crab left to eat. I was thinking of something less drastic. Think you can handle one of these?" He indicated the wooden rod in his hand. "It takes a little hand-eye coordination, but it's fun."

What new torment was this? Why was Hunter pretending he wasn't delighted by the reappearance of that microphone? It seemed especially cruel to her that he could toy with her this way.

You win, she wanted to shout. *I'm crying Uncle. Don't you want to gloat?*

She had to bite back the sudden urge to cry. Embarrassed by the thought that her emotions might unravel at any moment, she looked away. Some of her quiet frustration must have begun to communicate itself to Hunter, because he rose from the table. When he stood directly in front of her, she had to meet his eyes. It would have been too humiliating not to.

The silence was awkward, unbearable. He lifted one hand, as though his fingers would model her cheek in a caress. She flinched from the contact; she couldn't help herself. If he touched her now, she really *would* break apart.

He must have guessed her defenses were pretty well shot, because his hand drifted back down to his side. He studied her for a time in a painstaking way and finally said, "Come stone crabbing with me, Alex. We could both sit inside here all day and try to analyze what's happening between us, but right now I just don't have the energy for it."

"Hunter—"

"The microphone's not going anywhere." The words were sudden, fierce, as though too much of an argument from her would ensure his capitulation. "Please."

She nodded weak acquiescence. Her mind tumbled objections. Enough, it said. Make the damned call to Riley! I have to get away from you! The words, pale and cowardly things that they were, remained lodged in her throat. Hunter seemed in no hurry to send her back, and all she could hear was the high-pressured pump of her heart. A heart that took far too much pleasure in the idea of lingering.

IT WAS A MISTAKE and Hunter knew it. Nothing new there. Lately it seemed he'd been making a lot of them.

He should have called Riley. Ended this foolishness between them once and for all. A moron could have read the kind of signal Alex was sending—*I want out!* But he'd chosen to ignore it. Instead, he'd let his emotions work on him far better than any active sense of self-preservation, and now he had a feeling, way down deep in his gut, that he'd made a big mistake.

He watched her pick her way carefully through the ankle-deep water of the inlet. He'd had to coax her into probing the murky shallows with the tip of her crab pole—she was such a landlubber!—but she'd finally gotten the hang of it. He could tell she was having fun now, teasing the creatures out of their holes until they retaliated by grabbing the end of her stick. She still wouldn't pick one up, that was his job she'd said with an adamant smile, and he'd willingly agreed to chance the crab getting hold of him with its pincers. He suspected he'd have swallowed fire just to see that look of genuine enjoyment turned his way.

"Got one!" she exclaimed as one of the crustaceans clamped its pincer around her pole.

She glanced at him with a grin of triumph. The leafy buttonwoods hugging the shoreline had left the inlet in cool shade, dappling Alex's features in a lacy veil of tropical sunshine. The mellow light made her seem heart-robbingly young, more carefree and a little vulnerable.

Her look turned into one of playful censure. "Stop goofing off and get over here before he gets away."

Picking up the pail they'd brought, he sloughed through the shallows. The creature was pinned between Alex's pole and the muddy bottom. Its free claw ranged wildly, trying to find something solid to vent its frustration upon.

"Be careful," she cautioned and he tucked back an inward smile. No matter how many times he'd told her he'd been catching stone crabs since boyhood, she never failed to add the warning.

He removed the crab from beneath her pole and straightened. The dripping crustacean was a big one. As he reached for one of the claws, Alex sucked in air, squeezed her eyes shut momentarily and made a face. "Ooh, are you sure it doesn't hurt when you pull them off? It sounds so awful."

"They grow back," he explained yet again. He'd made the quick discovery that, while Alex loved the idea of a crab feast and found the hunting fun, she didn't have the stomach for separating the animal from its claws. "It doesn't hurt, and he'll have a new pair next season."

"How do you know it doesn't hurt?"

He cocked his head toward the crab. "Does it hurt, Charlie?" He wagged the animal back and forth as if in answer. "Tell the lady," he demanded. As though manipulating a hand puppet, he added in a high stage voice, "Oh, no, Miss Alex, it doesn't hurt at all. I'd

love you and Mr. Hunter to have my claws. That's
what I was born to do. It's my destiny."

Alex laughed, a sound so sweet and uncomplicated
it went straight to his heart.

She played along by asking the crab, "Are you sure
it's not your destiny to be in the theater? After all, a
talking crustacean . . ."

Hunter frowned at her in mock disapproval. "Don't
make fun of Charlie. He's—ouch! Son of a—"

The crab, less than impressed with this ventrilo-
quist act, had taken revenge at last. Its claw had
clamped onto Hunter's hand. The animal went sail-
ing as he dislodged it with a shake. It landed in the
shallows with a *kerplunk.*

"Damned thing got me," he complained.

"Let me see," Alex said sympathetically. Her head
was lowered, but he could tell she was working hard
not to laugh at him. The curve of her mouth was
breathtakingly soft, lush with whimsy.

He extended his hand. "I haven't had one get hold
of me since I was sixteen. Wait till I find him again.
His claws will be the first ones in the cooker."

"Serves you right. He probably didn't like being
made fun of. And you weren't very good, you know.
I saw your lips move."

"Every crab's a critic."

"It barely broke the skin. I think you'll live."

In spite of that prognosis, she didn't turn loose of
his hand. With her head still lowered in frowning
concentration, her fingers rubbed gently at the spot.
Her touch was like a shock. He felt the electricity of
that contact all the way up his arm.

"Alex . . ."

He didn't know what he intended to say. All he knew was that he suddenly didn't give a damn about crab claws and minor scrapes. Alex was touching him, touching him the way he'd dreamed about being touched for three nights now. And he didn't want her to stop.

He took her hand and she looked up at him in a surprised, shaken way. He moved closer, and the wind-dusted fragrance of sun on her skin made his head reel. He thought he should say something now— she was looking a little unsure and hesitant—but all his best dream-speeches had deserted him.

Vaguely, he realized there was one question he wanted an answer to. "Why did you return the microphone, Alex?"

Her cheeks darkened. "Why didn't you use it?"

His fingers found the velvet softness of her inner wrist, where the pulse throbbed with warm life. "Guess neither one of us can figure out what we want."

"What *do* you want, Hunter?"

To the note of curious desperation in her voice he offered a half smile of sympathetic understanding. Did she really think he was any closer to being able to deal with any of this than she was? "The same thing you do, Alex," he replied quietly. "The very same thing."

He would have pulled her into his arms then and kissed her. Really kissed her. All his convictions of the last few days had decayed beyond salvation. But the unexpected honesty of his words seemed to throw Alex into confusion. Her expression shifted into a frown and she backed away from him. "Hunter, I''m not good at this sort of—" her features clouded over in sudden pain "—oooh."

"What's the matter?"

"I've stepped on something sharp."

Intimacy yielded to concern as Alex leaned heavily on her crabbing pole to take the weight off one foot.

"Let me look at it," he said, and she gingerly lifted her bare foot. Along the side of her heel bright blood welled and dripped, zigzagging a path down her wet instep to merge with the inlet water. "You've sliced it, probably on a broken shell. It doesn't look serious, but we'll have to put something on it."

She nodded and limped awkwardly toward her beach bag and sandals. He wondered if she was as disappointed as he by this unexpected turn of events. He didn't want to see her hurt, but the greatest part of his awareness was still focused on how a simple touch from him could throw her breathing into a series of sharp gasps.

He stopped her as she tried to make her wounded foot fit into a sandal. "Don't. You'll leave a trail of blood from here to the cottage." He tapped the back of his shoulder. "Hop on, I'll give you a piggyback ride."

"You can't do that. I'm too heavy."

"Gee, I think I can manage."

She shook her head, but gave up the idea of wearing the sandals. With footwear and beach bag in hand, she started hobbling down the path. "I couldn't. It's silly."

"It will take you forever that way."

"It's not far."

He gathered the bucket and poles and caught up with her. "Far enough. Don't be pigheaded, Alexandria. Let me help you."

"Oh, all right." She sounded petulant, like a thwarted child about to throw a temper tantrum.

"Did you bring a towel?" he asked.

"No."

He withdrew one from his own beach tote, handed it to her, then stuffed her sandals into his bag. With some artless maneuvering, they managed to get Alex situated on his back, his arms wrapped around her knees, her one hand barely hanging on to the back of his shirt for balance. Even holding both their beach bags, the poles and bucket half filled with crab claws, she weighed next to nothing, he thought.

"Stick your foot up here," he commanded, and when she did he took the towel and wrapped it around the cut, continuing to hold on to it with one hand while his other hand boosted her fanny farther up his back. "If I keep the pressure on, the bleeding will probably stop by the time we get to the cottage." When she didn't say anything, he angled his head around, but his view of her was no more than one silky shoulder. "You okay?" he asked.

"Yes."

"Comfy?"

"Just go."

He'd gotten no more than ten feet down the path, when he realized what the problem was.

It had been honest good intentions that had made him suggest the piggyback ride. But now, with the heat of Alex's body pressed next to his, those good intentions were turning into great ideas. None of which had anything remotely to do with administering to the wounded. Her slightest movement threatened to make a shudder pass through him, an uncontrollable response to her nearness that told him that, like everything else where Alex Sutton was concerned, this idea, too, had been forged from less than brilliance.

She shared that knowledge; he knew it. She was too quiet, too determined to keep contact between them at a minimum. He sensed her straining away, even as she struggled to keep a precarious balance by hugging her legs around him more tightly. He might have said something to her, if his tongue hadn't been so thick in his throat and his pulse hadn't been running like surf.

Damn, this was getting ridiculous.

"Stop wiggling," he said through gritted teeth, a valiant effort to salvage some control out of the situation.

"I'm not."

"Well, stop whatever it is you're doing."

The cottage had never seemed so far away.

CHAPTER NINE

THE CUT HAD STOPPED bleeding by the time Hunter lowered Alex to the living-room couch. He encouraged her to stretch out with her foot propped up. She didn't say a word as he gathered items from the medicine chest in the bathroom, then set about the business of cleaning the wound.

It was a small and precise injury, not in a spot likely to cause much future discomfort, though you'd have thought otherwise, given the expression of solemn intensity on Alex's face. She sat there, looking as transparently uncomfortable as he felt. He had a pretty good notion it had nothing to do with the tiny cut.

Under the guise of offering help, he was able to continue manipulating her foot, and even that minor contact brought ridiculous pleasure. He was going to be almost sorry when the chore was finished and he lost the legitimate excuse to touch her.

"Bandage, or something more elaborate?" he asked from his end of the couch.

She shrugged. "You're the doctor."

He placed an adhesive bandage over the wound, then made a show of slowly brushing stray particles of sand off the top of her foot. His fingers settled on the dainty knob of her ankle. "How does it feel now?"

"Better." And then, in a self-consciously soft voice, "Much better, thank you. You have a very gentle touch."

He met her compliment by lifting his gaze to hers, confronting the uncertainty in her eyes with undisguised wanting.

You don't know how gentle my touch can be, Alex.

She settled back on the couch, but he noted she had pulled one of the throw pillows from beneath her and now unconsciously clutched it across her breasts, as though forming a tangible barrier between them. He smiled at that unmistakable, last-ditch effort to erect some sort of defense. He knew in that moment that he was going to take her here, on a silly, sagging excuse for a couch that had seen way too many seasons at the beach. He was going to make slow, sensuous love to her, with her foot freshly bandaged and the wind-dried salt still clinging to their skin.

His hand tightened around her ankle, just enough dominance to keep her from turning away her glance. His eyes held hers, steady, and probably full of the longing that bubbled just beneath the surface of his emotions. "The doctor prescribes rest," he said in a husky whisper. He bent his head to place a kiss against the bandaged cut. "Rest, and a little tender loving care."

She gave a little gasp, but he knew the difference between surprise and pleasure. He let his fingers travel up the length of her leg. His hand skimmed her thigh, and even as he encountered the hem of her shorts he was already lifting himself over her, balancing himself with his other hand braced against the back of the couch and one knee pressing into the cushion beside her body.

He lifted her chin with one finger until he could almost see himself in the twin dark pools of her eyes. "Kiss me, Alex. Reasonable doctor's fee, don't you think?"

Her lips twitched, expressing a willingness to meet this invitation to love-play. "Do you demand this sort of payment from all your patients?"

"Only you, Alex," he replied in a voice that boasted the rough texture of sandpaper. "Only you..."

At first, his mouth moved against hers lightly, no more than a feathery touch full of promise. But a moment later, he increased the pressure, glorying in the way she rose to meet it. He kissed her again, and again, varying the shape of their contact by angling her jaw with his free hand placed against her throat. His sensitized fingers felt the whimpers that fluttered up past her larynx.

Putting her acceptance of him to a subtle test, he let his weight bear down, just a little, until her body molded against him. The silken glide of her legs against his stirred his excitement to new heights and made for dizzying contact. "Alex, are you protected?" he asked softly, stroking her ear with his tongue.

Her head swiped back and forth against the couch cushions as she grimaced in frustration.

He smiled down at her. "It's all right. Lie still."

She felt him withdraw, but only for a moment or two. When he returned, she immediately recognized the package from their grocery-store encounter. With a light laugh, she asked, "Don't you want to save those for your hot date?"

"I think you *are* my hot date," he replied, and in no time he was touching her again, making her forget everything but the feel of his hands on her flesh.

In a slow, delicious sweep of movement, his fingers found the swell of her breast. He began to edge apart the buttons of her blouse and cocked a crooked grin at her. "Tender loving care, Alex. Listen to the doctor."

Alex's reply was a mere gasp of sound as his lips found the valley of her breasts. "Yes. Just what the doctor ordered . . . oh, Hunter."

He quieted her with the soft touch of his lips.

Involuntarily, she lifted against him, so that she was hardly aware of the moment when his proficient fingers unhooked her bra and slid the straps down her shoulders. The lavender scrap of lace and satin—the very same one she'd been embarrassed to know he'd touched that first day—was easily discarded along with her blouse. Her own hands, eager yet unbearably clumsy, slid under the waistband of her shorts and panties, kicking away the material in frenzied haste.

Hunter's mouth explored lower, following the trail left behind by her abandoned clothing with his lips. Each caress was a brand against her flesh. Each hot convulsion rippled through her limbs like flame. She was burning, burning up. And she would be glad to be incinerated to smoldering ash if it meant Hunter would take her now.

His weight increased, but it was warm and welcome, like burrowing under a downy comforter on a snowy night. He groaned as he shrugged out of his clothes, as if dissatisfied with the fumbling slowness of his fingers. Then he was naked at last, and had she possessed breath in this state, he would have taken it away.

How beautiful he was, how godlike, each bone knit just so with muscle, smooth, almost satin in places. The crisp fleece of hair covering his powerful chest was marred only by that mysterious scar, the slight imperfection of flesh that made him a man and not a god at all.

Need consumed her. Her legs eased open, prepared to accommodate him. Hunter shifted, nestling into the warm, wet, sensitized core of her femininity with his own heat. She quivered, shivering with anticipation and unendurable longing. Wanting. Needing . . .

"Hunter, please . . ." Her voice was no more than a shaky exhalation, no more than a dreamy breath.

Their gazes found each other. A smile tipped the corners of his mouth. "You're shaking. Are you cold?" His mouth nipped and stroked. "Shall I get a blanket?"

Alex's head snapped back and forth against the couch cushion. "No, I'm hot..." Dear God, was that his tongue playing games with her nipple again? "You know I'm burning . . ."

She lifted a trembling hand to his face. Hunter seemed to absorb the wandering trend of her thoughts. He clutched her hand in his own, kissed it and held her fingers until the trembling stopped, a gracious captive. And then, between the stammer of her heartbeat and one wavering breath, he eased into her.

Almost immediately, she reacted. Alex was melting for him, making it so easy. The taste of her was strong in his mouth, the sunshine fragrance of her body imbedded in his senses. He wouldn't have let her go for anything, yet his body felt unfamiliar to him. A bubble of panic surfaced. *So long ... it's been so long ...*

He tipped past reason, no longer able to fight the mindless demands of his body and seeing no profit in pretending any longer. Instinct and desire drove him forward. With a hand that was shaking badly, he sifted damp tendrils away from her face so that he could find her eyes. "I'm the one who's cold, Alex," he murmured hoarsely. "I need your heat ... Warm me, sweetheart. I've been so cold, so long ..."

She responded by scattering kisses along his collarbone, nuzzling her face into the curve of his shoulder. She didn't want to be so embarrassingly eager, but she couldn't keep still.

In what she was sure was a disgracefully short time, she was following his lead. Her fingers furrowed into his hair, pulling him closer, pulling him into her. This was so good. This was wonderful. It was all pleasure. An electrifying feeling flushed through her, creating a low, powerful echo that grew and grew and grew ...

Pulsating with the need for his own release, Hunter was still cognizant of the moment Alex climaxed. After one soft cry, her lips parted in a whispery sigh. Along the straining muscles of his back he felt her fingers, kneading in slow, raptured circles. And then he was aware of little else, because desire took him firmly in hand, filling the empty spaces within his heart, growing larger and larger until that was all there was.

His last coherent thought was that he hadn't made so many mistakes, after all. Why had he fought it? This closeness felt so right, so good. His feelings for her had the force of instinct.

And the thing he'd dreaded the most—revealing to Alex all the pain and hurt of the past—had not brought him the twisting agony he'd feared, but rather a sweet, natural healing.

VIBRATIONS RUMBLED in Alex's ear, pulling her from the languid half sleep she had fallen into. She lifted her head from the hard wall of Hunter's chest. They were in his bed, though she couldn't remember the moment they'd made the transition from the couch.

The day had been spent in tender passion, exploring wondrous feelings and becoming lost all over again in the enchantment of each other's arms. Now the afternoon was nearly gone, and the air was a teasing veil of heat, scented with the perfume of pine and oleander.

The rumbling reverberated again. She glanced up at Hunter. The light was falling in broader and yet broader strokes across the bed, and angled sunlight had found his mussed hair, lifting honeyed tones from its thickness. He looked completely relaxed, his eyes closed as though he slept. But he wasn't asleep, and she knew it in the way his arms suddenly tightened around her body and his mouth curled in slight humor.

She let her hand drift across the hard expanse of his belly. "Is that your poor stomach making all that noise?"

His eyes slitted open and he stared down at her through the bars of his lashes. "I think we've missed lunch."

"We could have the crab claws for dinner."

"We could."

"Maybe we should get up."

"Maybe."

With lazy reluctance, she pushed herself higher in bed, until the top of her head was even with his chin. The wanton wildness of their earlier lovemaking was still with her. She let her hand wander down the length of him, letting her fingers play. She manipulated and massaged until the look of amusement on Hunter's face shifted into something else entirely. "Oh, my goodness," she grinned. "It appears you *are* up."

He made a low sound and bucked against her. "You wanton little tease..."

She tilted her chin, placing her mouth against the pulse that pounded at the base of his throat, lapping the sun colors with her tongue. "Are you hungry?" she purred softly.

"No. God, no," His voice had a winded sound, as though he had just engaged in strenuous exercise. "Not for food."

His hand tunneled into her hair so that she had to lift her head. His tongue began to brew ecstasy once more. Suddenly he pulled back, and his eyes looked straight and overpoweringly into hers. "I have a confession to make."

She planted a kiss along the warm column of his throat. "Confessions are for church."

"I'll feel better if I get this off my chest."

"*It* off your chest? Or me?" she asked, perfecting a playful sulk. "Surely not me?" She punctuated the question by sending her hand on a gentle odyssey, until Hunter drew in a shaky breath.

"Dammit, Alex, behave," he commanded in a voice rough with longing. "I'm serious, and you're killing my concentration."

With a sigh of reluctance, she pushed herself still higher in bed. "All right," she said primly. "Clear your conscience."

"I suppose I should just come right out and say it," he grumbled, and after a second's hesitation, he added, "I read your notebook."

He saw that he had her full attention now. "What?"

"Your notebook. I read it."

"When?"

"You left it on the couch the night we fixed the generator, and I just picked it up. I didn't realize until then that it was more of a...a private journal than anything else."

Myriad emotions flowed through the warm depth of her eyes. "You shouldn't have done that. It's...personal, full of things I don't want to share with anyone..."

"Well, at the time, I felt justified. I apologize for not telling you sooner, but I'm not sorry I read it. That night, I started to see you in a different light. You weren't just some snooping reporter after a story—"

She was uncomfortable with the conversation, and he knew it in the way she moved suddenly, tucking the sheet over her bare breasts as she sat up. A flush of color dyed her cheeks. She scooted to the edge of the bed. "I'm hungry. Why don't I fix us something to eat?"

His hand shot out to catch her forearm. "Alex, wait."

"Let's drop it. I accept your apology."

"I want to talk about this."

"Well, I don't."

She tossed her head, and long strands of hair obscured his view of her eyes. Without releasing her, Hunter tilted closer, determined not to let her leave the bed or avoid the discussion. "Why?" he asked softly. "Your writing is lyrical. Vivid. I'm not a literary critic, but there's something powerful and evocative about your work, Alex. It's certainly nothing to be ashamed of. Have you ever shown it to a publisher?"

"There's no reason I should. Writing is my way of doodling. A diversion for lazy, rainy days. It's not meant to be taken seriously."

"Really?" he refuted. "Longfellow and Keats might object to that sentiment."

Roused, she gave him a look that would have frozen water at twenty paces. She was gathering her defiance, and he thought how amazingly beautiful she seemed in that moment, full of radiant fire. "You know that's not what I'm talking about. In this day and age it's not a commercially viable way to earn a living."

"Who sold you that cynical load of garbage?"

"No one. A few short stories won't put food on your table or pay the rent. And poetry certainly doesn't—"

"Doesn't what?"

"Nothing," she said, pulling out of his grip. "This is a pointless discussion and I'd much rather—"

"Doesn't what?" Hunter pressed. "Make your family sit up and take notice? Get their respect? Is that so important? To measure up to the Sutton definition of how you should live your life?"

She swiped hair out of her face to eye him savagely. "You don't know anything about my family."

"I'm a scientist. I'm good at putting together the pieces."

"I'm not some specimen on a petri dish to be viewed under your microscope."

"I don't need a microscope to figure out the obvious. Your family's the reason you dogged me all over Fort Myers, isn't it? That's why you took out that boat, when you're scared to death of water. Why you cut the fuel lines and hid the microphone. It's not your editor you're really worried about pleasing. Sure, he'd be angry, might even bury your stuff on the society pages. But it's the Sutton seal of approval you're hungry for."

She looked momentarily stunned, then annoyed. "That's ridiculous. But even if it was true, there's nothing wrong with wanting your family to be proud of your work."

"Nothing at all," he said with a shrug of indifference. "As long as you don't sacrifice your own happiness in the process."

"I *am* happy," she replied in a displeased tone. "At least, I was until you started playing dime-store psychologist and ruined the mood."

He brought his hand to the back of her cheek, and when she tilted her face away he settled for capturing her fingers once more. "I don't want to ruin anything, Alex. I just want to encourage you to explore other possibilities."

She lifted her lashes to look him squarely in the eyes. "Why?"

He wasn't sure how she would accept what he was about to say, but she was looking at him with a full gaze that saw everything. She'd probably know if he tried to back away now. He took a fortifying breath. "Because you don't have what it takes to be a hard-boiled newspaper reporter."

She tried to wrench her hand out of his grasp, but he held on. Throwing him an angry, frustrated look, she snapped, "Just what makes you such an expert?"

He gave her a self-deprecating smile. "I've spent an awfully long time running away from people like that. Believe me, I know how ruthless you have to be." He looked down at their entwined fingers, then turned her hand over to run a fingertip along the lifeline that bisected it. "The woman I . . . I've wanted to make love to for the past three days couldn't ever remain impartial and uninvolved." He touched his lips to the center of her palm. "She's passionate. And caring. And so sensitive to another person's pain that she's willing to make it her own. The great journalists in this world keep their distance, Alex. They're only observers of life. They can't afford to be anything else."

"I'm not nearly as noble as you make me sound," she refuted. Her chin lifted. "And I'll settle for merely being good."

His smile broadened. "Just don't lose sight of what makes you who you really are. They're the qualities that make you so—" he kissed the inside of her wrist, where her pulse ran fast and warm "—irresistible."

She drew in a sharpened breath as his mouth sketched a path up her arm. "You still shouldn't have read my journal," she chastised.

"You're right, I shouldn't have," he agreed. "Let me make it up to you."

"How?"

Against her neck, she felt his lips stretch in amusement. "We'll think of a way."

Opening her eyes later, much later, Alex lay curved against his chest and watched the first stars appear in the sky. She and Hunter were marooned in moonlight. The silver light etched the flowing pattern of his cheekbones, the hard curve of his shoulder, the muscled length of one leg that had escaped the sheets. Everything within her felt melted down and fluid.

Beside her, Hunter sighed heavily and said, "I think we made a mistake."

Something jolted in her soul. She lay suspended in fear. In a nonchalant voice that she forced out with all her remaining self-control, she asked, "What do you mean?"

"We should have put those crab claws in the fridge. The cottage is going to smell like a bait shop."

She lifted herself onto one elbow and punched him lightly on the chest. "Dammit, Hunter, that's not funny!"

"What?"

"I thought you were going to say *this* was a mistake. That we shouldn't have...that you regretted making love."

He dragged her against him. "I know all about regrets, Alex. This feels too good to be one. The only mistake I made was not doing this sooner."

"You could have, you know. I've been eaten up inside wanting you to touch me."

She caught the gleam of starlight as he smiled. "I've been eaten up *outside,* letting mosquitoes have me for dinner, staying away from you rather than coming inside and facing the inevitable."

"You make me sound like a dose of castor oil."

His fingers tipped her chin so that he could find her lips with his in a soft, potent kiss. "You're good medicine, Alex. Like an elixir of life."

Her hand found his cheek and lay there. "Hunter, what we've shared today..."

"Shh...please, sweetheart," he said, laying a finger against her love-bruised lips. "Don't let the reporter in you start to put labels on this yet. I'm still trying to absorb the fact that I'm not cut out for the life of a monk."

It was her turn to grin. "Oh, I'd say long-term celibacy is definitely out of the question."

"One day at a time. All right?"

"If all the days are like this," she agreed.

There was something, something deep inside of him, a corner of inner darkness. What was it that he was so reluctant to let her see? She had to know. He had learned the trick of shielding himself, but she was teaching him how to share. At least she wanted to believe that was what was happening between them.

Are you any good at this, Alex?

I can help him.

He's not making any promises.

I don't care. I want to help him.

Why?

The realization came with such deep certainty that anything, anything at all, seemed possible.

Her hand caressed his deeply muscled torso. Her fingers traced the scar that lay hidden among the crisp hair. So close, so close to his heart. Another centimeter nearer might have taken his life. None of these past hours of exquisite pleasure would ever have happened. How horrible a thought—never to have known Hunter. Her heart ran hot with tenderness. She wanted to wrap him in warmth and shelter... and love.

I love him.

She pressed her lips to the incision, imagining that she could feel the throb of his heartbeat against her mouth. "Don't ever let anything hurt you like this again," she said. "I couldn't bear it."

His breath caught and held, and she felt him go still. She lifted her head to try to gauge his feelings, but in the darkness she could make nothing of his expression. "Will you tell me how you got this?"

For many uncounted moments there was only silence. Then, like a man suddenly coming awake, he said gruffly, "There's nothing fascinating about the story."

"Then you shouldn't mind telling it."

"Alex . . ."

Some sixth sense warned her to start out with something less traumatic. "What did you do after the Cavanaugh investigation was over?"

His shoulders lost some of their stiffness. "I assume you did your homework before coming over here. Your newspaper kept a reporter on my trail often enough back then."

"I know what the computer files say. I want to hear it from you."

He sighed and settled her against him. Staring up into the darkness, he said, "All right, Lois Lane, I guess you can't think any worse of me than you already have." He let one hand sift through her hair; she felt the slight, tingling pull against her scalp. "After the trial, I didn't have a job, and I couldn't get one. My family was . . . gone. I had a few close friends who supported me, but not much else. What I *was* left with was a small degree of fame. After spending years quietly protesting the environmental abuses I've seen in this state, I thought my sudden celebrity might be useful."

"It also got you labeled as a kook."

He laughed. "After what I went through, do you think I cared what people thought? Especially those who had reason to be wary of the attention I was bringing down on them. Remember Senator Kale?"

"The poor man with twenty-eight broken refrigerators in his front yard?"

"I dumped them there to protest the landfill bill he was trying to slip through the senate. One for every point in his proposal. That bill would have ruined some of this state's best wetlands, but no one seemed to give a damn. The publicity and embarrassment made him back off."

"You've had failures, too."

She felt his shrug. "It depends on what you mean by failure. When I tried to free that dolphin from the real-estate pond it was confined in, I got arrested and charged with malicious mischief, but the day I got out, there were a thousand people waiting for me, showing their support. Eventually, the real-estate company was convinced it didn't need to sell lots by offering people the opportunity to swim with a captive dolphin." His voice became ironic. "Strictly speaking, I failed, but they ended up setting the animal free."

With one finger, she traced the line of that terrible scar. Except for one involuntary twitch of his chest muscle when she touched him, Hunter didn't make a move. "And is this one of your failures?"

"Yes."

"When we were on the beach, you said you got it nine months ago, so I'm assuming it's also why you disappeared from the public eye for that length of time."

"Yes."

"What happened?"

His fingertips, which had been stroking the side of her face, tapped the end of her nose. "You certainly have the Sutton persistence for a story."

She pushed herself upward, brushing her hair away from her face in an attempt to make eye contact with him. The moonlight sparkled in his gaze, and she thought she glimpsed wariness there, as well. Calmly, she said, "If you think the only reason I want to know is because I want a story, then we really have made a mistake and it's time to use that microphone to call your friend Riley."

With a roughened groan, he hauled her against him. "Come here, Alexandria."

She was very aware that he wanted to kiss her. But he didn't. Instead, he brought her close enough that the murky shadows yielded up his features at last. "I had a run-in with a shrimp-boat captain," he said after a long silence. "He was using illegal nets. I snuck out to the boat in the middle of the night and destroyed his equipment. When I confronted him, he tried to argue his point with a knife."

"He stabbed you."

Hunter nodded.

"Why would you confront him like that?" she wondered aloud. "You had to know the situation could turn ugly. He might have killed you."

He smiled tightly. In a carefully neutral voice, he said, "Yes, he might have." The words seemed forced up from some well of sorrow deep within him.

She frowned. Something about his matter-of-fact tone unnerved her. The implication behind those words made her look at him more closely. He met her gaze directly, but in the austerity of his expression there was no light.

Sudden knowledge fretted at the corner of her mind, then settled in with brutal clarity. It hit her, what he'd wanted from that confrontation with the boat captain. She could not bear the thought, and yet, it seemed so obvious.

With hardly breath to utter it, she gasped out, "You wanted that man to fight you, didn't you?"

She tried to watch the harsh words settle in, but he made a sudden movement, as though unable to endure her eyes on his. "I was on an empty treadmill in those days," he acknowledged in a husky voice. "The idea of taking out my frustrations in a physical confrontation did have a certain appeal."

And did you hope that his aim would be a little bit better than it was? She was afraid to ask the question, but more afraid not to. Her heart was tight in an anguish of suspense. The darkness seemed alive and full of knowledge, but Hunter's features were expressionless, save for the black points of torture she could see in his eyes.

"Hunter . . . ?" she began hesitantly.

CHAPTER TEN

SHE NEVER HAD a chance to complete the question.

Instead, Hunter suddenly took her into his arms with a kind of desperate hunger that told her more vividly than words that he knew where her thoughts had taken her. In the soft, dim magic of the night shadows he teased her lips with his, stroked her body with fingers that touched as lightly as a dove's feather, making her shiver with need.

Distractions, she thought sadly. Such wonderful distractions. She caught the drift of his intentions easily; he wanted to give her no chance to pursue her question.

Go slow, her brain coaxed. If that portion of the conversation was really at an end, then accept it. For now.

So she curled against him, letting his hands take her to a place where only the present mattered.

Morning came at last, and hunger reasserted itself. While Hunter showered, Alex slipped back into her borrowed swimsuit and fixed breakfast. Settling on scrambled eggs, she stood at the kitchen counter and slapped cream cheese across the bagels she had found in a package in the refrigerator.

The kitchen shared a wall with the cottage bathroom, and as she listened to water surge through the pipes, every sound Hunter made seemed magnified for her enjoyment.

Her active imagination was more than willing to conjure up the memory of his naked body—water sluicing down those well-muscled thighs, bubbles trapped amid the dark hair that matted his chest, his strong hands lathering a circular, soapy path across his rock-hard stomach, just the way he had charted a course across her breasts during their lovemaking. Oh, what a fool she'd been to laugh off his suggestion of showering together for the practicality of satisfying their hunger!

Realizing that she'd spread entirely too much cream cheese on one of the bagels, Alex marshaled her wayward thoughts. She was supposed to be preparing a quick, simple meal, not indulging in fantasies.

The shower stopped running almost at the same moment she finished pouring herself a glass of milk. "Breakfast is nearly ready," she called. "Do you want milk or orange juice?"

"Milk's fine. I'll be out in a second," he promised.

She began to set the table, which seemed to have become a repository for all their beach gear from yesterday's crab hunt.

She tossed the beach towels in a corner for washing later and set the metal crabbing poles against the front door. Wrinkling her nose against the smell, she lifted the bucket of crab claws. Uncertain of their fate, she opened the front door, and set the container on the outside deck.

The morning was already too hot, and the sun seemed eager to dazzle and distract. She shaded her eyes against its glare as she took a desultory glance around the island. Nothing moved in the heat. She returned gladly to the cool interior of the cottage.

Lifting Hunter's duffel bag from the table, she remembered that he had placed her sandals inside, along with her tanning lotion and sunglasses. The shoes lay on top of his things, but the glasses and lotion had sifted to the bottom of the bag, and as Alex dug deeper, her fingers encountered something hard and unyielding.

When she pulled it out, she was stunned for a moment, but she quickly recognized it. Hunter's work on biological warfare had been well documented. The pictures she'd seen of the anti–nerve gas injectors had carried too chilling an implication for her to forget what they looked like. This small plastic case, or one very similar to it, had promised lifesaving protection against an enemy bent on teaching the United States a thing or two about war.

If it worked.

Alex wet her lips, finding that her knees had gone suddenly weak. Dropping into a chair, she set the injector case carefully on the table, as though it might be a sleeping snake that could awaken at any moment.

What was Hunter doing with this particular set of injectors? He'd given her the impression that he wasn't actively involved in research anymore, and certainly not interested in reopening old wounds. Was this a contaminated batch? And did it have anything to do with Leo Isaacson's death? The questions went round and round in her head.

She lifted the lid and removed one of the injectors. Slim and cool, the barrel nearly fit the palm of her hand. Such a small thing, really, and yet so full of life.

If it worked.

"Did you find what you were searching for?"

She couldn't prevent a guilty start. She jerked her head up to see Hunter leaning in the doorway, his arms locked over his bare chest. He looked marvelously male, barefoot and dressed only in jeans, water from his recent shower painting his hair a liquid gold. She remembered the beauty of his eyes, which were sometimes filled with light, suffused with wonderful promise. But right now, he was staring at her in a strangely indifferent, sterile way.

She could imagine what he thought, seeing her there. But nettled by his implication that she had deliberately searched through his things, she said emphatically, "I was *searching* for my sandals. So you can stop looking at me that way."

"What way is that?"

"Like you've just caught the cat trying to take a bite out of the canary."

"My father used to say that a guilty conscience was its own accuser." He paused, as if to allow that statement time to cool. His eyebrows knit as he tilted his head. "Do you have anything to feel guilty about?"

"No. Do you?"

"Lots of things. But none of them involve what you're holding in your hand."

He watched her almost cunningly, as though trying to find his advantage. She thought how easily they could destroy what had been shared before, but she couldn't let him put her off this time. She just couldn't.

"If I asked you," she said quietly, "would you tell me how you got these?"

"No."

"Why not? Because you don't trust me to keep your answers from ending up in print?"

The air throbbed with tension. He continued to watch her with keen, undaunting eyes. "You should have seen your face when I walked in, Alex. Like you'd just discovered the Holy Grail. Admit it, you could already see the boys in the pressroom typesetting your headline."

Feeling as though she were imprisoned in some horrible and fatal trap, she ducked her head. Her fingers wrapped around the barrel of the injector she'd removed, and the plastic felt cold and deadly against her palm. "All right. So I could." She lifted her chin, refusing to allow him to scatter her poise. "I've never pretended that I didn't want a story out of you. But you have to know that after last night, I'd never print anything that could cause you more harm."

In a remote, relentless tone, he said, "Don't confuse lust with trust."

Stunned by this unexpected piece of brutality, she rose. "Is that all it was for you?" she said in a low, unmetered voice. "Oh, God, I'm such an idiot..."

He made a move toward her, but she lifted her hand in a defensive gesture meant to keep him away. It didn't surprise her to see that the hand she extended trembled.

With a half-spoken curse, Hunter took a cautious step forward. "Alex, I'm sorry. I shouldn't have said that. Making love to you was the best thing that's happened to me in a long, long time, and what I said just now about lust—that was bull."

Alex's heart was pounding so hard she felt sure that her voice must shake. "Then why did you say it?"

"Because as wonderful as last night was, it's made me wonder what you'll expect from me now. I don't distrust you, but I can't share this."

"Why?"

"Because Leo Isaacson's death is looking more and more like murder." His voice dropped to a low caress of sound. "And you're becoming too important to me to take a chance on anything happening to you."

"Nothing's going to happen to me."

"You're damned right," he said with new determination. "Because you're going to put that injector case back in my duffel bag and forget you ever saw it."

"Hunter, I can't," she said, shaking her head. "You know I can't."

"Yes, you can. Walk away from this, Alex. Forget about what your editor needs, or your family expects. I'll help you get any other story you want, but not this one. Put the case back."

"What are you going to do with it?"

He drew a deep breath. "I've given it some thought lately. It can't hurt to run a few tests, see if the injectors are tainted. If they are, I'll get them to the right people."

"And that's it?"

"What *should* I do? File another lawsuit with even less proof than I had four years ago? No, thanks. I've had my turn at bat, and I think I'll sit this game out."

"You're not that kind of person. You could never sit idly by and do nothing if—"

"You don't know the kind of trouble that kit can bring a person, Alex," he interrupted. "I do. I know what I'm asking. But put it back." He threw a winsome grin her way. "For me. Please."

He had a special talent for touching the raw places within her. She could hear the double thump of her heartbeat as she looked at him with quavering bewilderment. Could she believe him? Would he have said *anything* to keep her from pursuing this line of investigation? What would he do if she refused?

As it happened, she never found out.

Like a thunderclap on a still morning, the front door suddenly burst open. Alex turned to find a stranger outlined in the bright sunlit doorway. He took a quick, prowling step forward, and she realized in less time than it took to blink that he was dirty, sunburned, disheveled and holding a gun.

His eyes darted like startled fish between the two people in the room and the plastic injector case that still sat on the table. "Let me settle this for you," he said in a wild, dangerous tone. "Give it to me."

There was a threatening pause while the sudden shift in the situation settled over them. With her heart jumping in her chest, Alex glanced toward Hunter.

If he knew this intruder, or was afraid of him, he didn't show it. He did, however, seem remarkably unperturbed to suddenly be facing a man with a gun.

"Richard!" Hunter actually greeted. "This is a surprise. My God, you look like hell," he complained in a conversational tone. "What have you been doing with yourself?"

The man's dark eyes blazed with overwrought excitement. "I'm not talking to you."

Hunter ignored him. With a nod in her direction, he said, "Alex, this is Richie Cavanaugh, Charlie's son. He usually looks more presentable than this." He glanced back at the gunman. "Was it Charlie's idea for you to come here, Richie?"

"It doesn't matter whose idea it was. You've got one hell of a miserable sandbar here, you know that, Garrett? Between the heat and the bugs, and running out of food, I almost gave up."

"You should have come to the door," Hunter replied with an unsympathetic shrug. "We could have talked, and you could have reported back to your father, less the sunburn and sand in your shorts."

Richie gave him a sneering grin. "Sure we could have. And I suppose you would have given me *that*—" his gun waved toward the injector case "—as a parting gift?"

"Well, there are limits to hospitality."

"So who gave them to you? My brother-in-law?"

"You don't really expect an answer to that, do you?"

"Doesn't matter. If there's a leak there, my father will plug it." He turned his attention back to Alex, who had watched this interchange between the two men with more than a little uneasiness. "Now, hand over the case."

She shook her head. "No."

"Give it to him, Alex," Hunter cut in sharply.

"Hunter—"

"It's not worth losing our lives over." He cast a speculative look Richie Cavanaugh's way. "Assuming, of course, that Richie doesn't intend to do anything stupid like killing us once he gets it."

"I just want the case," the younger man said quickly. He straightened, as though trying to invest his posture with some sort of earnestness. His effort failed miserably. There was nothing trustworthy in Richie, and when Alex met Hunter's gaze, his eyes told her he was no more fooled than she was. Then why was he willing to give up what might be the only evidence they had?

Her hesitancy had done little to assuage Cavanaugh's temper. He looked tense and gathered together like a cat about to spring. "No more crap. Bring it here to me."

"Do it, Alex," Hunter commanded.

With the feeling that her heart was taking up an uncomfortably large portion of her chest, Alex slid the case off the table and dropped it into Richie Cavanaugh's outstretched palm. He motioned her away with his gun, and quickly slipped the container into his shirt pocket.

She backed against the dining-room table, panic beginning to burn at the edge of what remained of her poise. *Now what? What do you want me to do,*

Hunter? How can I help get us out of this? In desperation she telegraphed her fear, looking into Hunter's flinty blue stare. His glance jumped down to her hand, then back to her face, then to Richie again.

You idiot! she cursed herself, realizing that her other hand was still curled around the autoinjector she had removed from the case. It was small enough that Richie might not realize she had it, and he hadn't bothered to look inside the container before he'd pocketed it. If she could hide it somehow, without his notice...

"Did you kill Isaacson?" Hunter asked.

"Shut up."

"The police have figured out it wasn't suicide. It's only a matter of time—"

"I said, shut up!" Richie yelled. As though he needed the welcome release of violence, he fired the gun randomly into the room. A bullet plowed into one of the couch cushions, sending up a tiny snowfall of stuffing feathers. Then he trained the gun back on Hunter, looking oddly pleased.

Alex's knees felt as limp as sun-softened candy, but Hunter appeared to be unperturbed. He turned his head to note the damage, crossed his arms over his chest and slanted Richie Cavanaugh an annoyed look. "That's my favorite couch," he said in a tone that suggested freezing boredom with a child's temper tantrum. With a heavy sigh, he added, "Okay. Now that you've subdued the furniture, what's next?"

Richie stiffened, and went bright red with fury. In his unkempt, uncertain state, he really didn't seem much of a threat, but she wondered if it was wise of Hunter to irritate a man holding a gun.

"Now the three of us take a little walk," the young man said.

"Where?"

"First to your storage shed to pick up a shovel, then to my boat. After what I've been through the last couple of days, I don't mind shooting you, but I'll be damned if I'll dig the hole for your bodies."

Hunter shook his head. "Bad idea, Richie."

"I don't think so. By the time someone discovers your bodies, I can be out of the country. I've had plenty of time to work it out in my head, and no matter what Pop thinks of me, I'm not staying here to take the heat for something that was really an accident."

"If that's true," Alex interjected, "then there's no need to do this. I can help you. My paper can make sure your side of the story gets told. Don't let your father convince you there's no other way to handle this situation."

"My father doesn't—" He broke off with a heavy, hard-jawed look. "I'm my own boss. Now shut up and get over here."

"Let her go, Richie," Hunter said in a tight voice. "She can't do you any harm without that evidence in your pocket."

The gunman gave him a look of sly pleasure. "What's between you two? Here I thought you didn't like each other, and all the time you've been trying to persuade her out of her underwear, I'll bet." He gave Alex a venomous look. "I've been out there sweating and starving for days, and you two have been sheet-wrestling, haven't you?" He had started to breathe in long, deep waves. "Now, *get over here!*"

Alex moved slowly to stand in front of him, praying that Hunter had some plan in mind to keep them alive.

Richie suddenly brought his free hand up and slapped her, hard, then pulled her to him so that her back was against his chest. Not a whisper of space lay between them, and Alex could feel the barrel of the gun wedged against the underside of her breast. The gunman's sweaty, stubbled face lay beside her cheek in sickening, overheated familiarity.

Hunter took a step forward, but Cavanaugh moved quickly, like a cornered dog, jerking the gun in his direction to bring him up short. "Don't move, Garrett. I swear, I'd rather kill you *now*. You two lecture more than Sunday preachers in a roomful of sinners." He rubbed his cheek against Alex's, abrading her flesh. "When I tell you to move, honey, you'd better do it without an argument."

She kept her eyes averted, concentrating on the sight of Hunter, who looked tense, his eyes narrowed and unreadable.

"What's the matter, Garrett?" Richie taunted. "Don't you like me touching her? Scares you, doesn't it?" He let his free hand drift across the top of her breasts, dipping into the loose swimsuit to fondle one nipple. "I'm not such a kid anymore. You need to show me a little respect."

Over the terrible plunging of her own heart and blood, Alex heard Hunter say in a tone richly steeped in sarcasm, "A few years hasn't made much difference that I can see. You're still the same molting little weasel you always were.''

Too stricken to breathe, Alex waited as their captor absorbed the insult. He continued to back them into the doorway, but his gun hand was shaking. Alex was filled with the sick conviction that Hunter had pushed him too far.

In a gasp of raw, thick confusion, Cavanaugh shook his head and said, ''You're crazy, Garrett. You ought to fear me, man.''

''Actually, Richie, I'm thinking of killing you,'' Hunter retorted in a calm, quiet tone.

There was a sinister stillness in Hunter's bearing, and the profound certainty of his words seemed to take Richie aback. His superficial composure slipped, taking with it his confidence. The hand across Alex's chest suddenly loosened.

Alex seized the moment. She had no intention of going to an unmarked grave without a fight. Noticing the metal crabbing poles that still stood propped beside the front door, she allowed Richie to inch out of the cottage, carrying her backward in that awkward shuffle that tied the two of them together. The moment she found herself in the doorway, she slid her hand down her side and reached blindly for the pole.

She heard Hunter curse, but already her arm was swinging the metal rod against Richie's leg. It connected with a sickening thud. Richie howled with pain and rage as his leg crumpled, throwing both him and Alex off balance. She tugged out of his grasp easily, but the gun was turning in his hand, finding her...

In the next moment, Richie went barreling out the open doorway, landing on the outside deck with Hunter on top of him. Alex had fallen on her hands and knees. She lifted her head, watching the two men struggle. Richie was younger, but his state of exhaustion was no match for the hard, punishing precision of Hunter's blows.

The gun was nowhere in sight. Then, like a magician's rabbit produced out of a hat, it suddenly rose between the two men, clutched in Richie's outstretched hand. Fear stung through Alex's system. Coming to her feet, she cast around for the crabbing pole. She snatched it up, ready to lay another blow on Richie's gun arm the moment an opportunity presented itself.

The men had stumbled to their feet—a panting, grunting blur. Alex searched for an opening, but could find none.

Hunter landed a blow under Richie's chin, and, thrown off stride, the younger man suddenly lurched right into her. Unprepared, she went flying backward, the crabbing pole cartwheeling out of her hand. Pain flared in her back, there was a splintering sound, and the earth tipped. Then her legs were pedaling air.

Somehow it registered in her brain that the deck railing had given way under her weight. She dropped into the silver spume, which pressed around her like a living thing, filling her nose and mouth. A straitjacket of water encased her. A lifetime of fear took her by the throat. She kicked toward the surface, but the tide battered her against the pilings of the stilt cottage, tossing her every which way in the current, until she had no idea which direction was up. Numbness began to spread through her body.

Where was the peaceful, floating dream-death she'd heard so much about? Where were the significant events of her life, flashing past her brain for final inspection? The only picture her mind could resurrect was Hunter, holding her against his chest in the lagoon, promising that he could teach her to swim. As the burning in her lungs became a fiery suffocation, and she relinquished the last bubble of breath, Alex thought it was a damned shame that he hadn't come up with the suggestion of lessons a day or two sooner.

CHAPTER ELEVEN

"OF ALL THE IDIOTIC, lamebrained things to do... Come on, Alex, snap out of it!"

The words rose and fell in Alex's numbed brain like the crackling sounds from a dying radio. She wished someone would turn it off. The blackness was much more pleasurable. Nothing within the blackness could touch or terrify her.

"I'm not going to let you fade out on me, Lois Lane. What about your story? What will the Suttons think if you pull a stunt like this? Damn you, Alex, listen to me! I'll tell them you couldn't cut it as a reporter. I'll tell everything I know about Isaacson to some journalism major right out of college. I swear I will. Wake up, dammit!"

Was that frantic howl of rage truly Hunter's? And why was he handling her so roughly? All she wanted was to be left alone. Her mind was working without pattern, drifting and swaying. But he wouldn't stop. He was making her angry, still trying to bully her into doing what he wanted. Well, it wouldn't work, and she would tell him so.

"Please, Alexandria, I can't go to another funeral for someone I— That's it, come back to me! That's my girl."

Alex opened her eyes. The first twist of the kaleidoscope revealed nothing but a soup of colors. Then she saw Hunter kneeling beside her, misery and concern etched on his tired face. She realized he was soaking wet, and she was amazed to find herself in the same condition, back on the cottage couch.

She frowned up at him. "I'll ruin the cushions," she said, surprised when the words came out in a hoarse whisper.

Hunter's mouth stretched into a smile, and he lifted one of her hands to his lips. "It was time to buy a new couch, anyway." His voice sounded husky, unused, and for a long moment he turned his face away. At last, he sucked in a shaky breath and asked, "How do you feel?"

"What happened?" she asked over a cramping sense of disorientation.

"Just rest," he commanded. His delicate, searching touch trailed across her forehead, moving wet strands of hair away from her face, and against her chilled cheek his fingers felt warm and gentle. "I won't leave you," he said as she closed her eyes.

The curious caress in his voice seemed to lap the outside of her body in a hazy glow, delicious. She smiled, letting herself swim out of contact with the room.

When she woke again, he was still there beside her. She didn't think much time had elapsed. Although she was now cocooned in a blanket, Hunter's hair and clothes were still damp. She remembered everything—finding the injector kit, Richie Cavanaugh's threats against their lives, the moments of struggle in the water, when she was sure he had won, and finally, Hunter's voice, refusing to leave her alone in that endless, black world...

"For someone you what?" she asked unexpectedly.

Hunter gave her a puzzled glance. "What?"

She looked at him with sudden, dark interrogation. "You said, you couldn't go to another funeral for someone you..." Her words trailed off as she waited for him to finish the sentence. "Someone you what?"

His eyes were softened by an amusement that was seductively tender. "Someone I think ought to have better sense than to get herself killed."

"Oh." She had hoped...she didn't know what she'd hoped, but a vague disappointment sliced deep.

She felt flat and leaden against the couch cushions. In spite of the way fatigue pulled at her, she levered herself upward. Hunter moved to help, placing a hand behind her head. The nerve-rich flesh at her nape tingled under his touch.

"What the hell were you trying to do?" he asked, scanning her with a worried gaze. "Why didn't you stay back instead of dancing around that moron Cavanaugh like a cavewoman wielding a club?"

"I was trying to keep him from killing you."

"I had the situation under control. Lord, I wanted to throttle you."

She lifted her head, lacing her tone with sarcasm. "Pardon me for trying to save our hides."

"You don't know Richie. He's a sniveling coward who wouldn't know how to drive nails into a snowbank. By the time he got around to shooting us, I'd have had him in tears, begging us to take him to the police and fix things with his father.''

''It didn't look that way to me. Where is he?''

''He pounded down the stairs the moment I jumped over the railing after you.''

''You let him get away!''

He sat back on his heels, and she felt his wry amusement at the accusation. ''I suppose I could have let you go down for the third time. Maybe you'd have grown gills.''

Heat gathered in her cheeks. ''Sorry.'' In a voice that was a miniature of her own, she added, ''Thank you for saving my life.''

He gave her a soft, silky grin. ''You're welcome.''

She realized that she had begun to shake, little quakes of reaction to the fear that was finally releasing its hold. Hunter seemed to understand. One of his hands lifted to stroke the soft flesh beneath her ear. Caught in the throes of embarrassment, and rather ashamed that he was forced to cater to such foolishness, Alex trailed the tip of her tongue over her lips and gave him a rueful look. ''I thought I was going to—'' Her voice sounded so frail and pathetic to her own ears, she broke off.

''Alex,'' Hunter whispered thickly, letting his fingers massage the stiffness from her flesh. ''If you wanted another swimming lesson, all you had to do was ask.''

She looked into his wonderful forget-me-not eyes that were rich with understanding. ''I was so scared.''

His hand slid against her cheek, where the ache from Richie's slap still lay. ''*I* was so angry.''

Catching her chin, he tipped forward to bring his mouth lightly against hers. She emptied her mind of everything except Hunter, and felt the intensity of his touch, felt it as if she was being surrounded by warmth, cradled in a shivering sweetness. Her fear dissolved, replaced by a heavy thrill that ran down her nerves, as though life had come stealing back into her veins.

He shifted back at last, letting his gaze travel over her slowly. With a blissful sigh, she smiled at him. "Now what do we do?"

"I've called Riley. He should be here soon."

"I guess Cavanaugh got away with the injector kit."

"Afraid so."

Suddenly, she began to laugh. Hunter stared at her uncomprehendingly. Words spilled out amid little gasps of mirth. "Oh, Hunter...that stupid, stupid boy...how could he...?"

"Are you all right?" he asked in a concerned tone.

She wiped a tear of amusement from her eye. "Yes, I'm fine. Really. Richie took our evidence," she said, as if that explained everything.

"It looks that way," he agreed cautiously, his features still blank.

Alex grinned. She shoved the blanket away from her body. Lifting one hip, she slid her fingers beneath the hem of her swimsuit. A moment later, she removed her hand. The injector she had removed from the case lay in her palm. "All except this one," she said on a note of triumph. "I wondered what I was sitting on that was so uncomfortable, and then I remembered this."

Hunter plucked the injector from her hand, and pulled her into his arms. "You understood! I thought maybe it got lost in the scuffle or bounced off the deck into the water." His eyes were alight with eagerness and hope. "Alex, this little beauty could hold all the proof we need."

"I thought you wanted to sit out this game?"

He touched his hand to the back of her bruised cheek again. "That was before that idiot Richie Cavanaugh showed up and started playing dirty."

THEY SHOWERED and changed into dry clothes. Alex rejected Hunter's insistence that she rest and instead began emptying the refrigerator and cupboards of perishables. Not knowing when, or if, they would return, he shut down the cottage generator, bled the water pump and latched the louvered shutters back in place. By the time Riley arrived with new fuel lines for the incapacitated boats, they were ready and waiting for him.

While Hunter replaced the rubber tubing, he briefly explained what had happened. Riley met the news of Richie Cavanaugh's threatening appearance with his usual dry interest.

The only time he looked at all surprised was when the boats were ready, and Hunter drew Alex protectively against his side. "Can you tow the rental?" he asked. "Alex isn't crazy about open water, and I'd like her to stay with me."

Riley's glance skipped back and forth between them. "Sure. Do you think it's safe to go back to your house?"

"Richie seemed to think the injectors were the only proof we had, so I wouldn't think he'd be looking for more trouble. But I should probably stay away from there for now, just in case someone's watching the place for Charlie and hasn't been called off yet."

"The manager's apartment over my store has been empty since Dave quit," Riley offered. "You two could stay there."

"What about my things at the hotel?" Alex said. "I'd kill for fresh clothes. This outfit is going in the dust-rag pile when I get home."

"We'll manage something," Hunter promised.

With those tentative plans made, they headed to the mainland. The early-afternoon air was hot and cloying, but the chop in the bay sent a spray of saltwater against the bow and made Hunter's cruiser bounce like a child's toy in a bathtub.

Alex's stomach rolled as she sat next to him in huddled misery, trying to focus on the horizon. Her fear was like a dark cave inside her where her spirit was lost. Unable to get a grip on it, she closed her eyes and prayed for the trip to end.

She felt a soft touch against her face and lifted her lashes. Having guessed the reason for her absolute silence, Hunter was caressing her cheek in absentminded commiseration, his eyes never leaving the water. She turned her head into his hand, laying a kiss along his knuckles.

He glanced down at her for a moment. "We'll be there soon, sweetheart," he said over the motor's racket. "Try to keep your mind off the water."

She fought to summon a smile but was forced to settle for a brief nod. "I'm sorry to be such a hen-heart."

He gave her a full look that saw everything. "In case you've forgotten, you're the lady who took on Richie this morning."

She didn't feel worthy of that praise right now. In fact, her body felt as though it had been put through a cider press. She tried to concentrate on the man beside her instead of the lurching sway of the boat.

It wasn't as difficult as she thought it would be. He had such beautiful colors in him, she thought. Salt mist glistened in his fair hair like cold sunshine. His eyes were pure blue and piercingly beautiful, and there was a gleam in his sun-toned flesh like new honey. She looked at him with a long, scrutinizing gaze and knew that she loved him with passion and a fierce abandon. The sight of him, in this moment, was fixed in eternity for her.

No matter what happens now, no matter what lies ahead, I will always love this man.

They reached the marina without incident. In one easy movement, Hunter lifted Alex out of the boat. Riley, bless him, must have realized she was unsteady. He whistled and tossed a set of keys to Hunter that could be passed on to her. "The apartment's up the stairs at the back of the store. Why don't you start a pot of coffee, Alex? We'll get the boats settled and bring up all this stuff."

With a grateful smile, she took the keys and hurried down the walkway. The men watched her go, listening to the brisk tempo of her retreating footsteps.

When she had disappeared into the marina store, Hunter turned toward his friend. "Thanks. I owe you one. After everything that's happened today, I think she's about done in."

Riley began setting provisions on the dock. "She looks it. I have to give her credit, though, she's got plenty of pluck. And it looks like the two of you have reached an understanding."

"Uh-huh."

"Yep," Riley added, "I figured once you stopped fighting so hard, you'd see she wasn't half-bad."

"When did you become such an expert on women?"

"The other day at your house. When you didn't have the sense to invite her in instead of trying to get Buster to scare her off." He lifted fishing equipment to the dock, then straightened to eye Hunter with idle speculation. "You and Lois Lane getting serious?"

Frowning, Hunter braced himself against the slight tip of the boat. "I've only known her a week, Rile."

Riley shrugged. "You fell for Julie the first day of college orientation. Remember?"

"That was different. My testosterone level was higher than my I.Q. Every time I looked at Julie, I imagined her naked in my bed."

"And you don't with Alex?"

"The hell I don't," Hunter replied roughly. "That's part of the problem. When I'm around her, I feel like a randy stallion."

"So?"

"So I *should* be thinking with my head."

"Why? Because you're not a college kid? Because
Charlie Cavanaugh gave you a healthy dose of the real
world, and you don't trust your instincts anymore? Or
because you lost one great woman, and you're not sure
her ghost would like it if you found another?"

Hunter dropped the box he was holding on the dock
with a bang. "That's a damned lousy thing to say," he
snapped in a dangerously narrowed tone. "You know
Julie wasn't like that."

His friend seemed unperturbed. "No, she wasn't.
She was generous and caring and honest. Alex re-
minds me a lot of her. But Julie's dead, Hunt. And
throwing yourself into the grave after her wouldn't be
her idea of carrying on. I've been wanting to say this
for a long time, and whether it gets me neck deep in
still water with you or not, now's as good a time as
any. You need to dig yourself out of that hole and start
living again, pal."

Full-blown anger raged within Hunter, but he
maintained a dead silence for several long moments.
Riley was his best friend, but even friendship had its
limit. He had no right to question the way Hunter
chose to grieve for Julie.

And yet...

In an agony of irritation and misery, he knew that
part of him was turning away from those memories,
rejecting the horrible nothingness his life had become, to find enjoyment in the soft, da Vinci eyes and
dark-haired grace of Alex Sutton. He had known it
today, when he'd thought she'd been stolen from him
by the gulf. Touching her cold lips with his trembling
ones, he had done all the right things, but his senses

had been entirely apart from him. In those moments when he'd thought he could not revive her, he'd felt as though something had died within him.

He hadn't felt that way since the news of Julie's death had reached him. And he had *loved* Julie.

Was he in love with Alex Sutton? No, he couldn't be. He had no qualms about his feelings for her. He *desired* her. She made him go white-hot, molten, every time she touched him. He cared about her, enough to want to keep her safe as he had not been able to keep Julie. But that was a long way off from the clear, sweet purity of the love he had once shared with his wife.

He became aware of Riley watching him, and the anger foamed out of him like a sudden surf-rush. It wasn't his friend's fault he'd been sending such mixed signals.

He loosened his stance, and gave Riley a look of wry amusement. "Are you through?"

Riley refused to take offense. "You know, you've got to continue to live, no matter how many skies have fallen."

"I hate to sink your boat, Dr. Freud, but I've already had a doctor with a wallful of diplomas who told me things like that. And in a lot fancier terms, I might add."

Riley grinned and shrugged. "Yeah, but I'm cheaper."

RICHIE CAVANAUGH STOOD in front of the wide windows of his father's office at Cavanaugh Laboratories. The company occupied the top three floors of a Washington, D.C., complex that boasted a helicopter pad on the roof, an uninterrupted view of the Jefferson Memorial and an extensive workout room in the basement, complete with Jacuzzi and racquetball court.

It was a pricey address with tight security, and Richie, who bore the results of his fight with Garrett like a world-weary boxer, was still amazed he'd been allowed on the elevator. More than one passerby had gaped and given him a wide berth.

He turned away from the view as the office door opened, and his father walked in. Richie had asked his father's secretary to page him off the racquetball court, and Charles Cavanaugh didn't look pleased by the interruption. He tossed his racquet on his desk as he slouched into the leather chair behind it. Red-faced from exertion, he used the towel around his neck to wipe perspiration from his face.

Without preamble, he said, "It's about time you showed up. Where have you been?"

The bold excitement Richie felt over his recent escape withered in the face of this displeasure. He swallowed hard and tried to sound confident. "You wanted whatever Garrett had that he could use against us. Well, I got it, Pop. Nearly got myself killed doing it, but I came through for you."

His father's gaze flicked over him contemptuously. "Why does your face look like that? No, don't tell me. It'll only be something ridiculous, I'm sure." One wiry, dark eyebrow rose as Richie moved forward. "Why are you limping?"

"The woman with Garrett whacked me with a metal pole."

"And did you kill them?" Charles asked mildly.

"Pop, I couldn't," Richie said with a quick sweep of his tongue across his dry lips. "I swear, it was all I could do to get away."

"Dammit, Richie! I told you I didn't want any more trouble from Garrett. He's a loose end we can't afford."

"He's not going to be a problem," Richie promised, trying to keep his voice steady. Reaching into his shirt pocket, he placed the injector kit in the center of the leather desk pad. "This case was all he had."

Charles picked up the kit, then slowly turned it over in his hands. "He told you that, did he?"

"No. But—"

"This kit comes from the batches they produce in Virginia," Charles said, reading the manufacturing labels. "You know what that means?"

"Ken's developing a conscience again."

"I warned Melissa not to marry him," his father said almost to himself. "I knew the day I stood up at church and gave her away that he had no backbone."

"What are you going to do?"

"I'll handle it." Charles flipped the catch on the front of the kit, lifted the lid, then looked up at his son. "Richie, have you looked at this case?" he asked in a quiet voice.

Panicked by something in his father's tone, Richie looked down at the kit. "Just to see that there were injectors in there. Why?"

"This model holds six. There are only five here," he said carefully, as though explaining something complicated to a child. "Tell me you lost one, or that it got broken somehow. Tell me you threw it in the Potomac River." His voice rose as he brought his fist down on the top of the desk. Both the injector case and Richie jumped. "Just *don't* tell me that Garrett has it!"

"I was lucky to get away at all," Richie said wildly. "Garrett and the woman were all over me—"

"You were the one with the gun, weren't you?"

"I was going to shoot them, I just never got the chance. The two of them—"

Charles waved away any further argument. He emitted a heavy sigh and rubbed his beefy hands across his face. "Saint Mary, I don't know what I could have expected... And just where are they now?"

"I left them on Garrett's island. By now, they're probably back on the mainland."

Charles moved from behind the desk to the liquor cabinet that was built into the far wall. With his back to his son, he poured himself a large drink, then downed the contents in swift gulps.

He took a deep, fortifying breath and said in a tight voice, "Find out, Richard. Find *them*. Use whatever resources you need from the Fort Myers office. In the meantime, I'm going to talk to Ken."

"And then what?" Richie asked as a worm of nervousness began slowly inching up his spine.

Charles turned around, and his dark eyes were sharp and unforgiving. "Then I'm going to get on a plane and meet you down there. I'm going to do what I should have done in the first place—take care of Garrett myself."

"Pop, I've been thinking—"

"Don't."

Richie knew there would never be a good time to say what he wanted, so he chose to ignore his father's sarcasm and forged ahead. "I don't think I can do any more. I don't want to go to jail, but I can't do the things you want me to."

He had expected his father to erupt in anger, but to his surprise, Charles looked remarkably unmoved. He turned his attention out the huge windows. After a time, he said softly, "There was a parade down there in the park yesterday. Some veterans' thing. I watched from up here—all those old men trying to keep from passing out in uniforms that are too damned tight for them now. I saw some uniforms from Lyle's outfit down there. Do you think any of them knew him?"

Richie's scalp prickled as his father's face turned toward the bright sunlight pouring through the windows. His features seemed like wax lit from within. A dreary weight of anxiety settled over him.

"When your brother was killed," Charles went on, "I didn't think I'd survive. Your mother, God rest her soul, grieved herself into an early grave. He had such promise..."

His father turned slowly, seeming to see his son for the first time. Richie hated the way his veins tingled as Charles came to stand only inches from him, the tense disquiet within him that shattered his poise and broke him down. His father placed his hands on his shoulders. When Richie attempted to move away, the grip tightened.

Charles let his head droop forward, until his forehead lay against Richie's. "I'm not going to let the government take my only remaining son," he said quietly. "You made a stupid mistake with Isaacson, but I can fix it for you. You just have to trust in your old dad. You understand, Richie?" Like the lick of a snake's tongue, one of his father's hands stroked his face. "You understand, son?"

"Pop—"

Charles backed away, his attitude becoming brusque once more. "Just do what I tell you, and everything will be all right."

THE APARTMENT ABOVE the marina store was a small two-bedroom unit with thin walls, noisy plumbing and a window air conditioner that blew a blast of arctic air worthy of a penguin habitat. It was plainly decorated, but comfortable.

Over a late lunch of take-out Chinese food, Alex, Hunter and Riley sat around the dining-room table of knotty pine and planned their next move.

"It's been days since I've checked in with my editor," Alex said as she plunged her fork into a carton of lo mein. "Ernie's probably worried sick."

"Tell him you'll be back in Miami by late this evening," Hunter said.

"Why would I tell him that?" Alex asked in some surprise.

"Because I want you to go back," he explained. "You should be safe there, and I won't have to worry about you."

"I think it's time to call in the cops," Riley interjected matter-of-factly around a mouthful of moo gui gai pan.

Hunter was more skeptical. "And tell them what?"

"That bastard tried to kill you!"

"It's Richie Cavanaugh's word against ours. All we have is one injector, which may or may not be suspect. And even if it is, Charlie could say I monkeyed with the contents. He'd have no trouble convincing anyone it was just more sour grapes on my part. Let's face it, I don't have a lot of credibility when it comes to making accusations against Cavanaugh Labs." He flung down an empty packet of soy sauce with a grimace. "I've got to have something concrete."

Alex exchanged a glance with Riley. Considering the results of Hunter's last attempt to bring Cavanaugh to account, they both understood his reluctance to jump back into that nightmare again. The injustice of it choked her with bitterness, but more overpowering was the tender, protective tide that rose within her. Hunter could be gentle or fierce, demanding or generous, but he never ceased to be a man she could love with all her heart, if he would let her. Now, when he needed her help, she couldn't desert him.

"I'm not going back to Miami," Alex stated. She lifted her chin determinedly and refused to flinch from the look of displeasure in Hunter's eyes.

"Alex, let's not argue about this..."

"Yes, let's not. I'm staying."

"There's nothing you can do here except get in the way."

"That's not true."

"Alex, Hunter is right," Riley added his support to his friend. "You'll be safer in Miami."

Calmly, Alex turned toward Riley. "I nearly drowned today. A man held a gun against my side and threatened to shoot me. I can't get any more scared than I've already been. If you think I can go back to Miami and pretend none of that happened, you're wrong. I'm going to see this thing through to the end, and if either of you try to shut me out, I'll just traipse after you on my own. I've done it before."

"Still looking for that story, Lois?" Hunter asked.

Alex recognized the sarcasm in his voice. She crossed her arms. "As a matter of fact, I am. And the one I end up writing might surprise you."

He rubbed his mouth with a napkin, balled it up and tossed it on the table. In a tone that sounded profoundly cynical, he said, "I suppose I can keep a better eye on you if you're not following behind me like a friendless pup."

She governed the impulse to smile. "All right," she said in a businesslike tone, eager to put this issue behind them and move on. "We need more proof. Can you get another injector kit?"

"I couldn't get within twenty feet of the plant here in Fort Myers. Besides, I don't think the kit came from this lab. Since so much attention was focused on the Florida branch before, I can't imagine Cavanaugh would be stupid enough to let it continue to produce diluted batches."

Alex flipped through her journal to scan her notes. "You said Ken Braddock gave you the first one. Where would he have gotten it?"

"Probably the Virginia plant. It's the closest to their main office. And," he said, his eyes suddenly lighting with a gleam of excitement, "not that far from Washington, D.C."

"Where Isaacson worked."

"And died." Hunter finished her thought.

Riley sighed. "Do you think Braddock will furnish you with another kit?"

Hunter shook his head. "I don't know. He bolted like a startled sheep when the pressure got to him. He says he won't back down this time, if..." Hunter reached across the table to pick up the single injector they'd managed to keep out of Richie's hands. "If this one turns out to be bad."

"Then the first thing we should do is find out what's in that injector," Alex said. "If it's bad—as Braddock must have suspected—we contact him. How do we find out for sure?"

Hunter pursed his lips in thought. "There's a biologist I'm still in touch with from the old days. He might loan me his lab for the necessary tests."

"I'll come with you," Alex said eagerly.

Hunter shook his head. "It's ten minutes up the beach from here. While I do that, why don't you have Riley take you to your hotel to pick up your things, then call your editor?"

"Why?"

"Because we may not have time later. I'm guessing Richie is on a plane back to daddy. He didn't notice that missing injector, but Charles will, and he'll want to know what happened to it. Which could mean he'll be back looking for us before we know it."

Hunter pocketed the injector and dug through his things for the keys to his truck, which still sat in the marina parking lot. He bent down to her, giving her a slow, luxurious kiss, then ran his finger down the line of her nose. "Don't get in any trouble without me, Lois," he told her. "*I'm* the only one who's allowed to put you in a panic."

She sat very still, staring at him as the blood ran faint in her veins. "Hunter..." She wet her lips, uncertain how to go on. *I love you, I love you.*

"I know, I know. Be careful."

No, that's not what I was going to say, she wanted to tell him, but he was already out the door, pounding down the stairs.

THE TRIP down the beach to her hotel didn't take long, but it passed in absolute silence. Riley drove her rental car, and Alex sat with her hands entwined in her lap, hardly seeing the glimpses of beach, gaudy tourist shops and hotels passing in front of her eyes. It took a conscious effort to force her stiff, cold fingers to relax. Convincing Hunter to let her help had been one thing; now the reality of the danger they were in was beginning to hit home.

At the hotel, Riley insisted on accompanying her to her room, where she hastily swept everything into her suitcase. It seemed such a long time ago that she had stayed here. How different she felt now from the woman who had naively plotted the best way to meet Hunter Garrett. In only a matter of days, she had found love and denied death. How quickly the focus of her life had changed.

She checked out, with Riley at her elbow. No one stopped them or asked any questions. Once she was back in the car, the tension started to slip away, and by the time the two of them returned to the apartment, the odd little skip of her heartbeat had nearly disappeared, too.

But talking to her editor produced its own kind of stress.

He began the conversation with the inevitable question. "Where have you been?"

"On assignment," she replied, trying to gauge his attitude.

"Don't give me that. It's Fort Myers, not the Australian outback. Why haven't you checked in?"

"I've been out on an island in the gulf. Garrett has a place there, and I've spent the last few days with him."

"He's talked to you?" Ernie sounded pleased.

He's done more than that, Alex thought, and was glad Ernie wasn't there to see her flush. "He's been very cooperative."

"Anything we can use on the Isaacson story?"

"I think so."

"Good. The D.C. cops are saying it's definitely murder. Get back here so we can meet with Hawthorne on how to play this."

"I can't."

There was dead silence on the other end of the phone for several long moments. Then, "What do you mean, you can't?"

"Ernie, there's more to it than just Hunter's slant on Isaacson's death. Things have happened—" She broke off, uncertain just how much to reveal.

"What things?"

"I can't talk about it right now."

"Are you in trouble?"

"I'm not sure," she hedged, then, sensing his dissatisfaction with her answer, she added, "I mean, not at the moment. But what I've found out could make it very unpleasant—"

"How unpleasant?" The editor's tone became wary.

"Ernie, if someone threatened one of your people, would the paper back us up?"

"You listen to me, Sutton," Ernie said, his voice taking on fatherly importance. "This isn't *All the President's Men* we're talking about. If you've got trouble, you get your sweet little inexperienced fanny back over here."

"I appreciate your concern, Ernie, but—"

"Concern, hell! Do you know how many lawsuits we've got Legal working overtime on? We've been in court more times this year than a bunny's been in clover. One more and Jessup will have us both scanning the classifieds. Now get back here and file the nice simple report I asked you to write."

"I can't."

"Alexandria, I'm not kidding—"

"I've got to go, Ernie. I'll call you," she promised quickly over his spluttering objections and hung up the phone.

She was looking through her notes at the table, wondering if she'd even have a job when she finally got around to writing her story, when Hunter entered the apartment. His features were maddeningly unreadable as he sat the injector directly in front of her.

She looked up at him optimistically. "Well? What's in it?"

"Atropine citrate and pralidoxime chloride."

"Which is..."

"Exactly what it should be," he said with a hard stare that conveyed a gray, gritty hopelessness. "There's not a damned thing wrong with it."

CHAPTER TWELVE

"I'M SORRY, sir. Mr. Braddock is out of the office at the moment. May I take a message?"

Hunter shook his head at Alex and Riley, who sat at the dining-room table, a hopeful audience. *"Still out,"* he mouthed. Into the receiver, he said, "Thanks, anyway. No message." He hung up, and with a grunt of exasperation complained, "The guy's got better hours than a banker."

"Do you think it's a bad sign?" Alex asked.

"You mean, do I think Cavanaugh's figured out that injector case came from his own son-in-law and has done something to him?" Hunter shrugged. "I don't know. I just don't know."

"Maybe you can reach him at home," Riley suggested.

Directory assistance yielded no home phone number for Braddock. Hunter took a deep breath and set his jaw. "Ken gave me another number, but I left his card at my house. There's no choice. If I'm going to persuade him to furnish us with another test kit, I'll have to go home and get it."

"I'll go with you," Riley said.

"No. If anyone makes trouble, I don't want to pull you into it, too. Besides, I'd feel better if someone stays with Alex."

"I can take care of myself," Alex objected.

"I didn't say you couldn't," Hunter said with the ghost of a smile. "I just said it would make *me* feel better. And I know how to move around my place in total darkness, so I can be in and out in five minutes."

For the second time that day, Alex found herself being left behind by Hunter. It didn't seem right that she should have to say goodbye again so soon.

She walked him down to his car. The late-afternoon sun threw their shadows before them, and the sugar-pink light bouncing off the water made the marina's rambling wooden facade look glamorously tropical.

Before he got into his truck, Hunter pulled her into his arms for a quick kiss. Then, as though he saw something in her face that disturbed him, he frowned and tugged on a lock of her hair that lifted on the breeze. "You worry too much."

"I don't think *you* worry enough."

"Alex, you heard what Richie Cavanaugh said. Killing Isaacson was an accident. He's not really cut out to be a murderer."

"What about his father?"

"What about him? Charles would be crazy to harm us, knowing the cops would connect your investigation with my allegations four years ago."

"So maybe he *is* crazy," she argued. "We could still end up dead."

His eyes shone with affection as he tucked the wayward strand of silky hair behind her ear. "We won't."

"Hunter..."

"Let me guess," he said with an indulgent laugh. "Be careful."

"I wasn't going to say that."

"No?" He lifted one eyebrow. "What, then?"

"I suppose it's really stupid to admit this, but I think I'm in love with you."

His grin faded immediately as his eyes darkened. "Alex..." He shook his head slowly, and whether it was a denial of her feelings or his own disbelief she didn't know. "You shouldn't..."

Defensively, words tumbled against each other. "I do a lot of things I shouldn't. Just ask my family. Or my editor. My friends will tell you—" She broke off, aware that she was rambling, aware that Hunter's reply was probably the beginning of a kind, careful rebuff. His eyes held the wary appraisal of a man trying to disarm an intruder with a loaded pistol and it was, she thought, almost more than she could bear. "You're not going to let me in, are you?" she said softly. "I can't get close to you because you're a one-woman kind of guy, and that one woman was your wife. Does that pretty much sum it up?"

"No. It doesn't," he said with a slow, thorough look. He enfolded her hand in his and ran his lips across her fingers, never taking his gaze off her face. "You're very special to me, Alex. In ways you'd never guess. I'm just not sure now is the right time to talk about love and relationships. We're both under a lot

of stress. Don't let the situation push you into saying
something you'll regret later."

His calm practicality aggravated her. "I'm not in the
habit of making impetuous declarations of love."

He gathered her drooping chin. "I didn't think you
were. When this is over, we'll sit down and talk this
through. All right?"

She nodded and tried to offer a resigned smile,
though she couldn't make it work and had to turn
away at the last moment to pretend interest in the
traffic that growled in the nearby street. Hunter
backed his truck out of the parking space with a
crunching spew of bleached oyster shells. She returned his goodbye wave with one of her own, and a
moment later, he was gone.

HIS ATTENTION WANDERED as he wove his way
through tourist rental cars prowling the beach strip
and the inevitable date-night traffic near the malls and
cinemas.

I think I'm in love with you.

Damn her, he thought. Why had she said it? Why
couldn't she have just let things be? But no, she'd
stared up at him, her face radiant, that wild little catch
in her voice as she'd spoken. Beautiful—so beautiful
his heart began to pound against the wall of his chest.
It had been all he could do to keep from pulling her
into his arms. Forget the past, forget Cavanaugh Labs
and all the insanity.

*You've got to continue to live, no matter how many
skies have fallen.*

Riley had been right, of course. Hunter knew that.

There was only a small part of him that still held on to the past, and he was beginning to think that almost none of it had anything to do with his feelings for Julie. He had loved her, but she was gone, and he could not bring her back. An awareness of the outside world seemed to be spreading within him. And all the sunshine on Eric's Island couldn't give him the inward expansion and warmth he felt when he was around Alex. It made him almost angry. He'd come all this way, only to discover he hadn't made himself immune at all...

So why hadn't he told her that?

Instead, he had remained silent, afraid that by voicing his thoughts he'd bring about a new cycle of pain. With love came grief, and he'd had enough of that. So he'd deliberately forestalled her, pacing his words so that they didn't sound like denial, knowing she was hurt by them, anyway.

What could he offer her?

Nothing.

His life was in shambles; the situation with Cavanaugh was growing more and more perilous. His gut was in a tangle of tight horror at the thought of any harm coming to her. He should have already put her on a plane back to Miami, bound and gagged, if necessary.

A kid in a red sports car cut in front of him, forcing Hunter to brake suddenly, bringing him back to earth. The boy roared away into the night. Hunter shook his head, wondering if he'd had so little common sense at that age.

Common sense. He could use a stiff dose of it now. He'd made miscalculations before with Cavanaugh. He couldn't afford to make new ones. When he got back to Riley's, he'd have to make Alex see that she *must* return to Miami.

Just in case someone had been left to watch his house, Hunter parked his truck at the corner of his street and walked the rest of the way. He moved silently through the shadows, staying out of the pools of illumination that came from the overhead streetlights.

The oppressive heat of the day was gone, and the air was a pot pourri of scents—the earthy smell of freshly mown grass, hamburgers on a grill, the faint perfume of the neighbor's roses nodding in the stray breeze. The occupants of the homes he passed had settled in for the night, to dinner and television. He had moved to this neighborhood of empty nesters and retirees shortly after he'd lost Julie and Eric, longing for the return of some kind of tranquillity to his life. Now it all seemed dreary.

His own house lacked distinction, and was a prime example of its owner's lack of interest. It needed paint, and the yard was becoming a jungle of aggressive shrubbery. Funny how he'd never noticed before just how much he'd let the place go. If he came out of this scrape with Cavanaugh alive, he promised himself he would invest some time in fixing it up.

No vehicles were parked near the house, and there wasn't a soul in sight. Still, better not to take foolish chances. He moved along the connecting backyards of homes three doors away. He didn't much like the idea of skulking around the neighborhood, but he knew it was safer.

Entering by the kitchen door, he made his way through the house. Even without the benefit of lights, he could see that an intruder had been here before him. Someone—maybe Richie Cavanaugh—had gone haphazardly through the place.

Hunter didn't know why he had hidden Ken Braddock's business card, but he was glad now that he'd taken the instinctive precaution. The card was still tucked inside the conch shell that sat on one of the bookcases.

He was about to make a hasty exit, when he spotted a square of white paper lying just inside the front door. He scanned it quickly with his flashlight. It was actually two pieces of paper, the first, one of those self-sticking notes the parcel companies used to notify customers that a delivery had been attempted. Only yesterday a package had been left for him with the neighbors next door, the MacAllisters. Beneath it was a note in the spidery scrawl of Maggie Mac-Allister.

Hunt,
   Hope you had fun.
   Mac and I have your package. Will trade for a dinner of snook, red snapper or, if the fish

weren't biting, flounder from Bartocci's Fish Market. We'll bring the wine. See you when you get back.

Maggie

P.S. Hope you remembered to water your plants this time!

Hunter smiled. Mac and Maggie were the only people in the neighborhood he'd bothered to get to know, mainly because neither of them would give up when he'd initially rejected their overtures of friendship. They were both retired schoolteachers, nice people and good neighbors.

He wasn't expecting a package from anyone. But if he stopped by their house to pick it up, they might know if any strangers had been in the area, showing an interest in his place.

The lights were on in Maggie's kitchen, and from their backyard he could see her pouring iced tea into two glasses. He knocked on the door, and she looked up with surprise, and then a smile of recognition.

"Hunt Garrett, what are you doing sneaking around?" she asked as she let him in. "And what are you doing back so soon?"

Her face was a wreath of wrinkles, though in her features there was a glimpse of the beauty she'd been. Hunter smiled at her. "I'm not, really. Just forgot something and had to return for it." He held up the scraps of paper she'd left for him. "I got your note."

"Oh, your package! Let me get it for you."

She disappeared into the next room, where her husband sat slumped in a lounger, his favorite game show blaring its theme music in an effort to combat his deafness. A TV tray in front of him bore the remains of dinner.

The old man turned his head to acknowledge Hunter with a nod. "You catch anything over on the island?"

More than you could begin to guess, Hunter thought, but aloud he said, "A few sheephead. Nothing that would make you jealous, Mac."

The old man snorted in a harsh laugh of pure ridicule. To the television he said, "No, no, you nitwit. What's the Panama Canal? Don't you even remember the category?"

"Have you seen anyone hanging around my place while I've been gone?" Hunter asked loudly.

"No. Why? Who's the archbishop of Canterbury?" Mac shouted before the game-show contestant could answer.

"Just thought it looked like someone's tried to jimmy one of my front windows," Hunter said. "Kids, maybe."

"Oh, for pity's sake, where do they get these people? What's the Cape of Good Hope, you numbskull?" Mac turned in his chair as the show went to a commercial. "You gonna call the cops?"

"No. There's nothing concrete to go on."

"Well, if I hear a peep from your place, I'll have the police here lickety-split. If it's kids, that ought to rattle their slats."

"Thanks, Mac," Hunter said, though privately he suspected the entire graduating class of Fort Myers High School could march through the MacAllisters' living room without Mac hearing them.

Maggie returned bearing a package about the size of a briefcase. The room was too dark to make out the sender's name. He followed her back into the kitchen, leaving Mac once more calling out answers to the television.

"Would you like a glass of iced tea?" Maggie asked. "I've just brewed a fresh pot."

"Sure," Hunter replied absently, sliding into one of the kitchen chairs, taking the parcel from her.

His mouth had turned to sawdust as a fierce thrill flowed through his limbs. The return address was Washington, D.C., and the sender was Dr. Leo Isaacson. Suddenly, he couldn't wait another moment to open the package.

Hunter tore off the plain brown wrapping. He was hardly aware of Maggie MacAllister setting a glass of iced tea in front of him. Excitement ran through his blood like a current of fire. It couldn't be. And yet...

He lifted the lid off the cardboard box.

Notebooks.

Personal papers scribbled in the hasty hieroglyphics of scientific language, all of it painfully familiar to Hunter.

And beneath them . . . an injector case from Cavanaugh Laboratories.

On a soft exhalation of breath, he lifted the case out of the box. He could tell by its weight it held a full complement of injectors. Taped to the case was a note.

H—

If my latest findings match the ones you came up with four years ago, it looks like your old friend Charles is still up to no good. See what you think, then give me a call so we can discuss this. He'd have a hard time making a case against *both* of us, don't you think?

I.

The note was dated the day Leo Isaacson had died. Almost in a trance, Hunter replaced everything in the box, then simply sat and stared at it.

He didn't need to convince Ken Braddock to send him another test case of injectors. He didn't have to worry that the authorities wouldn't believe his accusations a second time. It seemed too good to be true, yet here it was in front of him. Isaacson's own test findings reaching out from the grave to accuse Charles Cavanaugh.

He surfaced from his thoughts as Mac swore loudly at the television. Maggie had returned to Hunter's side and was watching him keenly. "My goodness," she ventured, "you're as white as a sheet. I hope it's not bad news?"

Satisfaction filled his soul and he found he couldn't control his grin. "Maggie, this has been . . . the most incredible twenty-four hours. Today, a terrific woman told me she thinks she's in love with me. And this package..." He shook his head like a man coming out of a dream. "No, it's not bad. This may be one of the best days of my entire life."

"That's...wonderful, Hunt," Maggie said, clearly confused, but more than willing to be happy for him.

Mac was grumbling loudly because his game show had been interrupted. One of the local newscasters was trying his best to deliver a bulletin without much actual information to go on, a fact that only irritated Mac more. "Why don't you come back when you actually *know* something?" the old man complained.

Hunter rose, casting Maggie a what-are-you-going-to-do-with-him look of commiseration. Scooping up Isaacson's case, he was about to leave when some of the news anchor's words began to penetrate his subconscious. Frowning, he turned his head slowly toward the MacAllisters' darkened living room.

The television station had cut to its reporter on the scene. Behind him, flames leaped into the air as firemen rushed to hose down a twisted pile of lumber.

"...but we'll keep you updated as more facts about this terrible fire become available. Right now, all we know is that the explosion at this marina is responsible for at least one death, and that the injured have been taken to a local hospital. The fire seems to be under control now, but Chief Avery believes the building will be a total loss, as well as several boats in the marina basin which caught fire as a result of falling debris. Arson investigators have been called to the scene and we should have an update soon...

A wave of nausea rolled over Hunter. His strength dissipated as he stood suspended in the doorway of the MacAllisters' living room. He felt disconnected from everything but the fading voice of the news anchorman.

The flickering swim of light in front of his eyes flashed as the bulletin ended and programming switched back to its regular schedule. "Which marina, Mac?" he managed to articulate.

"What?" the old man asked.

"Where...where was that explosion?" Hunter asked, though in his heart he already knew the answer. He knew...

"Someplace down south of us," Mac replied. "I don't know, probably one of those marinas down by the public beach. Why?"

"Hunt," Maggie said beside him. "Are you all right?"

He felt too stricken to breathe, much less reply. Somehow, he was able to nod, and he left the room. Somehow, he managed to stumble out of the Mac-Allister house.

The initial shock left him as he ran back to the truck. Blood burned through his veins like fire now, until he thought he could actually feel the fine flame running under his skin. Fear was a monstrous pain inside him, devouring control and rational thought. He punched buttons on the radio, then pounded the dashboard in frustration when no station seemed to be carrying more information.

"Please...please...please..." The word was a necklace of sound, slipping through his stiff lips like a prayer.

He zigzagged through traffic, trying to fix his thoughts on practical matters. It wasn't Riley's place. It *couldn't* be Riley's place. Hunter had only been gone little more than a couple of hours.

But the only two things he could think of were that he'd left Alex to the Cavanaughs' mercy, and that Riley had done nothing to deserve this except remain his friend.

If he'd had some small hope that his worry was groundless, it died as he hit the beach strip only blocks from Riley's marina and saw the red glow in the sky. Sirens wailed in the distance, and traffic slowed to a crawl, fanning his sense of helplessness. He screeched the truck to a halt in a parking lot, jammed Isaacson's package into the storage locker behind the driver's seat and set off in a loping run toward the marina.

The scene was chaotic. Knots of tourists stood along a roped-off area, and only grudgingly yielded ground as he pushed his way through. The fire's glow gave their features a ruddy illumination, so that they looked like imps from hell watching demons dance.

He ducked under the wide tape that kept bystanders at a safe distance, and a cop grabbed his arm.

"My family was in there," Hunter barely managed to utter the explanation. "Which hospital were they taken to?"

"Stay right here," the officer ordered. "I'll find out for you."

Hunter nodded absently. The scene before him nearly slapped the breath out of his lungs. Even at this distance, the heat was an unbearable furnace. The fire department seemed to be concentrating on the area around the marina's gas pumps, anxious to keep the fire from spreading any farther.

He didn't care if every boat in the basin went up, if the whole block ignited. His eyes wouldn't be coaxed from the sight of Riley's store, or what had been the store. It was no more than charred lumber, broken glass and twisted metal, a hissing, smoldering pile of spent history. Flames still shot toward the night sky, but the walls and ceiling had collapsed inward, or been pulled down to help suffocate the blaze. Only a small team of fire fighters worked to douse the rubble.

The apartment above the store was...gone. Consumed by the fire's bright greed as though it had never been.

Like a sleepwalker, he moved forward. He had to *know*. He stumbled over something hard and blinked blearily as he bent to pick it up. In the smoky darkness, he could barely see, and at first he thought the object was nothing more than discarded trash. Then his face froze as he recognized it. Oh, God, he recognized it.

It was Alex's journal.

Warm to the touch, the book still smoldered. The pages were singed and slightly damp. The full implication of its charred condition sank into his heart and left his sanity teetering.

I think I'm in love with you...

"Alex," he breathed hoarsely.

The night breeze carried his voice back to him. His eyes watered from the smoke, and everything turned into a smear of red and black.

HE LOST TIME, precious time, when the cop directed him to one of the local hospitals. When he got there, he discovered that a pileup on the interstate had forced the emergency room to send the ambulance to another hospital. It took a maddeningly long time to find out which one.

By the time he got to the right hospital, it seemed as though an eternity had passed. Hunter raced down the emergency-room corridor to find the place in pandemonium. Doctors, technicians, cops, the families of patients—there wasn't a spare seat in the house on a busy Friday night.

He came to a skidding halt as he recognized Riley's parents standing in front of a young doctor who was in earnest conversation with them. The older couple nodded mutely at something he said, then Mrs. Kincaid started to weep. Mr. Kincaid pulled his wife into his arms.

The sight of their pain knifed through Hunter's composure. His breath departed with a force as fear exploded within him. On legs that felt like wet paper, he moved away from the emergency room. He had to get control of his emotions; he couldn't face Riley's parents like this, especially if the news was as bad as it looked.

He slid into the first open doorway and realized immediately he'd entered the hospital's nondenominational chapel. Dimly lit, boasting no more than a dozen pews and a small window covered in diamond panes of colored glass, the room was quiet and empty. Hunter stood beside the double doors, his hands splayed against the wood. He pressed his forehead to the cool paneling, concentrating on taking deep breaths.

Instead, he found himself praying—a desolate, desperate litany that repeated itself over and over again in his head. *Please don't let them be dead. Please, God. Don't let them be dead. Not Riley. Not Alex. Please, not Alex...I'll do anything...just please don't...*

A great weakening wash of anger and doubt splashed over him. What right did he have begging God for anything? He'd spent the last few years cursing Him. He'd made too many mistakes, too many miscalculations. God didn't have much patience with fools and skeptics. And now Cavanaugh had found the perfect weapon to use against him.

This may be one of the best days of my entire life.

What a joke, what a foolish, terrible joke those words seemed now. Moments after he had uttered them to Maggie MacAllister, his world had come crashing down.

I could be in love with you.

He heard Alex's voice again, as if she stood beside him and whispered in his ear. He was haunted by the picture in his mind of her sweetly earnest face, shining up at him in trust and love, open and honest, while he...while he...

A knot of dread seemed to have taken up permanent residence in his heart, and he had to squeeze his eyes tightly shut to control the painful spasms that suddenly racked his throat.

Why had he left himself open to this kind of hurt again?

It was just like before.

All the light and warmth had been taken away, and he was going to walk out into that emergency room and talk to one of those calm, impersonal interns, who would tell him with practiced compassion that his life was over.

He opened his eyes to stare down at the tips of his shoes. The sneakers were nearly black with soot and grime, dirtying the rose-colored carpeting beneath his feet. He didn't belong in this clean, peaceful sanctuary. This was a place for people with hope. And he had none.

He turned, trying to find some sense of equilibrium. A small sound, something between a sob and a sigh, caught his attention. He realized suddenly that he was not alone. A visitor sat huddled in one of the front pews, her body nearly bent double as though in pain. She lifted her head. One hand shoved through her hair in an impatient gesture. It was lovingly familiar, and with that first snap of recognition his heart suddenly floated up in his chest as light and dizzying as a helium balloon.

"Alex . . . oh, God, Alex . . ." He tried to say more, but his lungs were too jealous of his breath to provide the words.

Somehow she heard him. Her head turned; her eyes widened. She rose, moving into the artificial lighting of the multicolored window so that she looked like a jeweled ghost.

"Hunter," she gasped as she came toward him.

His eyes roamed over her restlessly like a blind man granted sight, seeking every subtle change, the possibility of damage. She was pale and dirty, her hair a disheveled tangle down her back, and then suddenly she was in his arms and he was finding out for himself, touching her with shaky, gentle haste, too joy-filled to be proficient, just eager, so eager to put the frightening, detestable world of expected sorrow away.

He wished he could hold her forever. His face pressed into the curve of her neck, where the smoky scent and reality of her filled all his senses. She was shaking against him, murmuring incoherent words into his shirt.

"Shh," he whispered into her soot-streaked hair. "I'm here, Alex. I'm here."

He placed his hands against her head, capturing her face. Her eyes were full of tears, the dark lashes spiky with glistening wetness. He stopped her trembling mouth with his own, soft and questing at first, his desire submerged beneath an overwhelming need to comfort her.

Tenderness welled within him, filling the cold, barren places that had been there such a short time ago. His kiss became deep, penetrating, and she rose to meet it, her breath becoming one with his.

At last he pulled back, frowning at her in concern. "Are you really all right?" he asked.

He saw what he had not before, the fresh bandage around her forearm. "Only a minor burn. It was Riley who—" She stopped as her voice developed a distinct tremor.

Hunter sucked in a shaky breath. "Tell me," he commanded.

"After you left, Riley suggested we go out for burgers. We were just coming back up the walkway of the marina... Riley was making jokes about his cooking...and then it just..." She scowled, and tears slid down her face, leaving streaky paths against her smoke-blackened cheeks. "Everything went crazy. I ended up on my knees. When I looked up, the whole place was roaring. All these pieces of burning debris kept lighting on my clothes and hair." Her fingers plucked absently along the sleeve of her blouse, as though cinders were still eating holes through her clothing. "Riley was lying a few feet away. There was...there was a beam across his chest, and it had set his clothes on fire." She gazed up at him with stricken eyes. "I couldn't put the fire out, Hunter. I tried, but I couldn't." The words ended on a rising note of pain.

He sensed she was going into shock, and he gripped her shoulders tightly to keep her grounded to reality. "It's all right, sweetheart, I know you tried." Cautiously, he added, "I saw the report on television. What about Riley? They said one death..."

She touched her bandaged arm gingerly. "They made me ride in the ambulance. Riley was already there, and I sat beside him while the paramedics tried to revive him. He was so still and white. His face and hair didn't seem burned at all. Don't you think that's strange?" she asked in a vague tone.

Grief was seeping back into Hunter's system. "Then he's dead... Damn that bastard Cavanaugh to hell..." His voice trembled and fell away.

"The paramedics said it was too late. When we got here, the doctors starting working on him... and they found a pulse."

His heart skidded to a halt. Working to get past her shock, he raked tangled strands of hair away from her face, forcing her eyes to meet his. "Alex, what are you saying, sweetheart? Is Riley alive?"

"I just told you. The doctors think he has a chance. His parents are here, did you know that? They're thinking of flying him to a burn center in Houston."

His moment of fear dissolved. Alex was alive. The report had been wrong and there was hope for Riley, after all. Cavanaugh hadn't won. Not yet. "A second chance, Alex," Hunter said softly. "Oh, God, I didn't think I'd get one..." Hungry for the wondrous comfort of Alex's embrace, he pulled her back into his arms and kissed her. Then he took her hand in his. "Come on, let's check on Riley."

They left the chapel, returning to the bright confusion of the emergency room. Hunter cast a glance down the corridor. At the far end, Riley's parents stood talking to two men.

With his fingers still laced in Alex's, he took an abrupt right turn and headed out the front doors.

CHAPTER THIRTEEN

"WHERE ARE WE GOING?" Alex asked as Hunter pushed her into the passenger side of his truck.

"Anywhere away from here."

"Why?"

"Because I'm not ready to try to explain any of this to the police."

The truck swung into Fort Myers traffic, and Alex turned her head to glance back the way they had come. "Riley—"

"There's nothing we can do for him right now. And his parents are there."

She started to say something, then closed her mouth as she took one look at Hunter's face, illuminated by the lights on the dashboard. His features were fixed like steel, leaving little room for argument.

She straightened, realizing suddenly that he was driving with a particular destination in mind. "Now where are we going?"

"There's a discount store somewhere up this road. I want to get there before it closes."

"We're going shopping?" she asked with an incredulous look.

"We can get a room at a motel, but we're going to need more than just the clothes on our backs."

"What about your place?"

"I don't want to chance going back there yet."

Alex glanced down at the ragged, sooty mess that had once been her best silk blouse. "I can't go into a store looking like this. Can't I just give you my sizes and wait in the truck?"

"Not a chance," Hunter replied with a determined shake of his head. "I'm not letting you out of my sight."

In the store, he entwined her hand in his and led her through the crowded aisles with all the haste of a game-show contestant who'd won an hour's shopping spree. Alex kept her gaze locked on the floor most of the time, knowing that her shabby appearance garnered more than a few curious glances from the other shoppers.

Without stopping to try on anything, they each pulled jeans and T-shirts off the racks, underwear, a new purse for Alex to replace the one that had been salvaged from the explosion by some thoughtful fireman, a full supply of toiletries, a first-aid kit and knapsack from the camping section, soda, instant coffee and snacks. Hunter paid for everything with a credit card, which the cashier scanned skeptically before returning.

He drove down the crowded avenue that ran along the beach until they reached the neighborhood where small businesses and individual homes fought for space behind the sand dunes.

Finally, he pulled into a small motel called the Shamrock, where an overhead sign blinked a neon green four-leaf clover. Answering Alex's questioning look, Hunter said, "Maybe it'll be lucky."

The choice was better than either of them expected. The truck could be parked directly in front of their room, which was small, but clean.

"It's very... green," Alex said, noting the excessive use of the shamrock motif.

"It won't have to be home for long."

How long? she wanted to ask. *What do we do now?* But the day's events were catching up to her fast, and those seemed like questions meant for more focused moments. Right now, all she wanted was a long soak in a hot bath and some sleep. A weary sigh escaped her.

Hunter caught her hand and pulled her to him. "You look like hell," he said, giving her a smile that robbed the words of offense. His fingers brushed along her cheek. "I know what you need. I'll finish unloading the truck, and then I'm going to call the hospital to check on Riley's condition. Don't get out of the tub until the steam starts peeling the shamrocks off the wallpaper."

She gave him a grateful look, dug through the plastic shopping bags until she found shampoo and a handful of other things, then disappeared into the bathroom.

When she came out, barefoot and dressed in a baggy nightshirt, Hunter had turned down the sheets and sat propped with his back against the headboard of the bed. A stack of papers and a notebook she'd never seen before lay across his lap. Alex settled on her knees on the opposite side. She raked a comb through her damp hair, cocking her head to survey the scribbled notations on the pages of the notebook.

"Where did you get these?" she asked.

"I'll explain later. You're too tired to make sense of anything tonight."

Recognizing the truth in that statement, she gave him a worried glance and captured his hand. "How's Riley?"

With a grim look, Hunter closed the notebook with a snap. "I talked to his folks. He's stabilizing, but he has third-degree burns over his chest, one hip and leg. He hasn't regained consciousness, but the doctor says that's a blessing, really. There's going to be a lot of pain..."

His golden hair was trapped in the lamplight, and a gleaming lock of it had shifted against his forehead. Almost without thought, Alex fingered it back. "He'll be all right, Hunter. I just feel it."

"It shouldn't have happened," he replied through teeth he clenched so tightly that she could see the hinged movement of his jaw. "The Kincaids wanted to know if I knew anything about the explosion. I couldn't tell them."

"No, of course not."

He lay a gentle finger against the fresh bandage she'd placed on her burned arm. The bedside lamp cast a soft, mellow glow in his eyes as he looked up at her. "I thought I'd never see you again."

"But I'm right here beside you," she reassured him, tilting forward to touch her lips to his. She nibbled lightly at the corner of his mouth, but though it quirked at the invitation, he didn't open to her.

His hands clutched her forearms, and he set her apart from him. There was a tormented look in his eyes. With a husky roughness in his voice, he said, "Tomorrow is going to be a busy day. You need to get some rest."

She was disappointed, but she nodded and slipped between the sheets. "What about you?" she asked with a yawn.

"I'm going to take a shower, then I want to read through these notes for a while. Will the light keep you awake?"

"Not likely. I can hardly keep my eyes open now."

"Don't try," he said, snuggling her closer to his side. "Just rest, angel."

His hand played among the tendrils of hair that curled around her face. The light, rhythmic movement was like a narcotic, sending her into deeper layers of exhaustion.

She closed her eyes, listening to the pattern of her own breathing as it settled. Her bed at home had never felt this good. After such a long, traumatic day, she probably could have slept on the cold ground. But this was so nice . . . wonderful . . . with Hunter close . . . touching her . . .

Her body felt heavy and disconnected from the harshness of reality; her mind drifted into a twilight realm. Snatches of the day floated through her brain, moments both brutally frightening and deliciously sweet. "Hunter . . . ?"

"Hmm?"

"We're safe here . . . aren't we?"

"Very safe," he reassured her, his voice a low rumble near her ear. "I'll be right here."

She liked the way his words made her feel, warm and protected. Her senses began to shut down. Just before she faded out of consciousness completely, she thought Hunter murmured something else, but she was beyond the ability to sort through reality and dreams. All she could muster was a foolish smile of contentment.

SHE DREAMED of the explosion.

Everything jostled together in a dark, fathomless flood of images—cinders plucking at her clothes, Riley smiling back over his shoulder at her one moment, then just...*gone* the next...into a blinding flash of red and gold. The heat, oh, the heat, seemed to melt and sizzle the flesh right off her bones. Hunter was there, trying to pull her out of the hellish pit of flames that threatened to consume her, but his fingers kept slipping, slipping, and she was falling back, falling away from him until he couldn't reach her and the hungry fire was licking at her heels...

"Alex... Wake up, sweetheart. You're having a bad dream."

Called to the surface of sleep, she struggled awake. Light flared beneath her eyelids, and she squinted and turned her face away from the intrusion.

A gentle touch along her shoulder made her open her eyes. She frowned, hardly able to comprehend where she was, and caught sight of the bedspread, its design fisted in both her hands. Clusters of shamrocks, spilling out of golden pots over and over again.

She stared at the cheap print with its silly message of good fortune, feeling bleak and terrified.

The luck of the Irish. Good luck.

Was there any left for them?

She couldn't restrain it; a single tear slid along the side of her nose. She turned into the shelter of Hunter's embrace, sensing that he was watching her, waiting for her to be aware. Murmuring words of comfort, he drew her close, and she burrowed against his naked chest. His presence pushed back her panic, and the slow thudding of his heartbeat echoing in her ear brought a soothing, mesmeric calm.

Hunter's hands stroked along her back. "Alex, please don't cry...please, sweetheart. I'm right here, and everything's going to be all right."

"No, it's not. I'm not Irish," she said in sleep-confused misery. "Are you?"

"Not a drop," he replied, and she heard the indulgent smile in his voice.

"You see? Everything's working against us."

"Not quite everything," he replied mysteriously. Then added, "Would it help to know that I have an old rabbit's foot stuck in a drawer somewhere at home?"

"No."

"I suppose not. And how lucky can it be, anyway? It didn't help the poor rabbit."

Coming fully awake at last, she smiled. Hunter was completely naked beneath the covers. His skin carried the soft, clean fragrance of soap, the warm, innocent scents of sleep. It felt so good to be cradled in his arms again; she didn't want him to ever let her go.

Pale light poured through a crack in the curtain. "What time is it?" she asked, laying a kiss against the curving scar that hid among the crisp hairs of his chest.

He angled away to read his wristwatch. "Nearly six. There's no need to get up yet. You should try to sleep a little longer."

"I can't." The joy of having his flesh against hers tickled through the eroticized patchwork of her nerves. She let her lips and tongue play upon one pebbled nipple. "Can you?"

She heard his breath halt, and then come more quickly against the top of her head. "Not when you touch me like that." He groaned. "I'm trying to remember that you need to rest."

"You're what I *need*," she whispered.

In response, his wonderful touch threaded through her hair. He charted the structure of one ear with his finger, then brushed an unhurried path down the arch of her throat. Her flesh hummed with delight under the subtle movement of his hands and her blood beat up in waves of desire.

He touched the collar of her gaudy nightshirt. "Do you really need this?"

"Not if you can keep me warm."

He rolled suddenly, carrying her with him until he lay on top of her. Luminous early-morning shadows surrounded her, but all Alex saw were Hunter's eyes, brilliant with laughter. "I'll make you warm," he said, stroking her cheek with the back of his fingers. "I'll make you *hot*."

His mouth descended on hers, an impassioned demand that she met with impassioned need. Instinctively, she curled the tip of her tongue to tentatively stroke his. The kiss spun out, until they were both struggling for air.

Hunter drew back at last, searching her heated gaze with a curious frown. Burning ash from the explosion had left a red mark the size of a dime against her temple. He touched his lips to the spot. "Your poor, beautiful skin," he breathed against her forehead.

His fingers slipped beneath the hem of her nightshirt to slide it upward. Cool morning air drifted across her exposed flesh. He kissed her breasts, nuzzling out the places that pleased her by the sound of her sighs, as though he had set himself the challenge of memorizing and healing every tiny injury. "Every inch of you is so precious," Hunter murmured. "Like a treasure I want to wrap up and hide from the outside world. How can I bear to let you go?"

You don't have to, she wanted to say, but she couldn't, because her throat ached from the pressure of holding back a cry of delight.

"Alex, help me. Help me to be gentle with you."

Nearly lost, she gasped out, "Hunter, please . . . I don't want you to be gentle . . . I just . . . want you . . ."

As though sensing the moment when desire became necessity, Hunter took a new lead. He helped her tug the nightshirt over her head, then settled his hardness against her hot, agitated body.

"Alex . . ." His voice, no more than a ragged whisper, ran to her like fire, and then he plunged into her, pulling her hard against him.

Her arms curved around his long, tapering back and buttocks and she felt the contoured strength of his muscles straining to deepen the connection between them. The throbbing power of his thrust forged them into one and left them tangled in a knot that only orgasm could untie.

Like the thrill of pure intoxication, the deep, easy rhythm swiftly captured them both. He drove harder and harder against her tight warmth. As from a distance, she heard him repeating her name and words that were the shape of his desire.

She felt the pulsing tremor of his fulfillment, and her pleasure, fed by his, grew. In place of urgency, there was a sense that this could last forever. She felt the fine flame running under her skin, hot, so hot, and her body, shimmering like mist in separate shining cells, unfolded its secrets at last.

THEY DOZED until morning was firmly upon them. The powerful fear and hopeless dread of last night was temporarily stilled and tamed by the luxurious bond that had been forged as dawn had stolen sweetly into the room.

Locked in his arms, Alex listened as Hunter called the hospital. He cradled the phone between his ear and shoulder as he spoke to the nurses' station, letting his fingers trail a lazy path along the tops of her breasts.

"How is he?" she asked when he replaced the receiver.

"Better," he said, lifting her knuckles to his lips. "He might not need to be flown to a specialized burn center, after all."

"That's wonderful," she cried. When Hunter leaned forward to gently brush his beard-stubbled chin against the line of her jaw, she added, "Ohhhh . . . so is that."

He tipped her face up, and she surrendered meekly as his lips moved with inflaming expertise along the curve of her neck. His voice dropped to a deep strumming as his tongue stroked the hollow of her throat. "Alex . . . do you care about me?"

Her heart skipped a beat, then another. "What?"

"Yesterday, you said you could be in love with me. What about now?" His voice softened. "What about today?"

The sudden depth of his look made her shy, but it was foolish to repudiate the obvious. Wasn't her body embarrassingly quick to respond to his simplest touch? "I love you, Hunter. Today—" she punctuated that acknowledgment with a nibbling kiss "—tomorrow—" her tongue coasted an unhurried pace along his upper lip until his mouth parted "—always," she whispered, kissing him deeply.

When they broke apart at last, he said, "I'll consider that a yes." He gave a fluid laugh, and her attention was pleasantly diverted by Hunter's own mouth, playing so expertly against hers that the merest twitch was like a delicious caress. "Will you do something for me, Alex?"

"Anything . . ."

"There's a plane leaving Fort Myers for Miami this morning. I want you to be on it."

She froze, like an actress who'd forgotten her next stage direction. Shock closed her throat, so that it was several long moments before she could respond. She pushed out of his embrace and levered herself against the headboard, putting herself out of his range.

Damn him! Everything in her wanted to scream a denial, but she knew in her heart he had exploited her emotions with the efficiency of a warrior. She hated the suspicious brightness forming behind her eyes.

"Alex—"

With one outstretched arm, she blocked his move to capture her again. "Don't!" She swiped hair out of her eyes. "Why didn't you just tell me last night?" she managed to say in a censorious tone. "You could have gotten a lot more sleep."

"Alex, listen to me—"

"Why? So you can sweet-talk me into seeing things your way?"

"The decision doesn't require any more discussion." He blew out a breath and drew back. "You're going."

"You think so?" she challenged fiercely. "You're going to attract an awful lot of unwanted attention in the airport if you try to put me on a plane against my will."

"You won't make a fuss."

"How can you be so sure?"

"Because you're not crazy enough to jeopardize us both with a public display," he said, the words carrying a faintly desperate edge. "And I don't believe you'll make this any more difficult for me than it already is."

Her eyebrows lifted. "Keep talking. I'm feeling less generous toward you by the minute." She sensed his frustration, as deep as her own. But the hurt was welling up in her, great dark waves of it, threatening to spill over into foolish, impotent tears. She shook her head. "Whatever your plans are, Hunter, I'm not going to let you go through this alone."

He gripped her shoulders tightly. "Sweetheart, look at yourself. You've been through hell. Don't you get it?" he pressed in a quiet, silky tone. "*Alone* is the only way I can face Cavanaugh. He nearly got to me through you and Riley, and I won't give him another chance. For the love of God, don't you know how far I'd go to protect you from him?"

There was a wealth of meaning ladled into his tone, but her unhappiness was too much to allow her to yield that easily. "No. I only know that you don't want me in your life. What is it, Hunter? Am I still too untrustworthy, or are you so hung up by the past that there's no room for me in your future?"

She might as well have struck him. His posture altered, his body tightening in every muscle. "It isn't either one of those things. Don't you understand—"

"No, I don't," she cried with a miserable, wild shake of her head.

He bent forward, until only a breath separated them. "Listen to me," he said softly. "Everything about you is special to me, but if I let Charles Cavanaugh hurt you again, I don't think I'll be able to survive it."

"Hunter, I can't leave you—" Tears clogged the words, and her head dropped against his shoulder.

"Yes, you can," he whispered in her ear with searing tenderness. "Do you remember asking me about the knife fight I had with that shrimp-boat captain? You wanted to know the truth, and I put you off. I won't anymore.'' He placed his hands on either side of her head, tilting her face up so that he could meet her eyes.

In a hard, relentless tone, he said, ''After I lost Julie and Eric, I just wanted everything to be over. I couldn't get up the courage to do it myself. When that crazy bastard attacked, I saw the knife coming and I thought—just step into it. Let him do what you haven't got the guts to.''

A hot, drenching surge of horror rose within Alex, sending her pulse hammering. She could see the black depths of disintegration in Hunter's eyes as he spoke haltingly, half-lost to memory. ''He put a good-size hole in my chest and took a grappling hook to my boat. Riley got me to a doctor we knew who kept my name out of the papers, and I ended up in a hospital up north, listening to some shrink lecture me about death wishes. But life still didn't seem worth the effort.''

His eyes never left her face. ''And then you showed up at my door. You made me feel angry and confused, and more alive than I've felt in a long, long time. But my life right now is too shaky a foundation to build any kind of relationship on. The only thing I'm certain of at the moment is that I have to put all this business with Cavanaugh behind me. And I can't begin to do that unless you get on that plane. Go back to Miami and start writing whatever story you want. You'll be safe there, and I won't have to worry about you coming to any harm.''

"How can you be sure of that?"

"It's me Cavanaugh wants. And maybe after today, it won't matter."

"Why?"

"Because last night while you were taking your bath I called Donald Lefkin, the attorney who represented me four years ago. I've convinced him to try to set up a news conference so that everything that's happened can be brought out into the open."

She sat back, stunned. "How?" she asked in disbelief. "How can you without any proof?"

Instead of answering, he released her and rose. If she hadn't been so shocked by this latest revelation, she would have found thorough enjoyment in the sight of his naked body moving across the room, every fluid muscle shifting with lazy grace. He returned with the knapsack, out of which he removed the notebook and papers she'd seen last night. Finally, on top of all this he placed an injector kit that looked exactly like the one Richie Cavanaugh had taken from them. Hunter flipped the catch and the lid popped up to reveal twin rows of shiny injectors.

Settling back on the bed, he said softly, "This ought to get Cavanaugh a hundred years at Leavenworth."

For a moment, she felt robbed of movement or speech. It seemed so impossible, and yet... "Where did you get these?"

Hunter managed to look perfectly composed as he explained about Leo Isaacson's package being delivered to his neighbors'.

"I'm going to run the tests on them this morning," he said. "Just to be sure. But I seriously doubt that

Isaacson would have sent them to me if they were clean. By tonight Richie and his father could be in police custody."

"What if something goes wrong?"

"Then I'll still know you're safely away from here."

CHAPTER FOURTEEN

THE FLIGHT across the state was a short one—a few glimpses of the gulf as they circled the city, then nothing but grasslands and marsh as the Everglades spread beneath Alex's window.

She had thought that once she was in the air she would break down, perhaps let go of the knot of tears that she'd somehow held at bay all morning. She was desperate to be beyond it all, to know the peace and innocence of her life before Hunter Garrett had come into it.

Instead, she found herself paging through her journal. Hunter had handed it to her at the airport, and she'd seen in his eyes that he'd understood what it meant to her to have it back. But although the book was filled with such promising, beautiful dreams, she couldn't make pursuing those half-formed fancies work within the framework he had created.

Some of the pages were more damaged than others. The section of her notes about Hunter's public accusation, culled from the paper's Vutext, were crumbling around the edges and gave off the distinct odor of smoke. She hadn't known him when she'd jotted down these reminders to herself, and reading them now, they seemed so impersonal.

Garrett strictly on his own against Cavanaugh Laboratories.

C.L. pulled out all the stops, until even hearing-committee members who believed H.G. were skeptical.

Co-workers refused to testify against their bread and butter.

Wife nowhere in sight during eight weeks of bitter accusations on both sides. Where is she? Divorce? Look into this. Find out why Garrett chose to go through this alone.

Alone.

She knew now, of course, why Hunter had faced Charles Cavanaugh without a single soul in evidence to back him up. He'd been alone from the beginning of that fight, with Julie and Eric beyond his loving reach in some cold and distant grave in Norway. Without that familial network of support, he'd gone on a one-man crusade against the enemy. And lost. Horribly.

Alone.

How strange to think of the pattern repeating itself. Here she was on a plane, just like Julie and Eric, exiled to safety for her own good, while Hunter went off to slay dragons by himself.

She kept thinking of those first moments of awareness at the motel this morning, when his determined, ready-made speech had left the breath stalled in her throat. His features had been so curiously blank, as though he longed to keep his detachment polished, and was just barely managing it. But he had convinced her, he'd even been willing to let his words alienate her if necessary.

She brought her fingers to her lips to hold back an anguished cry. Outside her window on the horizon, the sun came bursting in like a skyrocket as the plane turned to make its descent into Miami, moving in solid brightness on the water below. Behind her, somewhere on the other coast, Hunter was preparing for a final battle against Cavanaugh.

Alone.

She realized suddenly that she couldn't let him do it. Her despondency dissolved. Whether he could ever return her love or not—it didn't matter. She and Hunter had come through the most horrendous things *together*. She couldn't desert him now. If she left Hunter, and he failed, she would never be able to forgive herself.

The moment stairs were wheeled up to the plane's hatch, Alex rushed down them. Weaving through human traffic, she found the flight counter, purchased a ticket and ran back to the boarding gate. The stewardess welcomed her back with an odd look, but feeling more confident and clearheaded with each passing minute, Alex smiled and took her seat. Impatiently, she waited for the commuter to refuel.

HUNTER HEADED for his friend's lab to test Isaacson's injectors. He took his time with the procedures so there could be no doubts, but the results were irrefutable. The contents were diluted to anemic proportions. He found a pay phone and called Donald Lefkin.

"That's terrific," the attorney exclaimed. "Isaacson's notes are powerful stuff, but the physical evidence will give the argument some teeth."

"Yeah, it's good news," Hunter remarked.

"So how come you don't sound happier? Something you're not telling me?"

"No, nothing. I'm just tired and hungry. And I want this to be over, Don."

"I'm working on it. As soon as I have something definite lined up, I'll be in touch. Are you still at that motel?"

"I checked out this morning. Maybe I'm just getting paranoid, but I'm not sure it's safe to go home yet."

"No, I wouldn't," Lefkin agreed. "I've done some checking. Ken Braddock's wife says he's on a hunting trip in South Dakota, and from what I can get out of my contacts in Washington both the Cavanaughs are out of town."

Hunter snorted, and in the reflection of the phone booth's glass he saw that his mouth was drawn into a line as grim as his resolve. "I'd bet money that Charles and Richie are right here in Fort Myers, doing a little hunting of their own."

"Well, sit tight, and stay out of trouble. I should know something by this afternoon. Be ready to show up where I tell you at a moment's notice."

"I'll call you," Hunter said.

"No. The office is closed for the weekend and you might miss me. Does your answering machine have a special code that allows you to pick up messages when you're away?"

"Yes."

"Then let me call you."

"Do you think that's wise?" Hunter asked.

The attorney laughed. "Don't worry. I know how to be appropriately vague."

After he hung up, Hunter went to the hospital. He avoided the waiting room, where he knew Riley's parents were sure to be keeping a nervous vigil, and hoped that he might be able to slip into Intensive Care. But the burn isolation ward was laid out so that visitors had to pass the nurses' station. He put on his most charming smile, but the woman in charge refused to be swayed. No visitors except the parents. He was forced to find comfort in the fact that Riley had been taken off the critical list and was sleeping peacefully.

There was nothing more he could do at the hospital. Realizing that he was ravenous, Hunter picked up a bag of fast food, parked in the strip-mall parking lot across from Riley's business and ate facing the charred husk of the marina store.

The place had the eerie desolation of a ruin. Snakes of trapped smoke continued to spiral up from the wreckage and yellow police tape still roped off the area.

The sight of all the destruction made his appetite disappear. Angrily he stuffed the remains of his burger back into the bag. His veins tingled with fine hatred for the Cavanaughs, but he slowed his breathing with the reminder that soon it would all be over.

Repeated disillusionment had tarnished his vision of the world, but he knew that he had enough now to put the Cavanaughs behind bars for a lifetime. There was nothing they could do to stop him. And when it was all over, maybe he could start to rebuild his life.

With Alex?

That was the part of the equation he was less sure about. She must be home by now—safe—but hating him for sending her away. He thought of the way she had looked at him in the airport, the life fading out of her eyes, replaced by hurt. It was an odd bit of irony, really, that in her face he could see all the misery that was in his own heart, as though the image had been reflected back through a mirror.

He made a call to Lefkin, but the attorney was out of the office and had left no messages on Hunter's answering machine. With time on his hands, he spent a couple of hours in a dark corner of a local tavern, nursing a single beer, setting down on paper all the events that had led up to yesterday's explosion.

He tried to make his test conclusions sound clear and concise; scientific facts generally bored the media to tears, and he didn't want their attention wandering for a single moment. The explosion and Isaacson's death would guarantee an audience. Lefkin's involvement would help, too. The attorney was well-known in the state for taking on high-profile cases.

Lefkin was still out of the office when Hunter made his next phone call. He rang his home to retrieve his messages, and Donald's voice came on.

"Hunt, we're all set for tonight. Call me around five and I'll brief you on the details. For something like this we'll need as much credibility as we can get, so plan on a jacket and tie, and if you're still wearing your hair long, get a haircut. Talk to you soon."

Hunter was about to replace the receiver when the machine beeped again, indicating another message.

"Hello, Hunter. We haven't spoken in a long time, but I imagine you'll recognize the voice. I believe you have something I want, and it just so happens that I have something you might be interested in. You really ought to call me. I'm at 555-3782, but not forever, so please don't wait too long."

The shock of hearing Charles Cavanaugh's voice went through Hunter like an electric charge. The man must be desperate, to be calling him. Did he know about Isaacson's evidence, or was he only fishing for the missing injector out of Braddock's kit? His nerves stretched taut with curious uncertainty as he dialed the number Cavanaugh had left.

The phone was picked up on the second ring by the man himself. "Well, well, Garrett," Charles said mildly. "I thought you and I had finished with each other. Now here you are pestering me again."

"What do you want, Cavanaugh?" Hunter said in a tight voice.

"I should think that would be obvious. Richard brought me a gift—five little collector's items—but it seems you held one back without telling him. I'd certainly like to have it."

"That's all you want?"

"Oh, yes. Quite simple, really."

Hunter drew an easier breath. Evidently, Cavanaugh had no knowledge of Isaacson's package. Hunter leaned further into the phone booth and said, "You can go straight to hell, Cavanaugh."

The older man didn't seem fazed. He sighed heavily and replied, "Still tilting at windmills, I see. It appears you haven't learned a thing."

"You'd be surprised."

"Perhaps," Charles said calmly. "Richard was at the hospital today, checking on your buddy Riley. I believe he just missed you, according to the nurse."

For the first time, Hunter felt a prickle of alarm. His hand tightened on the receiver. "Stay away from him."

Cavanaugh chuckled. "Of course, dear boy. With all those people flocking around him, it's quite impossible to pay a little visit. That's why I was so pleased when Richie came back with even better news."

Hunter wet his lips and swallowed hard. "What are you talking about?"

There was a brief pause, the sound of the phone being transferred hand to hand, and then the soft, ragged breathing of someone else. "Hunter?" Alex said in a tentative voice, and then the receiver was snatched away.

For a moment, Hunter's heart refused to take a beat as a white flame of fear ran along his nerves. Blood surged through his veins in scalding bursts.

Cavanaugh came back on the line. "The lady sends her regards," he said smoothly.

Frightened anger spilled over into Hunter's voice. "You son of a—"

"Now, now. There's no need to be ugly. This can be a simple business transaction. As attractive as she is, we have no interest in detaining the lady longer than necessary. You bring me that last item, and Miss Sutton goes home with you."

"Where?"

"Your old stomping grounds, the warehouse outside the lab here in Fort Myers. We'll meet you at seven this evening."

"I'll be there."

"Oh, I don't suppose I need to tell you, but please make sure you come alone. If we see anyone who looks remotely like the police, I'm afraid we'll have to forget the arrangement . . ." In a threatening tone that chilled the sunshine into moonlight, he added, "And . . . dispose of our merchandise."

The line went dead in Hunter's ear, and the world seemed to dissolve away from him.

It gave Hunter an eerie sense of déjà vu to drive through the front gates of Cavanaugh Laboratories. Years ago, he had come here with Julie at his side, the two of them newly married and fresh out of graduate school. The company had offered them jobs that seemed challenging and on the cutting edge of technology. The world looked fresh and exciting, and they were going to change it, or at least make it a safer place.

But the last time he had been here, that world had turned its back on him. He'd cleared out his things with a feeling of disgrace and isolation gnawing through his self-esteem, Julie and Eric no longer there to make him feel as though the fight was worth winning. He had not stepped foot on Cavanaugh property since.

Now he was back. It seemed as though he had come full circle.

He'd had to call Donald Lefkin and cancel the press conference, of course. How could he stand in some hotel meeting room and spout his claim against Cavanaugh Laboratories with Alex's life in danger?

Somewhere in the building in front of him she waited, with both the Cavanaughs her impatient jailers. They could hurt her. They might already have done so. As Hunter got out of his truck, he thought how easily he could see Richie and Charles dead.

The flare of sunset painted the warehouse walls a golden orange. Hunter checked his watch. Seven o'clock exactly. He didn't want to be late. Men like Charles Cavanaugh had no respect for you unless you could frighten them a little. But with Alex's life in the balance, he wasn't about to risk being late for their meeting.

The place was deserted. Charles Cavanaugh had always believed in heavy electronic security, but it didn't surprise Hunter that the huge sliding door to the warehouse yielded easily as he pushed it back. No doubt the video cameras and alarms had been turned off.

He slid the door back into place. It blocked out the twilight efficiently, and it took a moment or two for Hunter's eyes to adjust.

It hadn't changed much in the years since he'd last seen it. Though piled high with boxes labeled for shipment and the usual assortment of forklifts and machinery, there was no smell of old dust about the place. Whatever else Cavanaugh was, he believed in keeping a clean house.

There was a light coming from the manager's office on the second floor. Shadows bounced wildly as someone moved around up there. Hunter headed in that direction, his footsteps hollow on the concrete floor, then he stopped. He didn't want to get too far away from the only exit.

"Cavanaugh!" he shouted into the cavernous unknown. "I'm here. If you want the injector, you come to me."

The words echoed and died. For long uncounted moments, there was no response. A trickle of sweat skipped down Hunter's back as he stood in the dusky shadows and waited. Then another. If he had underestimated Cavanaugh...

Lights went on. Not enough to chase away the darkness completely, but enough illumination that Hunter had no trouble making out Charles Cavanaugh standing at the foot of the office stairs. The man came forward, until no more than a hundred feet separated them.

"Where's Alex?" Hunter demanded.

"Where's my injector?"

In response, Hunter reached into his shirt pocket and held up the injector between two fingers.

Cavanaugh smiled, and without taking his eyes off Hunter, turned his head toward the office. "Richard!" he called. "You may bring the lady downstairs."

The office door opened, and Alex was suddenly standing there, with Richie Cavanaugh pressed close behind her. The barrel of a gun was no more than a deadly shadow between them. They made a slow, awkward descent, eventually reaching Charles's side. Richie looked nervous and uncomfortable.

"Are you all right?" Hunter raised his voice.

Alex nodded. Her face was pale and shining.

"Come here, Alex," he said, but when she made a move toward him, Richie stopped her with the movement of his gun.

"Not so fast," Charles interrupted. "The injector, please."

Hunter held it up to the light. "When Alex is halfway to me, I'll toss it the same distance."

"Fair enough," the man replied with a shrug.

Strung tight with apprehension, Hunter watched as Alex began crossing the distance that separated them. His eyes were locked on hers, an invisible tether pulling her closer to safety. When she had reached the halfway point, he bent down and sent the injector skimming across the concrete. Both the Cavanaughs came forward to collect it. Richie handed it to his father, who looked the injector over carefully, then deposited it in his jacket pocket.

Alex had reached Hunter's shoulder. His hand came up to cradle her face in a delicate, searching touch. "Lois Lane," he said softly. "What am I going to do with you?"

He pulled her to him for a brief moment.

"I'm so sorry," came her muffled response against the front of his shirt. "I messed up."

"It's all right," he reassured, then set her slightly in back of him, one hand laced through hers. "Everything will be fine." He straightened and faced the Cavanaughs. "That's it, then. I wish I could say it's been a pleasure."

He and Alex were only steps away from the huge sliding door, when Charles's voice halted them. "One moment, if you please." They turned, discovering that the older man had drawn his own gun and was now pointing it at them. "As much as I hate to spout melodrama, I'm afraid we can't let you leave."

Richie's head swung toward his father. "Let them go, Pop. We have what we want."

"Be quiet, Richard." Charles came forward until only a few feet separated them. "Do you know, Garrett, I've spent years wondering when you'd show up again. I always knew you would. You have that crusading mentality that insists on righting perceived wrongs. What took you so long?"

Hunter had pressed Alex against his side during Charles's approach, and he hugged her even closer now. "I guess it just took me a while to find something worth fighting for again."

Charles turned his catlike smile on Alex. "Ah, of course. Love makes us fly in the face of all danger, doesn't it?" He looked back to Hunter. "Unfortunately, it can also lead to foolish decisions, such as your coming here. Surely you know I can't have you popping up in my life every few years?"

"I assure you," Hunter said in an amiable, unperturbed tone, "this will be the last time."

Charles gave a short bark of a laugh. "Finally, we seem to be in agreement! I'm sorry, you've left me with no choice."

"Did you kill Ken Braddock?"

"A member of my own family—certainly not! I have, however, sent him on an extended hunting trip with an associate of mine who has instructions to make him aware of the hazards of selling out his own father-in-law." He grimaced. "Painfully aware."

"Killing us would be a mistake, Cavanaugh."

"Really? How so, may I ask?"

"Leo Isaacson sent me a package on the morning that Richie was stupid enough to kill him. Lots of personal notes on how you've been tampering with the anti–nerve gas vaccines."

"The same meaningless theories you expressed so long ago?"

"They're not going to sound too meaningless coming from a man whose suicide is under investigation. Plus, he included a little bonus. One of your kits. Full of diluted injectors."

The words fell into a pit of silence as both Cavanaughs digested them. With a gasp, Richie had come striding forward to stand beside his father. Charles blinked quickly, but gave no other sign that this news had taken him aback in any way. "You're bluffing," he said at last.

"You know I was never much of a gambler," Hunter refuted.

"Pop," Richie broke in. His face was white, a horrible, working mask of anxiety and desperation.

"Shut up!" Charles snapped, and then more calmly, asked, "And where is this damning evidence against me?"

"I gave it to my attorney this afternoon with instructions to bring it here at seven-thirty." As though on cue, a sweep of bright lights traveled over the high windows of the warehouse door, then the sound of car doors slamming. In the distance, the wail of police sirens sliced the night air. "That will be them," Hunter said, then glanced down at his watch. "A few minutes early, but I might be running slow."

Charles stiffened, his supreme confidence starting to dissolve in front of their eyes. "He brought the police?"

"Better than that. He brought the press and the television media, Charles. Fully briefed." Hunter pursed his lips. "The way I figure it, you two can surrender now, and take your chances with the courts..."

"Or I can shoot you."

"You could. But in a few minutes, you're going to have to explain to millions of viewers why you're walking over two dead bodies to get out of here."

The warbling trill of a cellular phone echoed against the aluminum walls. Hunter motioned toward the bulge in Charles Cavanaugh's coat pocket. "If that's a lookout you've got posted outside, he's probably calling to let you know a media circus is already setting up camp."

Cavanaugh made no response, and the cellular phone rang and rang, until its frantic summons finally died and left the four of them alone once more. There was a tense silence as both Cavanaughs obviously tried to absorb the seriousness of the situation. Hunter had to give Richie credit. He seemed to know before his father that any further threats would be pointless.

"It's over, Pop," he said in a sunken sound of defeat. He slipped the safety back on his gun and tossed it away. Prying the second weapon from the older man's tight grip, he dropped it to the concrete and tried to put his arms around his father.

"No—no," Charles whispered, his head swinging back and forth between them like a trapped fox cornered by dogs.

Hunter felt no sympathy for the man. Before he lost the advantage, he stepped up to the warehouse door and wrapped his fingers around the handle. "Do you watch much tabloid television, Charles? America loves it, and you're about to become the lead story."

Everything happened quickly after that. Hunter jerked the door back on its sliding track. As he had hoped, Don Lefkin was there, standing beside at least a dozen media people. Cameras went up like saluting soldiers and flashes strobed. He pushed Alex blindly forward, out of harm's way into the mass of microphones and reporters scrambling for a better angle. The night was filled with the sounds of police sirens and shouts for attention.

"Mr. Cavanaugh, look this way!"

"Richard, did you kill Dr. Isaacson?"

Under the harsh lights, Richie's face was washed out with fear, yet he looked oddly resigned, almost relieved. "It's all right, we'll get through this together, Pop," he said, still struggling to calm his father.

Charles's eyes were wild, filled with raw rage. "No—I won't. No—no—you coward! Noooo!" his voice rose.

Suddenly, he seemed to collapse in his son's arms, bending low so that his hand swept across the concrete to scoop up the gun Richie had let fall. It came up, and Hunter didn't know whether Charles intended to turn it on himself, Hunter or the crowd in front of him. He lunged for it, but Richie Cavanaugh was there ahead of him, yanking on his father's arms until the weapon disappeared between them.

The gun roared, sending shrieks of fear through the crowd. Like a puppet that had been jerked by its strings, Richie Cavanaugh stiffened, then slid bonelessly to the floor at his father's feet.

There was a flickering second of shocked silence, then a cacophony of raised voices. Cops pushed their way through the wall of journalists and television reporters, shouting for everyone to get back. "For God's sake, Jerry, keep that tape rolling!" someone snapped behind him.

Alex was at Hunter's side again, her hands fisted in his shirt as he wrapped his arms around her. In stunned horror they watched Charles Cavanaugh fall to his knees in front of his son's inert form.

"Richard...Richard," the older man pleaded, his fingers imbedded like talons in his son's blood-soaked shirt. "Oh, my God, Richard, what have I done...?"

THE POLICE PLACED Hunter and Alex in protective custody. It became clear soon enough that they needed protection from the salivating pack of news hounds.

Blue uniforms formed a solid wall of humanity around the two of them as they were led to the cruisers. Donald Lefkin was pulled along in their wake, fielding questions.

As they waited to be whisked off, Alex looked back and saw Charles Cavanaugh being taken away in handcuffs. In spite of the calls for some sort of comment, he remained mute. His features looked as though the life had been drained out of them.

Seated beside Hunter in the back of the darkened police car, Alex remarked in a quiet voice, "He looks as if he wants to die."

Hunter threaded his fingers through hers, holding them tightly. "His life was over the moment he pulled that trigger."

She couldn't really read his face. He was cast in shadow against a background of white-hot camera lights. It haloed his hair and caught the curve of his cheek, which looked cold and carved in marble. "Are you all right?"

"It didn't have to end that way," he said harshly. "I was sure he would give up once he realized there was no way out."

"It's over, Hunter."

"Yes . . ." He turned his head away from her, toward the window, so that now she couldn't see his face at all and couldn't gauge his feelings. "Over . . ."

They spent long hours at the police station, telling and retelling everything to detectives and police stenographers. There was no time for private discussion between them. The only person they saw who wasn't wearing a badge was Donald Lefkin, who shepherded

them both through the process with the ease and determination of a drum major putting a field full of
band members through their paces.

Eventually, they were brought to a sparsely furnished interrogation room and left there. Alex sat in
a chair across from Hunter, exhaustion stealing into
her bones. She wished the room weren't so cold and so
unpleasantly olive green.

Hunter was silent and distant. What was he thinking? Was he angry that she had returned? It made her
heart and brain burn in upset and misery to imagine
that he was wishing her back in Miami.

His chair scraped back from the table so suddenly
that she jumped at the noise. He paced the length of
the room a couple of times, then lounged against one
wall.

Alex waited, resting her head on her hands.

"Why did you come back?" Hunter asked.

"I had to. I just couldn't let you go through it
alone."

"I told you that was the best way."

She sent him an exasperated look. "Well, I thought
about that. But it seemed to me that's the way you've
approached everything unpleasant in the last few
years. I just wasn't willing to calmly walk away while
you went off and possibly got yourself killed."

He stirred, a small indication of displeasure. "Instead, *you* nearly got yourself killed."

"It wasn't my intention to get caught," she said,
refusing to let his annoyance affect her reasoning.
"And I've said I was sorry. When I got off the plane,
the hospital was the only place I thought you might go.

But Richie was coming out as I was going in, and recognized me.''

After a long pause, he asked quietly, "Did he hurt you?"

"No."

The empty chair went sliding as Hunter sprang from his slouch against the wall. Startled, Alex jumped up and would have moved away from him if he hadn't captured her with his free hand. He swung her against the drab green wall, pinning her between his arms. "Dammit, do you have any idea what it did to me to hear your voice on the phone and realize Cavanaugh had you? Or when I saw Richie with his gun pressed against your side?"

Over her dismay at this abrupt explosion of speech, she found her own resentment. What right did he have to *feel* anything? He'd sent her packing quickly enough. "I suppose I should assume you were angry."

"That's too mild a word for it," he said, arching his neck back to draw a deep lungful of air. Quietly, he said, "I wanted to rip them both limb from limb. I nearly went out of my mind with worry, and when I finally had you by my side again, only one thought kept going through my mind."

Alex's head reeled with the power of his proximity, but healthy instincts of self-defense rose within her. "That if we ever got out of there, you were personally going to boot me back to Miami?"

He gave her a rueful smile and shook his head. "That I didn't want to let you out of my sight ever again."

She pushed his hand away when he tried to lay his fingers against her burning cheek. "I can't keep up with you, Hunter. You shove me onto a plane this morning and have me thinking I might never see you again, and now you say you never want to let me out of your sight."

He looked momentarily disconcerted, then he said with careful emphasis, "Alex, look at me." He waited until she lifted her eyes to his. "Do you know that I love you?"

She shook her head in mute distress. "That would be easier to believe if you hadn't spent so much time recently trying to convince me otherwise."

"Trying to convince myself, as well. But it doesn't seem to be working. I love you, Alex."

The words sounded like fragments ripped from his heart, but gradually a smile surfaced on Hunter's lips. "I love your courage. I love your face, with all its quirks and laugh lines. The little crease you get between your eyes when you concentrate. I love the way you say my name when I'm buried deep inside you. I love you even when you're trying to persuade me to see things your way."

She bit her lip. "You're making such a muddle of this, Hunter. What do you expect me to say?"

He gave her a fierce glance. "Say yes, dammit! I'm proposing marriage."

Her gaze raced over his face, the features that had come to be so dear to her. Torn between happiness and new worry, she said, "I'm not anything like Julie..."

"Of course you're not," he replied with a frown. "I fell in love with *you*, not Julie's twin. Yes, I'll always love her. She was a wonderful wife, and she gave me Eric. But love isn't something you only get one chance at. I want the person who's made me believe that. I want you."

She saw the pulse jumping in his throat, the white line that rimmed his mouth with tension. It took every ounce of Alex's willpower to resist that sweet, bullying speech. "Wanting is not the same as making a lifetime commitment, Hunter."

She watched sudden fear leap into his eyes. His supple, graceful hand moved along the side of her face, threading into her hair. In a low, uncertain voice, he said, "I know I deserve that, and probably more. But don't turn me away, Alex. I've been afraid of the hurt—running away from you—and all the time you've been the one who can make it right. You're the one who makes me feel whole again."

Her gaze rose, and she couldn't do anything about the tears glistening in her eyes. "I do love you, Hunter. I do..."

He pulled her to him in a rough caress, as though whatever had previously kept him in control had suddenly broken. "Oh, God, Alex, I think I'd rather chance death a thousand times than continue with a life I can't bear anymore." He touched her lips with a gentle fingertip. "One that doesn't have you in it."

His need for her was in his voice, raw and powerful. "You don't have to, my love," she promised softly against the drag of his mouth slanting across hers. "I'll be right here by your side. Always."

His kiss deepened. He stroked and held her, and it was only from the peripheral edges of a love-hazed consciousness that either of them heard the door open and close behind them.

Donald Lefkin cleared his throat, and they broke apart to glance his way. "Sorry," he said with a laugh. "I didn't realize you two were still conducting an interrogation in here."

"I didn't even need the hot lights and rubber hoses," Hunter said in a teasing tone. "She's just cracked."

"So has Cavanaugh. He keeps ranting something about the government being responsible for the death of his son. Guess he forgot who pulled the trigger in that warehouse."

Hunter frowned as a stray memory surfaced. "No, he had an older boy in the army. The first year I worked at the lab, we heard there was some sort of accident on the base. I remember thinking how ironic it was. Here we were, finding ways to save men's lives on the battlefield, and the head of the company couldn't do anything to save his own son."

Lefkin shook his head. "Well, looks like he thought of a way to get back at the army. The Defense Department's sending down some big guns to go over everything. Until they get here, the two of you can go home and get cleaned up. I just thought I'd warn you, every newspaper and television station in the state is on the precinct steps, waiting to get the story."

"Sorry," Hunter said to Donald, though his eyes never left Alex. "There's only one reporter who's going to get the exclusive on this, and she's right here in my arms."

EPILOGUE

THE SUMMER HEAT had hung on into October, and he was hot and tired by the time he returned to the island near sunset.

He changed into swim trunks and bounded down the cottage steps. Pushing aside the loose, hanging snakes of grapevines that sheltered the cove, he stepped onto the narrow ribbon of beach. His gaze traveled down the sand until he spotted Alex, wading in thigh-high water. She waved when she caught sight of him and began making her way to shore.

Hunter smiled. She looked beautiful coming toward him, like a mermaid released from the sea's captive embrace. As always, when he saw her, he felt the infinite, maddening intoxication of his senses.

My wife, he thought. *My love. My home.*

Once he had thought those words, and all the dreams they implied, were beyond his grasp forever. But in the three months since their marriage, he'd discovered how much more pleasure there was than pain, how many raw, empty places could be filled by her loving touch and gentle care. She had banished the cold bleakness from his heart, until he could no longer remember what it felt like to be lonely and incomplete.

Reaching his side, she lifted her mouth for a quick kiss. She carried the scent of sunshine, and her flesh against his was warm.

"You're late," she scolded without heat, then dropped to the beach blanket she'd spread.

He settled beside her, watching as she stretched her long tanned legs out before her, rubbing her toes together to remove the sparkling sand. "The sentencing took longer than expected," he said, trying to keep his mind away from the knowledge of how those legs could wrap around him in the heat of passion.

"How was it?"

"Grim. But it doesn't matter if he serves one year or a hundred. The outside world just doesn't exist for Charles anymore. I could almost pity him if I didn't remember all the pain he's caused every time I visit Riley."

Alex turned her head his way, giving him a troubled look. "How was he?"

"Better, physically. But still too withdrawn—for Riley."

Tilting her head as though deep in thought, Alex said, "When we go back to the mainland on Saturday, let's encourage him to spend a few days out here. Between the two of us, we can convince him it's time to get back in the game of life."

"Like you convinced me," Hunter said with a smile and leaned over to nuzzle Alex's neck. The wind-dusted fragrance of her skin made heat flood his veins.

Salt and sea and pure female. His hand tangled in her hair, and the lush life of it foamed over his fingers. "How about hitting the water?" he suggested with a low growl.

"I don't feel like a swimming lesson."

He let his fingers play across the line of her collarbone. "There are other things we can do out there besides swim, you know?"

"It'll be dark soon."

"Guess we'll have to do everything by touch, then." His fingers dipped to the top of her bathing suit, resting on the swell of her breasts that lifted with every breath.

He made a move to pull her to her feet, but she stopped him, a little frown of uncertainty marring the smoothly tanned skin. "Hunt, wait. We need to talk."

His brow rose over the smoky glitter in his eyes. "Now?"

"It's important," she said with a determined look.

"All right," he replied, trying to dampen his body's response to her nearness.

From the corner of the blanket she retrieved her notebook. It was a new one, replacing the sooty, fire-damaged journal she'd carried for so long. She flipped through the pages, and from where he sat he could see the sprawl of her delicate script.

"You've been writing," he stated, pleased that with Charles Cavanaugh's trial finally behind them, she'd slipped back into old routines.

"A little. Mostly a letter to Ernie, telling him one more time why I won't come back to the paper."

"He's afraid of losing you to the competition."

Alex's cheeks went pink. "That's silly. The story was good, but—"

"It was hard-hitting, thorough and came straight from the heart, Alex. It was beautiful. Hasn't the whole Sutton clan been telling you that?"

"You know that's not what's important to me anymore."

"What is?" he asked, certain of his position on her list of priorities, but wanting to hear it from her own lips, anyway.

With a shaky smile, she ripped a page from her journal and handed it to him. "You're the one who's always encouraging me to submit something to a publisher. See what you think."

He schooled his features into seriousness and tried to concentrate on the lines before him. In the fading light, he read:

My love for you is strong.
It's a sure thing, not a maybe.
Better catch up on your sleep,
'Cause we're gonna have a baby.

It took him a moment to absorb the significance of those words. Then his heart stumbled to a halt, and his gaze jumped up to meet hers. "Alex . . . ? Are you serious?"

"Of course I am," she said with a light laugh. "Aren't you always telling me to take my poetry seriously?"

"Don't joke about this."

"Believe me, I don't see anything funny about looking like a beach ball with eyes. The doctor says some time next April." Her smile broadened, but nervousness quivered through her voice as she asked, "Hunter, you're happy about this, aren't you?"

His hands came to each of her cheeks, trapping her head. "No. I'm thrilled. Why would you doubt it?"

"Well, this is one spark God blew on a bit quickly. We've only been married a few months."

"It will be fine," he said in a husky whisper. "A little girl I can teach to swim."

"Or a little boy you can teach to fish."

His heart skipped a beat as he thought of Eric, of how much he still missed him and always would. But how much joy there could be in loving a second child. "I can, can't I? This is so incredible. I just never dreamed..."

She touched the lushness of his bottom lip with a fingertip. "Really? I thought you were the scientist who was so good at putting the pieces together?"

"I'm not, Alex," he said, capturing her wandering fingers and bringing them to his lips. "Don't you know you're the one who specializes in that? You're the one who found my heart and had the patience and determination to put it back together again. All those ragged pieces—held in place by your gentle touch and spirit...and love."

She smiled up at him. Her hand was still a delicate captive within his own, and this time when Hunter tugged on her fingers, she rose and followed him into the calm turquoise waters of the gulf.

HARLEQUIN SUPERROMANCE®

If you've always felt there's something special about a
man raising a family on his own...
You won't want to miss Harlequin Superromance's
touching series

He's sexy, he's single...and he's a father!
Can any woman resist?

THE TROUBLE WITH TEXANS
by Maggie Simpson

Jake Evans knows exactly what his late wife's
sister is doing in Sotol Junction, Texas. She's checking
to see what kind of father he is. Michelle Davis will no
doubt be reporting back to her mother in Boston about
how eight-year-old Brooke is being raised. And Jake
had better keep that in mind, despite the attraction
developing between him and Michelle. If she thinks for
one moment that he'd allow the Davis family to take
Brooke away from him, she'd better think again.

Available in August

Be sure to watch for upcoming FAMILY MAN titles.
Fall in love with our sexy fathers, each determined to do the
best he can for his kids.

You'll find them wherever Harlequin books are sold.

HARLEQUIN SUPERROMANCE®

SHOWCASE

Special Books by Special Writers

Under One Roof
by Shannon Waverly

The Author: Two-time RITA Award finalist and
Romantic Times Reviewer's Choice winner, she's
got fans worldwide. Shannon wanted this, her tenth
book for Harlequin, to be a very special one. *It is.*

The Characters:
Spencer Coburn. Overstressed physician, divorced father.
He's currently the sole emotional and physical support of...
Stacy Coburn, his teenage daughter—his *pregnant*
teenage daughter.
Gina Banning. Hardworking, divorced schoolteacher and
only child. She's currently the sole emotional and physical
support of...
Joe Banning, her eighty-three-year-old father—her seriously
ill father.

The Story: One of the most moving, honest and *uplifting* books
you'll ever read. And it's just plain *romantic,* too!

Watch for *Under One Roof* by Shannon Waverly
Available in August 1996, wherever
Harlequin books are sold.

HARLEQUIN SUPERROMANCE®

RETURN TO CALLOWAY CORNERS

Remember the Calloway women—
Mariah, Jo, Tess and Eden?

For all the readers who loved *CALLOWAY CORNERS*...

Welcome Back!

And if you haven't been there yet or met the Calloways...

Join us!

MEET THE CALLOWAY COUSINS!

JERICHO
by Sandra Canfield
(available in August)

DANIEL
by Tracy Hughes
(available in September)

GABE
by Penny Richards
(available in October)

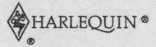

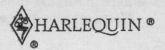

HARLEQUIN SUPERROMANCE®

**The book you've been waiting for
by that author you love!**

A Family of His Own
by Evelyn A. Crowe

Remember Matt Bolt, the handsome ex-homicide
detective in *Fathers & Other Strangers*? Remember Matt's
dashing and delightful brother, Jason? Well, Jason's
looking for *A Family of His Own*. And while
the setting's the same—West Texas—Jason's romance
is entirely different. That's because Jason's the kind
of guy who's never met the woman he couldn't
charm.... Until now!

**Watch for *A Family of His Own*
by Evelyn A. Crowe**

**Available in August 1996,
wherever Harlequin books are sold.**

Look us up on-line at: http://www.romance.net